WOR
STIFFS

LUCY LEITNER

FRESH
FLESH
SERIES
BOOK 4

NECRO PUBLICATIONS
2012

First Edition Trade Paperback

WORKING STIFFS © 2012 by Lucy Leitner
Cover art © 2012 by Travis Anthony Soumis

This edition © 2012 Necro Publications

ISBN: 978-1475211245

Assistant Editors:
Amanda Baird
C. Dennis Moore

Book design & typesetting:
David G. Barnett
Fat Cat Graphic Design
www.fatcatgraphicdesign.com

a Necro Publication
5139 Maxon Terrace
Sanford, FL 32771
www.necropublications.com

This is Book 4 in the Necro Fresh Flesh Series.

For my parents, who I can always turn to, even in the event of a zombie apocalypse.

Madre for help with everything from those douchebag semi-colons to these very words.

Padre for the hospital scrubs and the references. It's WS, by the way.

Richy for suggesting more machinations and abysses. And being my biographer.

Wendy for literally telling the world.

Sarah for answering the phone to celebrate and being a surprisingly adept clone.

Grandma, for giggles and terrible attempts at re-naming.

Carl Kurlander, for thinking that misanthropic misadventures make for good stories no matter how offensive students find it.

WORKING
STIFFS

Nestled uncomfortably between the perpetually clogged artery of the noisy highway and the fashionably depraved South Side, the Pro-Well Pharmaceuticals campus stood proudly as a beacon of hope in the sphincter of Pittsburgh. Though the parking lot surrounding the company's buildings was mostly gravel, the corporate headquarters was an immaculate memorial to redemption, four stories of pure American dreaming. From several yards away, Marshall Owens hubristically eyed his creation, the only baby that he would ever have. He watched it like a father, a doting one who micromanages his son's every move, who bribes the good girl from church to take his boy's eyes off the wild one with the eyebrow ring and multi-colored bracelets that brag of sexual encounters. The kind who would pull more strings than a puppeteer operating a marionette centipede to get the boy into a good school and would never let him spend a night in jail.

Marshall Owens looked at the beautiful blonde holding the microphone in front of him. Had things worked out a little differently, he thought, he could have had her. Though the TV news camera caught a face-to-face interview, Owens could see her eyes constantly flicker, moving back to the perfect, unscathed, unburned piece of corporate architecture behind him and blinking repeatedly as if that millisecond when her eyes were shut would help block out the vision of the scars and skin grafts that covered half of the Pro-Well CEO's face.

"It has been 15 years since Marshall Owens abandoned his parasitic so-called career as a meth dealer in Fayette County to turn his talents with chemicals to good use," Barbara Goodman said in that semi-nasal tone meant to be heard over a montage of exterior shots. "After working on prototypes for three years, Owens was finally given a grant to pursue his dream: to cure all that ails mankind." She smiled and addressed the CEO, asking, "And how far have you gotten on that goal?"

"Well, Barbara," Owens began, "it's a difficult road. It seems that as soon as we make strides on bird flu, the pigs start getting us sick. It's a perpetual cycle, but at Pro-Well Pharmaceuticals, we work tirelessly every day to find every possible solution to anything that kills, sickens, or just plain bothers mankind. Indeed, we're fighting everything from cancer to female cleft chins."

He had to maintain the image of charm, the charisma, not just so that beautiful blonde evening-news anchors would speak to him, but also so that they wouldn't even think to ask what was hidden behind the factory's walls.

"There you have it," Goodman said, relieved as she turned towards the camera, "From the monument of strength that is Pro-Well Pharmaceuticals, I'm Barbara Goodman."

The cameraman with the ripped black jeans and untrimmed goatee lowered the cumbersome news camera from his shoulder.

"So this segment will be on tomorrow night. I'm not sure exactly when, but sometime during our 6 p.m. evening newscast," Goodman said. "I can let you know the exact time once I speak with my producer."

"Oh, that's okay," Owens stated, resorting to the endearing assumed personality trait of modesty. "I can never watch myself on TV."

"Oh, you don't need to be concerned," she said hurriedly. "We made sure to keep you in the most flattering lighting to cov—" she caught herself, realizing that with all the training she'd undergone to learn how to talk to any subject on or off the record, she had never received instruction on political correctness when speaking with a burn victim who practically owned the city.

Owens smiled understandingly, another positive PR move. "Don't worry about it," he said. "I really should be getting back to work. Morton's toe isn't going to cure itself."

He grinned again, a terrible, off-putting, vile grimace that usually evoked too much pity to be associated with evil. That's just how someone with such severe facial burns smiles, his interlocutors convinced themselves, although joy had never looked so unnatural on anyone. Barbara smiled back at him, glancing above to the purple clouds surrounding the rapidly setting sun. She stuck out her hand to give him a hearty, professional shake, but he leaned down and kissed it. She trembled as what was left of his lips lightly touched her well-moisturized hand in the most uncomfortable way to learn that chivalry is not dead.

"Thank you so much, Mr. Owens," Freddy Mendez said as he lowered the Channel 13 News camera from his shoulder.

"Any time," Owens said, heading back to the Pro-Well factory, the smile erased from his scarred face.

He liked dealing with the press. Controlling the media, jumping in front of any story that may arise, that was part of the job, part of keeping himself out of jail. He reached the large metal door of the factory and quickly swiped the key card that he kept on a zip-cord attached to the belt loop of his Versace suit. As he entered the hallway that surrounded the clean production area, Harold was waiting for him, earpiece attached like he was a member of the Secret Service.

"Have they been fed?" Owens asked his loyal assistant.

"No, sir," Harold said in the baritone of a thug who cultivated the low frequency to add yet another reason for the other inmates to stay away even when he dropped the soap. "But Sven did pick up their dinner."

"From where?" Owens asked.

"Downtown. The jail," Harold replied as they walked down the hallway towards the clean-room entrance, in a perverse take on *The West Wing*.

"Another hooker?" Owens asked, stopping dead in his tracks.

"Yes, sir," Harold said.

"I don't care how much fun he likes to have with them beforehand. He has got to vary his locations or I'll take him off delivery detail altogether," Owens said furiously. "He'll be in here babysitting if that's how he's going to behave."

"I'll let him know, sir," Harold said, always welcoming an opportunity to reprimand his Nazi co-worker.

Owens started walking again, followed by Harold, who quickly shoved open the door to the employee locker room that was the final barrier between them and the production floor. Harold held the door open while Owens slipped into the room where Sven the protector of the white race and Michael the arsonist were waiting, holding the flailing arms of a thin young woman. Clad in a tight leather skirt, fishnet stockings and a top that more resembled a sports bra than a traditional shirt, the woman pulled and kicked and squirmed, but her efforts were overwhelmed by the strength of two recently released felons coming off of years of nothing to do but bench presses. Her feet slipping out of her pink patent leather stiletto pumps, she shook and screamed as black mascara tears rolled down her painted face.

Owens approached her, assuming the manner of the lean, reasonable gentleman who would never approve of the brutal treatment at the hands of these Neanderthal thugs who'd undoubtedly violated her during the abduction. As Owens came closer, she stopped screaming, her breaths now caught on top of one another, struggling for air. She shivered, making no effort to hide her fear as Barbara Goodman had so sweetly done. Owens smiled as he ran his hand over her greasy cheek. She shuddered.

"What are you going to do to me?" she asked between choked-back tears. "Are you going to—"

"Oh, don't worry," Owens cut her off. "Don't look so scared. I wouldn't dream of having sex with you."

She breathed a sigh of relief, "Then what do you want from me?"

"Nothing," Owens said. "If it was up to me, you'd never have been here."

"Then can I go? Please let me go. I won't tell no one," she pleaded.

"Unfortunately, that is not up to me," Owens replied. "See, there are others that want something from you."

"What do they want?" she asked, unable to control the tears anymore.

"You," Owens said.

He snapped his fingers, and the ex-cons pulled her around towards the doorway behind them. Harold quickly jumped in front of them and pushed open the door while Sven and Michael dragged the wailing, terrified prostitute who was attempting to plant her legs to the floor in futile resistance. She had shaken her wavy dark brown hair over her face during her pointless fight, but she managed to peer through her thick tresses at the factory workers. The machines were busy bottling, encapsulating and compressing, but their attendants were staring at her. They were all wearing hospital scrubs, and some even sported hairnets, but they were like no humans that she had ever seen before. Their skin was gray, their eyes blank portals of misty purple behind which all hope was lost, and many had developed grotesque lesions that made that man in the suit's burn scars much less shocking. They were all looking at her with vacuous expressions but obvious excitement as they simultaneously attempted to break free of the chains that shackled their arms to their machines and their legs to the floor. When they tried to move closer to her, the terrified prostitute could hear their rotting, yellow teeth clacking, chomping as if they were trying to eat the air.

Michael and Sven pulled her farther into the plant, amidst the stainless steel machines and the corpses manning them. She screamed again, beginning to kick and twist, but to no avail.

"Help me!" she shouted. "Please, somebody, somebody help me!"

"It's too late for you," Owens whispered into her ear as he pulled back her dirty hair from behind. "Your parasitic existence, feeding off the system will finally be put to use feeding someone else. You're all part of the food chain. See, these folks, they are above you, more useful. Their efforts here, they'll save the world."

The hooker screamed again, an aborted attempt at noise that was cut short by her own choked sobs.

"I've heard enough," Owens said as he shoved her shoulder blade and she lurched forward, falling to the floor.

She scrambled to try to stand up, but it was too late. The two zombies who were supposed to be bottling Owens's Be-Gone-Orrea had seized one of their rare opportunities for sustenance. They took advantage of the four feet of slack their chains afforded and jumped upon the young sex worker who could have so desperately used the pills they were packing. They bit the woman, ripping out large chunks of flesh with their decaying teeth. Had they still been able to think, they would have been surprised that their jaws, which were barely attached, had such strength that they could tear off her cheek in a single bite. They gnawed on her until the prostitute was merely a lump of bloody bones on the floor while the other zombies looked on with vapid expressions of envy.

The two corpses raised their heads, fresh blood dripping from their yellowed teeth, awaiting more—a dessert maybe.

Owens glanced down at the ravaged corpse on the white tiled floor and addressed Michael and Sven.

"Clean this mess up."

11:30 PM

To call Hank misanthropic would be an understatement. Hank hated everything. He hated people who used welfare cards to pay for frozen food. He hated whiteboy thugs who worshiped fictional Al Pacino characters and wore nightgown T-shirts and baggy male capris. He hated those Ugg boots and whatever Star Trek planet they came from. Every bespectacled male journalism student who read the *New Yorker* and used the word *pontificate*. He hated those lazy girls who pretend that their unshaven legs are a political statement rather than just a lack of effort. They were often the same girls who engaged in anti-establishment diatribes while in the middle of a swimming pool. He hated the red walls of the Male Box and the techno music screeching out of the archaic jukebox. He hated that no matter how many times he came to this place, they would always forget to freeze a bottle of Jim Beam for him. Shouldn't have been a problem, seeing as he was the only one who ever drank it. He hated that they stocked up on diet soda for the health-conscious clientele. He didn't believe in mixing drinking and dieting. He hated the stool pusher sitting next to him, even though Hank had fucked him last night.

The queer—Hank couldn't remember his name—kept smiling at him. It was definitely time to leave. Summer was gone, but it was still unseasonably warm, and there was a deliberate lack of air conditioning in the gay dive to facilitate a clothing-optional environment, leaving his Beam warm and unpleasant. But he had to come here. It was the only gay bar in the South Side. And the only one in the city that still allowed smoking. Hank rose from his seat, grabbing his half-full pack of Marlboro Reds from the bar. He threw a crumpled five-dollar bill on the worn surface that had once glittered as much as the fairies in the room, but now appeared to have reached the final stages of syphilis. Shoving the cigarettes into the pocket of his jeans, Hank saw the hopeful eyes of last night's stand on his right. Hank smirked, shook his head, and let out a breath of a laugh. *Dude*, he thought, *I'm not that desperate again.*

Hank hated just about everything, but he hated himself most of all. Gay—no, that was not something he ever wanted to be. And in his mind, he wasn't. He liked to think of himself as jailsexual, a prison homo. That's what his life had become: solitary confinement in his South Side dungeon. Maybe someday he wouldn't want to fuck men anymore, but today was not that day. Now, he was settled into this incarcerated existence dominated by the slave masters at work and the demands of his landlord and the utility companies. If he had the time, he would pursue writing dark, epic poetry and find another band, but he had become addicted to the call of happy hour. He had written several opuses in his head but had forgotten them by the time he was sober enough to type coherently. He was only 28, but he was already starting to forget all the plans he had made.

Pro-Well, where he slaved in anonymity from 9-to-5, had sucked his soul right out of his fingers as they typed inane technical copy for the regional pharmaceutical giant's website. So Hank felt that his bitterness had some justification. Yet he was not nearly as jaded as some of his co-workers. Judy came to mind, a vile specimen who took styling cues from Baby Jane Hudson and veritably hazed new employees. Hank prided himself on his ability to dole out his aggression in deliberate doses to those he deemed worthy of his sardonic rebuke: Politically oriented convenience store employees were a constant target. Judy was angry at time. Hank was angry at potholes, environmentalists, the *Twilight* saga, and Chesley Sullenberger. But right now, he directed his rage at Lady Gaga as she bragged about her poker face from the speakers. Whoever played this song had forfeited his right to have ears. Hank was never one for goodbyes, so he departed suddenly, leaving a bar of disappointed men in his wake. Only two days off a week and this is how he spent them. He would have kicked himself in the head, but he was not that flexible.

He pushed his stool in close to the bar, as was encouraged here, and walked across the hardwood floor of the Male Box to the exit—which also served as the only entry—in the rear of the members-only club. Shoving the door open, Hank inhaled the putrid sewage-filled air of the corner of Jane Street and 22nd. It was Saturday night, and he was dreading his imminent crossing of Carson Street. Through the throngs of collegiate sluts and all different colors of trash out for a night of booze sucking and ass grabbing. He lit a cigarette and commenced the short, yet mentally arduous journey home. The South Side housed an eclectic crowd; young trendies, octogenarian homeowners too stubborn to leave although their front steps were always drenched in vomit by the time they left for church on Sunday morning, and tattooed freaks of various musical persuasions. Yet they were all brought together by a mutual need to be in close proximity to enough alcohol to fill the neighboring Monongahela River and light it on fire. It was Mecca for those who knelt down three times a day facing the toilet, an area so self-assuredly festive that even the deaf sing karaoke. Indeed, Carson Street held a higher concentration of bars than Bourbon Street, and on any given night, each watering hole—from the glamorous to the grotesque—would house at least one man engaged in intense conversation with himself.

Taking 22nd Street, Hank arrived on Carson and spied the most detestable of all South Side rubbish: the parade of the fuck-o-lanterns, as he called them, the orange-complexioned sorority harlots in tight tops that boasted their unrepentant guts and short skirts that showed off their legs in the few years before cellulite and varicose veins crashed the party. The girls who'd already forgotten more in college than they'd learned. *Where was Ted Bundy when you needed him?* Hank asked himself. The girls could barely walk in those stilettos, and all five of them held little clutch purses. Hank hated those things. He'd carried way too many of those over the years. Karen, Julia, Angie, Jamie, Kayla—the list went on. Holding his girlfriends' purses had never made him feel sensitive or want to watch *Project Runway* or anything. It just made him feel more like the fag he always knew he was.

The fuck-o-lanterns stopped to pay a cover charge at one of the trendy nightspots that were popping up all over the area, contaminating Hank's pristine neighborhood, which was once filled only with tattoo parlors, dive bars, and old-man hangouts. Twenty-four-hour Sam's Diner was still intact, but it was littered with overgrown frat boys, jocks, people who felt an uncontrollable urge to sing Bon Jovi when they were drinking—the weekend warriors. Hank felt his war was waged every day. The food was greasy diner fare, and the waitresses were justifiably angry after being served more obscene pick-up lines in an evening than they doled out eggs. As he approached the pathetic neon lights of the diner, a group of jocks stumbled out of the glass doors.

"Yeah, I'll fucking kill you!" Striped Shirt yelled.

Yellow Polo responded, "With what? You've—you've got a butter knife!"

Hank didn't even care to stop this pollution of his streets. Let them carve each other up with their stolen cutlery, he thought. Survival of the fittest. He tried to walk by and ignore them, though he knew that, even if they were armed with unsharpened flatware stolen from the table, he could have taken either one of them out. He was a 6-foot-2 tattooed gay man who passed most of his time in rock n' roll dives. He knew how to fight. He was a bit of an anomaly in label-craving society, an enigma that no one really understood but everyone knew not to fuck with.

In one of the all-night diner's windows, a big white beard caught his eye. It was barely visible behind a veritable wall of grimy camouflage, green Mohawks, dirty spiked collars, and dreadlocks. The gutterpunks. They were still here in a seemingly endless summer of love-induced herpes to play one-string guitars and shout profanities at passersby who didn't honor their cardboard signs stating, "Need Money for Beer" and "Too Ugly to Work," giving it one last hurrah before hibernating in a squat for the winter. He hated these transients as much as he hated radio commercials with children's voices. One of the punks was wielding a small stuffed teddy bear clasping a red heart, a leftover from Valentine's Day sales. Hank pushed open the door, and a bell jangled and he entered the diner.

The walls of the all-night hangout had once been white but were now stained with coffee that had too often been liberated from porcelain prisons by some festive drunks. The place had a 1950s motif, with its confetti-patterned tables and sparkly red booths. Actually, now that Hank thought about it, it was more like a circus. But the animals on display were the customers, all barking and squawking and shoving food into their mouths without engaging in the civilized use of silverware. These creatures were out of control. He watched one particularly arrogant jock with a shaved head, pencil-thin goatee, and barbed-wire tattoo deliver an unnecessarily strong ass-smack to a waitress, causing her to drop a plate of nachos to the floor. Hank turned away from the mess of refried beans and gloating fraternity swine to concentrate on his original reason for entering this three-ring advertisement for temperance. He approached the table by the window where four bullet-belted, dirty junkies were hassling the General.

"What're you gonna do, Old Man? I've got your toys. I'll ransom 'em. Just give us your change and we'll be cool," a dirt-covered, dreadlocked squatter punk in a ragged Anti-Flag shirt demanded over the cacophonous noise of fifty ravenous drunks, waving the teddy bear in front of the General's emaciated Santa Claus visage.

"Hey, yeah. Okay," the General said in that strange drawl that could only be explained as totally fucking nuts.

Even through the thick, bright white beard, his lack of teeth was visible. He reached into his shirt pocket under the snipped pink carnation that he always kept pinned onto his black button-down. The flower was real, replaced on a semi-weekly basis with a fresher plant. The mystery of how he acquired the carnation only added to the enigma of the General, a riddle that no one really wanted to solve.

"Don't play their game, General," Hank barked from behind him.

The gutterpunks looked up at him, their stubble barely visible under the layer of filth that came with sleeping on the sidewalk in stark contrast to Hank's clean-shaven, Bruce Campbell-caliber chin.

"What the fuck you want?" the green Mohawk with the colony of eyebrow rings said through dirty lips and vivid white teeth.

"I want you to leave the man alone or I'll get the off-duty cop that's sitting at the counter to make sure you've gotta call your parents up at the country club to come down and post your bail."

Hank had struck a nerve. The dreadlocked one threw the Valentine's toy down on the table, and his filthy troops retreated from the General's table to resume their positions with the two pierced, hippie girls who looked like prime candidates for Manson Family recruitment on the other side of the room.

"Go back to your trust funds," Hank shouted to the table.

He had nothing but contempt for the spoiled 19-year-olds who lived on the streets while their rich parents pumped money into their bank accounts. And putting them in their place was liberating, a momentary escape from a life that Hank felt was becoming increasingly out of his control. Lately he'd begun to feel as inconsequential as a teleprompter to a blind man. Protecting the General was a mission to which Hank was deeply committed, even if it was just a way to alleviate the numbness. The elderly homeless man had never used the military to justify his madness. In fact, he had never claimed to have been in the armed forces, but because he sported a general's jacket he was called the General, for lack of a better name. Mostly he puttered away in anonymity while the more creative street schizophrenics cultivated bizarre identities. There was the bikini-clad transvestite in the ethnic grocery-filled Strip District, along with the mariachi maniac Sombrero Man in the student ghetto of Oakland, and, of course, the lost lady of Lawrenceville with a sunken face who stalked the artsy district's streets in a nightgown, searching for, well, no one was really sure what.

"Hank! Hey, yeah, hey. Thank you for saving my friends," said the General, holding up his bag of stuffed animals. "They are most grateful."

His white hair was cut even shorter than Hank's deep brown crop. An array of glow-in-the-dark, buy-by-the-gross party favors was strewn on the table, and a hot pink straw with an expandable pineapple was sticking out of his coffee mug. The General had been at the creatively named Bar, Hank thought, hitting on college girls again, trying to seduce them with stuffed animals. And if the overflowing grocery bag of plush was to be trusted, he hadn't done so well.

"Hey, General, let me walk you over to the Vets," Hank said, offering, as he always did, to escort the General to his favorite after-hours dive, the Scottish Vets, where the old man was safe.

He had made it a habit a few years ago to do so, every time he ran into the General, to avoid incidents like this. The General seemed to get his drinking money from disability or Social Security or some other government stipend and rode the buses all night to catch up on sleep. He was a staple of the neighborhood and added that eccentricity that had drawn Hank to the South Side in the first place.

The General had even been arrested a few months back for stalking Mario Lemieux's house to try to give the Penguins' owner advice on how to win hockey games. He was a colorful specimen, and Hank wanted to make sure that he stayed local for the entertainment value and for the opportunity to learn from a man who made his own strange way in life. Hank took the road less traveled to find that it was less traveled for a reason. The road that most people chose was a superhighway, complete with the flying cars that we've been promised since the '60s. But Hank's road was made of cobblestone, and it had a 25-mile-per-hour speed limit and some angry geriatric in golf pants with a radar gun yelling, "You're going too fast!" It was a one-way street that ended in a cul-de-sac where dreams went to slit their wrists.

"I, I've gotta get—where's the sexy young lady who was talking to me?" the General asked, his mad eyes searching the room.

"The waitress? I'll find her."

Hank headed towards the cash register, through the throng of sweaty young women, hungry after a night of dancing. Hank hated the dance clubs; to him they were the most egregious offense to the South Side, aside from the Cheesecake Factory, that haven for suburban parents to escape their Adderall-addled kids. He heard the weird voice behind him. And when he turned back to the table, he saw the General waving a pink stuffed rabbit with "I love you" embroidered on its chest.

"Hank, you—you're a very good man. You—you give this to your girlfriend."

11:49 PM

The members of the zombie chain gang did not have the same musical abilities as their enslaved predecessors. They expressed their melancholy in a chorus of groans and gurgles with all the enthusiasm of Eddie Vedder singing the list of side effects of the drugs the zombies were producing. Shackled to the stainless steel machinery of the Pro-Well Pharmaceutical plant, the slaves worked diligently, loading funnels with powder that would subsequently be compressed to pill form or loaded into capsules. The pristine white walls of the plant made even cannibal corpses seem monotonous, as they robotically repeated their actions day after flesh-hungry day. They sang the zombie blues. And it was a terrible song.

The chariot was swinging very low, but none of the zombies had a home to be carried to. They were vagrants, hobos, crazies, drug-addicted dregs, the forgotten residents of the city's irritable bowels. Some of the more confused derelicts had thought that a band of angels had already come for them when they were swept off the streets and into the clean white rooms of the Pro-Well Pharmaceutical plant. It wasn't heaven, but after the injection killed their minds and left them only as semi-functional shells of what they once were, it wasn't Hell either. Even if the afterlife for the damned was on fire as so many sources suggest, it wouldn't matter because a zombie cannot feel any pain. Indeed, several had failed to notice when a limb was torn off after being stuck in one of the dangerous industrial devices, like a door. What this place was, was purgatory. A state of limbo between life and death, with a bit of ravenous canni-balism thrown in for entertainment. So they couldn't mourn, they couldn't grieve, and they certainly could not sing. Instead, they came up with a chorus of monotonous groaning that, lay-ered atop the soft hum of the stainless steel machines, was not unlike the buzz of a vuvuzela philharmonic.

And it was eerily reminiscent of the solemn hymns sung by the choir in the church that the guard on duty, Stan, had once presided over.

Stan was growing accustomed to the sight of ravaged, dead human flesh sporting hospital scrubs, manning millions of dollars worth of bottling, packaging, and encapsulating equipment. During his years in the seminary, he'd fancied himself as a Mother Teresa figure, helping lepers all over the world. He planned to teach them to embrace their conditions, to accept Jesus Christ as their personal lord and savior, and to go on the inevitable reality competition in which the acolytes were all tempted by their former vices. He didn't think he'd have that much luck with the workers. Though they were technically dead, they were still moving, still working, without a pulse or a heartbeat or a single brainwave except for the impulse to feed. And that was the part that truly bothered Stan. Though the lepers could leave a trail of body parts in the sand, the others would not pick them up for dinner. But monitoring the zombies had really helped him keep the vow of chastity he'd re-sworn after the indictment.

Stan paced through the factory, careful to keep in the exact center of the rows between the lines of machines. In a manner that seemed as routine and predictable as their work, the zom-bies turned one by one to Stan, growling and flailing and biting the air as he passed. But chained to their machines, the fam-ished sort-of-dead hobos were unable to satisfy their hunger for the pederast priest, and as soon as he was far enough away that the few feet of slack their chains afforded them could not put them in striking distance, they returned to their tasks.

So they continued their wordless chant. They weren't asking for wages, benefits, approved overtime, vacation days. Just food.

Even if they had the brainpower to organize a strike, management could have easily swept up some new desperate vagrants and turned them into scabs with the prick of a hypodermic needle.

Sunday
2:30 AM

The General stumbled out of the Scottish Vets. He hadn't been there for too long and didn't really want to be in the bar anyway. That nice kid Hank had insisted on taking him. But the General was bored. Maybe he should go to the convenience store up the street. He should write another letter to Sidney Crosby to tell him that they need to use the goalie as a walking battering ram. That's how teams win playoffs. Or that Russian could hide the puck in his pads and slide into the opposing goal. *Those commies sure are a devious people*, he thought.

So the General formulated his plan. He'd go to the 24-hour convenience store up the street. It would surely have pens and paper, and he'd hand deliver the note to Sid tomorrow. Though everyone told him that the drunken mandolin player who lived above the Starbucks was not in fact the hockey star, the General would not believe their lies and decided to slip the note through his mail slot tomorrow.

He was so excited about drafting his battle plan that he stepped out onto the dark alley without looking. For a man who spent so much time on the city streets, he should have known better. To street people, being a bad pedestrian was suicide. Statistically speaking, he had used up his "Get Out From Under a Bus Free" cards a long time ago.

A black van slammed on the brakes and swerved to the left to avoid hitting the General. Startled, he dropped the bag of plushies. Kneeling down to pick it up from the gutter, the General felt a force on his shoulder blades that shoved him into the back of the van.

3:30 AM

Janice, aka Lucretia McNightmare, was out later than she'd planned, but she felt the morose bar crawl was necessary for a true creature of the night. Not to mention that she was starting a new job on Monday, and that would effectively put an end— or a momentary pause—to Wednesday-night tributes to The Cure. Maybe. After all, the job was mindless, one of those corporate gigs that were popping up with regularity on Craig's List. Data entry, spreadsheets, something like that. The kind of job that is the complete antithesis of the punk rock ideology she once believed in. But what other choices did she have? As a 24-year-old newly anointed Goth with a sociology degree, she didn't have too many options in recession-era Pittsburgh. Pro-Well Pharmaceuticals seemed to virtually own the town these days, and having enough job security to save up for her burial plans was the top priority.

But right now, it was getting down the relatively quiet Carson Street at 3:30 a.m. without incident. This place was packed with freaks when the sun was out, and now all the strange night prowlers were around. She was one of them, sort of. Well, not really. She had a college degree and came from an upper-middle-class traditional nuclear family, but she had always been drawn to the lunatic fringe. Ever since sophomore year of high school when she'd discovered electronic music and parachute pants, she had been adopting a new identity every six months or so in a different subculture. In the past three years, she'd been a hippie, a mod, a political punk, a raver, a rockabilly pin-up type, and now a Gothic princess. She pulled a clove cigarette from the pack in her vinyl, bat-shaped purse that held black liquid eyeliner, crimson lipstick, and a leather-bound copy of an Edgar Allan Poe anthology—essentials for a night on the town.

She approached the Subway—closed since midnight—as a bearded legless man in a wheelchair lingered in front with a paper soda cup in such disrepair that she presumed he bought it sometime around the Korean War. And she knew, even before he glanced in her direction, that he was going to speak to her. She was always the target of this. Why did her knee-high platform boots that laced up the sides, fishnet stockings, and long black fingernails with spider web decals always attract the complete nutjobs?

"Hey, sweetie," the presumably psychotic war vet called as she approached the gated storefront. She tried to ignore him. She was numb to South Side plight. She'd been broke with no hope of salvation for months before landing this daylight job, her dreams of ordering absinthe from Europe to sip in the cemetery put on the back burner.

"Hey, sweetheart, let me get some of that smoke!" the legless bum demanded. She kept walking. "Oh, come on. I'm dying here," he pleaded as he started to wheel after her.

"Leave me alone," she said to her unlikely pursuer. Quickening her pace, she continued on her way home. She only had a few blocks to go, and her gait was much larger with 5 inches of platform added to her 5-foot-3 frame.

"Give me some of that smoke!" came the undeniably deranged voice behind her. "I'll chase you for it!"

She heard the wheels of the archaic chair squeal as her legless hunter gained upon her rapid footsteps. She turned around.

"Seriously, leave me the fuck alone!"

But he kept coming, at Special Olympics gold-medal speed, when suddenly a white van swung into the empty metered space a few steps ahead of where she was standing. The legless nicotine addict's wheels stopped spinning as two young men in black suits stepped out of the vehicle. *Jesus*, she thought, *if they had sunglasses, they'd look like the Men in Black.* UFO cover-up officials *and* South Side bum exterminators? If this were the case, they would effectively cleanse the world of all its most colorful elements.

"Is everything all right here?" asked the tall suited man with his brown hair pulled back into one of those short, sleazy bail-bondsman ponytails.

"Fine," Janice said to the mysterious knights in the white Ford Aerostar. "This guy wants a cigarette."

She turned and continued her walk down Carson Street, keeping the brisk pace she'd started during the surreal pursuit. If a crazed, crippled amputee could put up that kind of chase, she would stand no chance against an able-bodied rapist. She should arm herself with a dagger, a crucifix, silver bullets—and even a Supersoaker in case she encountered the witch from *The Wizard of Oz*. She didn't turn around until she reached her small apartment three blocks away on the alley behind Carson Street.

But if she had just glanced back, she would have seen the sleaze with the ponytail and his blond crew-cut cohort tossing the bearded paraplegic into the back of the white van and driving off, leaving the wheelchair and aged soda cup like a foreboding omen for nicotine fiends to come.

5 AM

The clean-up crew had hit the South Side tonight, so this batch was quite colorful. The new guys they assembled were a particularly disparate, depraved display of degenerates. The hungry, the sick, the huddled masses of bums shuffled into the clean, white room hidden in the Pro-Well factory building in shackles, their hands and feet chained. But they weren't convicts; they were recruits. Or at least that's how he saw it. He, Marshall Owens, CEO of Pro-Well Pharmaceuticals, could see things however he wanted to and that would be the reality. That's what people would believe. Though he was in the business of health and wellness, he was more a doctor of spin than of medicine.

He stood atop a podium in a white lab coat, gazing down upon his recruits and his loyal procurers. Owens chose to believe that he was cleaning the streets, bringing back a sense of decency to the city while creating a viable workforce composed of men and women who would never have the self-discipline to work otherwise. It was like mandatory volunteering, like the charity drives he enforced in the office, forcing dregs to give back to the community they had been swindling for years with cardboard pleas. The parasites were finally helping society.

That's how he wanted his men to see it. For he'd delivered the same speech when he liberated them from the halfway house seven months ago. Second chances: That's what Marshall Owens was about. He wasn't sure if his men actually bought his rhetoric of reinvention, but their designer suits and hefty paychecks kept them happy and out of the criminal underworld. Just as he did with the drugs he manufactured at Pro-Well, Owens kept dangerous conditions from wreaking havoc. They were cured, at least until their prescriptions expired. Money was the true tool in creating a clockwork orange.

But Owens truly believed his own hype. He believed in hard work and advancing the human race with his products. He believed that the only way to create better pharmaceuticals was through intense experimentation. These recruits were the ideal specimens.

In his white coat, he stared down upon the newbies, a bizarre collection of dregs from the bowels of the city's drinking district. Bars outnumbered churches at a 12-to-1 ratio in the South Side, making the residents Dionysian revelers who never paid penance for their nightly sins. The recruits should have been flushed down the toilet with the rest of the vomit years ago, but they kept hanging on, stuck to the pipes like cooking grease. They wouldn't be driven away by gentrification and college students insensitive to the plight of the shell-shocked veteran who denounced his possessions during the Reagan administration to take on the image and persona of a mariachi musician with no band. Yet somehow, recently, after the shattered Yuengling bottles were washed away by the stream of public urination and the youth had returned to their crumbling apartments for nights of fumbling VD Russian roulette, the street urchins always wound up here.

Owens pointed to the gagged punk with the green Mohawk.

"Work," he stated calmly, and the dirty freak was ushered to the right.

The girl in the tie-dye with the dreadlocks shuffled forward.

"Work," he commanded, and his faithful servant Eric the online predator lecherously groped her exposed shoulder blades as he pushed her behind her green-haired friend.

"Fuck you! What the fuck are you doing to us! I'll call the—"

Her shouting was cut off by a leering, lip-licking Eric throwing a gag over her mouth. *Foul-mouthed and a parasite,* Owens thought. *Well she'll be silent evermore.* Her last words: He was almost curious how they would continue. Who was she planning to call? The police? That's what they usually say. And she didn't seem very creative. He had already amassed many of the young neon-haired specimens with the metal bolts through their faces. Travelers, mooching spare change off the citizens who had forgotten how to just say no. Transients were the ideal lab rats as their whereabouts were usually unknown and families failed to notice exactly how long they'd been gone. Drifters who floated from town to town, the young waifs whose fraudulent plight made them invisible to both the cause champions and the pitiless majority. And they were all so young and sturdy from walking. Once their dissension left when their minds did, they were the ideal workers.

Harold, the muscle-bound former crack dealer and current personal bodyguard, pushed another towards his podium—an older one with long thinning hair and tattered sweat pants. He looked like the type who feasted on garbage.

"Work."

Simon—whose rap sheet included extortion, racketeering, money laundering, and for some reason exposing himself at a Lane Bryant—carried the next one. A filthy creature with the grooming habits of a caveman and stumps where his knees used to be. Simon held him by the forearms as far as possible from his perfectly pressed suit. *Smart man. Style is important,* Owens thought. He eyed the specimen and chortled.

"Food."

Simon smiled and carried the subject to the left, so poised his shiny ponytail didn't even bob.

Owens enjoyed this part of the process. He liked being involved with the entire creation. His life's work. He had read somewhere that Josef Mengele used to stand on a platform in his white coat and point to the new arrivals, making a momentary decision of who goes to work and who goes directly to the showers. The Jews called him the Angel of Death. From their vantage point, that's what he was. But to Owens, he was a visionary, sacrificing the dregs for the greater good, for science. And Owens didn't kill anyone. At least, not directly. He gave the workers an altered state of existence that would transform them into productive members of society for the first time in their freeloading lives. He respected the military history of many to a degree, but thought that two tours in Vietnam did not offset the damage they'd wreaked upon society in the decades since the war. So they were repurposed as soldiers who would fight in his army, battling 24-7 the pesky ailments that plagued modern man.

The flesh-eating part was an unwanted side effect.

Sven, the giant of a white supremacist with rhetoric that could easily be silenced by the dollar, pushed the next specimen into the line. This one was older, frail, clearly unhinged. He wore an officer's coat over a button-down black shirt and black pants. Though his beard engulfed his neck and most of his face, his hair was cropped and combed. His dress was eccentric but clean, and he even wore a pink carnation pinned to his lapel. The man smiled at him, a giant toothless grin that denoted that he had no idea what was going on. Owens thought about this one. What to do with this supremely strange case?

"Work," he commanded from above.

Owens watched in awe as the General saluted him repeatedly, his hand jutting back and forth, smacking his own forehead as Sven pushed him to the right.

He was old and beaten down and obviously completely deranged, but Owens had a bit of esteem for this clean old bum. He would be a decent slave. And the workers really didn't need to eat that much anyway.

He was running low on laborers. He'd hit the jackpot last year when Pittsburgh hosted the G-20 summit, a gathering of the president and 20 international dignitaries, thus bringing all sorts of anarchic riff-raff to the fair city. Professional protesters who made their sub-living suing for police brutality had flooded the area to smash bank windows and object to everything from conditions in Darfur to the morning-after pill. All Owens had to do was send some of his henchmen down to their illegal tent colonies by the river before the police arrived and lure as many as possible into the vans. But working in a chain gang to operate the complex machinery of the pharmaceutical plant, eating only one hooker or war vet a night among the roughly 45 currently in his employ, the recruits did not live very long. Once a week, his men went on a collection run and brought them here to be injected with a virus that stopped their hearts and their minds but kept their bodies alive on the most basic level. Owens had pioneered this revolutionary science in the privacy of his lab, knowing that although most people would approve of his practice of cleaning up the streets and re-purposing some of society's most annoying members, the world would not be able to accept the reality of it.

The drug wreaked havoc on their skin, giving them grotesque gray complexions when the blood stopped flowing through their veins. They developed lesions, and their gums immediately contracted an advanced case of gingivitis and re-tracted from their quickly rotting teeth. Their appearances boasted the worst physical effects of leprosy, psoriasis, AIDS, and syphilis. Their skin scabbed and had a tendency to fall onto the polished white tiled floors of the plant. With their minds unable to formulate words, the workers could only make invol-untary guttural gurgles and groans that escaped from their ever gaping mouths. They moved with painful unease, like the small bit left of their minds was trying to recall how to walk. Owens was able to deal with their terrifying appearances because his scarred visage was not particularly pleasing and his troops were not new to inflicting disfiguring injuries.

Even Owens found the flesh eating pretty disturbing. But with any novel technology, there were glitches. He'd heard that the Haitians had been doing something similar for centuries, but he was a man of science, not voodoo.

7:28 PM

Hank didn't believe in celebrating Sundays. He didn't pray. He certainly wasn't pious. He believed in whiskey. Good whiskey. And that since Sunday was just another day of the week to him, he felt it was appropriate to start drinking good whiskey at 4 p.m., an hour earlier than his usual starting time because it was his weekend, damn it!

The other Bat Cave patrons didn't believe in Sundays either. At least not the seven who were there. But they didn't seem to believe in anything, least of all moderation. Hank did believe in self-control, especially before the sun went down. He ignored the other alcohol zealots—the leprechaun shouting obscenities at his fat girlfriend, the skinny cokefiend spewing misinformation to any listening—preferably female—ear like the two Match.com applicants sitting next to him who checked Hank out from time to time. He laughed it off with disdain.

Hank was a mystery at this bar, a quiet, sullen creature with striking musculature that denoted a lack of dependence on Pabst Blue Ribbon. The girls wanted him. They looked at him with those pathetic coquettish glances when he came down for happy hour three times a week. Sometimes they tried to talk to him. That was even worse. He hated those conversations, no matter how brief he made them. He wasn't ready to deal with female bullshit again. Especially not from Bat mattresses like those two. He'd rather enlist in the Kiss Army.

"Excuse me," said a voice behind him.

Hank turned to see what appeared to be five strippers. *Great, their day off.*

"Could you move over to the end of the bar, so all of us can sit next to each other," the short one in the stilettos demanded. Apparently she'd forgotten how to be nice when people weren't shoving one-dollar bills in her thong.

Calmly, Hank replied, "No."

"Why not?" asked the abrasive Amazon with the Betty Page bangs and the tube top.

"Because if I move, I can't see the TV."

"Come on. Please." The drugged-out blonde was trying her hardest to be cute. "What's your name?"

"Rosa fucking Parks. I'm not moving." Hank was particularly proud of this response and turned back to his drink.

So he concentrated on the television. Hank didn't believe in paying for cable, so he made sure to catch up on all the bad programming he was missing during his Cave visits. The Discovery channel was airing yet another special on shit-cleaners. On Thursday, it was reusable diaper washers. Today the host was shadowing guys who clean out yacht toilets. It must be the cruise buffets that made it look like that.

"Does it strike anyone else as odd that you can't say 'shit' on TV, but they can literally show it?" Hank asked no one in particular.

"Are you objecting to our entertainment selection, Hank?" asked Danny, the smartass bartender with the horror movie tattoos and ear gauges.

"Nope, just remarking on the paradox. I enjoy feces as much as the next guy."

"Oh, I know you do," Danny said with a wink in his best gay voice.

Hank laughed. He had no choice really, as he had set himself up for that one. There were only two people who could zing Hank: Danny and his pal Pete at work, who asked Hank if he needed to sit on a doughnut when he stumbled to his desk the Tuesday after Labor Day weekend. Danny, a fellow South

Sider, had often asked Hank pointed questions about the Male Box. Did it have a rear entry? Were the floors hard wood? Was there a special on cocktails? Reluctantly, Hank answered "yes" to each inquiry.

Danny started scrolling through the channels. Hank had always found the television selection amusing here. Surrounded by horror movie masks, autographed 8x10s of obscure scream queens, and the tattooed patrons, Hank found the animal and educational TV shows ironic. Danny stopped scrolling when he reached a newscast with the South Side in the background. Like Hank, he took much pride in his neighborhood.

And there it was: the egg carton as Hank called it, where employees were trapped in singular cages until they finally cracked. His office, the corporate headquarters of Pro-Well Pharmaceuticals. And there he was: the Penguin. Or the Joker, the Riddler maybe. All he knew was that the man was like a Batman villain, a disfigured power-mad freak hiding behind the guise of community revitalization. Two-Face was probably the name he was looking for, but Hank hadn't read enough comic books to get it right. The third-degree burn scars on the left side of Owens's face were what made him such a caricature of evil. And he always wore long sleeves and gloves, so anyone could ascertain that his face was not the only part exposed to the flame. He often carried a walking stick, like some dandy from days past. If he sported a monocle, he'd look like a grotesque Mr. Peanut. Those thoughts kept Hank from embarking on a Morningstar-wielding rampage even through downsizing, inquisitions, pay cuts, and the secret police that masqueraded as middle management.

Owens was speaking on the newscast, empty words spewing from his twisted, charred lips about how much money he had raised to combat cystic fibrosis. The fundraising just happened to coincide with the release of Pro-Well's new wonder drug that combined all the lung disease antibiotics into one, easy-to-swallow pill. The list of side effects made up half the copy that Hank wrote for the website.

"We're a long way from eradiating CF from the human genome, but we hope that this antibiotic will aid the day-to-day lives of all those afflicted with the disease. And with the $300,000 that we have raised in the past year, the Pro-Well labs will be hard at work developing a cure for this terminal condition. Imagine a warrant issued for your death on the day you were born. We cannot live in a society where murderers appeal their death sentences for decades and 20-year-old innocents are dropping dead all around us. The least we can do is ease their symptoms before the end," Owens told the reporter.

He was so rehearsed, so transparent that you could see the bullshit that coursed through his respiratory system, Hank thought. *How did no one else see him for the conniving businessman that he was? Were the Pittsburgh news media so desperate for a positive story that they'd spin this comic-book bad guy of a sanctioned drug dealer as a pillar of virtue? Had he pioneered a cosmetic powder that, when applied to the cheekbones worked its way into the cerebral cortex and controlled the mind?* For a moment, Hank found that a feasible explanation of this disfigured prodigy's success as a society darling à la the Elephant Man. Hank had never met the man, never stared the devil in the face as he liked to think of it, but he despised the deplorable office conditions endured by the employees while Marshall Owens paraded himself as a hero all over the 6 o'clock news.

Of course, Hank didn't know the half of it.

As a man of 28 living with an un-diagnosed, unmedicated case of severe obsessive-compulsive disorder, Hank had no sympathy for the masses dependent on Pro-Well's arsenal of prescription drugs. Among his many irrational phobias was the notion that if he did swallow a cure for his ailment, he'd grow forgetful and leave the coffee maker on one day. And when he returned from work to the scorched remains of all his earthly belongings, he'd have a real reason to check the "on" button, and the cycle would begin again, but he wouldn't have any stuff.

"How did the company raise the money?" the blonde journalist asked.

"It was through the generosity of the employees at the Pro-Well office and the production factory. It's not just the CEO of the company: Everyone at Pro-Well Pharmaceuticals, from the lab tech to the receptionist to the factory foreman, is deeply committed to finding a cure for this genetic disorder that claims lives far too early." He repeated the company name as if he was optimizing the broadcast's transcript for search engines—part of Hank's job.

If Hank had had a glass to slam on the bar, he would have done so in outrage. But Danny was refilling his whiskey, so, as always, he settled for a mere snarl at the TV. Hank was enraged. The "generous donations" were, in fact, mandatory. Every Friday, one dollar to the cause. In past years, the charity had changed every month, but Owens had been on this cystic fibrosis kick for a while now. Hank had tried to refuse to give to several charities, like the anti-rape fund, but Pro-Well just docked his pay instead, and he had created a fuss for no reason. It was difficult to argue that donations to charitable causes should never be mandatory. The women in the office were not pleased when he suggested that many employees may be pro-rape and thus should not be forced to compromise their beliefs. But now he had given up the fight, become a reluctant pseudo-philanthropist for a disease he knew nothing about. With each dollar bill he placed in team lead Wilbert's collection jar, he felt a bit of himself slipping away, his dissension all for naught.

Early in his stint at Pro-Well, Hank had launched into a vitriolic rant about the several company policies, particularly the so-called "team building" activities. He has been particularly bothered by an office cupcake contest that required the employees to purchase the ingredients on their dime and bake them on their time. Yet it provided a fun respite from the daily tedium of office life and the frosting-covered employees failed to notice that optical coverage. Hank, of course, saw this activity as the corporate soma that it was. The brave new drug, oddly enough, was one of the only medications that Pro-Well did not produce. But the parties and the mid-day charades breaks had the same lulling function in their ability to distract the employees from how painfully they were being screwed by the company. But now, his outrage melted to apathy then compliance and his fighting words turned into snide, mumbled comments.

"Can you get rid of this jackass?" Hank demanded.

"What, you don't like him either? Jesus, Hank you're really hard to please," Danny said, smiling.

"Turn the shit channel back on. I don't care."

But Hank lost interest immediately when he felt a soft hand and acrylic nail touch his right bicep. He whirled his head around to see the deranged smile of the terrifying Julie who'd been coming to the bar on a fairly regular basis. She had a tendency to get touchy. Hank hated that the way he hated flight attendants.

"What's the story behind this?" she asked, running her fake nails up and down the giant medieval scene in red and black ink emblazoned on Hank's toned arm.

"Birthmark," he said. And he returned to his beer.

Actually there was a story behind Hank's tattoos. He just preferred not to think about it because it signified his self-betrayal. While in college, Hank had begun collecting body art the way other students amassed road signs. It was supposed to remove his options, to veritably brand him unemployable in the vast corporate wasteland that was the modern workforce. His arms, legs, and back displayed a painful and expensive collection of reminders to never give up. He was a veritable bulletin board of motivation to succeed outside of the standard paths. Unfortunately, the extensive tattoos that were supposed to mark him as an unacceptable candidate for a job had backfired. Too many people of his generation had the same idea. His look was no more extreme than anyone else's. So he let himself forget their original meaning, let his hidden disappointment manifest itself in clever insults to strangers while every day the reasons for his body modification disappeared further and further into the abyss of denial.

If he hadn't blocked all that out with years of numbing 9-to-5 monotony, he would have recited his entire diatribe of angry self-loathing to Mrs. McFeely, but it was buried deep in his sub-conscious and it would take some serious excavating to remember who he had wanted to be before he let his rage define him.

7:45 PM

The abductions were taking their toll on Paul. It was one thing to clean the streets and procure cheap labor, but the grotesque mutations the recruits became once they left his hands…well, that was something else entirely. He felt like a naive SS officer, rounding up Jews to go take a shower, un-aware that they would be bathed in gas.

Being a man in black had its perks. The pay was good. The suits were cool. But the kidnappings—those he just couldn't take. He wasn't like the rapists and drug lords who made up the majority of Owens's team, just a simple drunk who had a few too many and went a bit too far with a girl who was a little too young. Haunted by remorse and humiliation, Paul was on a constant quest for his Holy Grail of atonement, but finding legitimate work was difficult for a convicted sex offender. So once again, he found himself locked in the same tireless pattern of sober self-hatred and boozy self-destruction. He'd done his four years, attended prison mass, prayed, bulked up in the gym to pass the time, and become a zealous 12-stepper. Plus, he had managed to stay away from the bottle in the eight months since his release. But he was having some trouble adjusting to what was happening to the men and women he captured.

The boss said he didn't kill them, but Paul had finagled his way into the factory a few weeks ago to see his captives hard at work, contributing to society, or so he was told. In the pro-duction room, he witnessed fifty men, women, and children chained together and to the machines, enslaved by their duties and their ghastly appearances. Paul recognized several that he had brought into this Hell. They looked cleaner now, sanitized, their grubby street clothes replaced with hospital scrubs, but their skin was rotting and covered in lesions. Several were missing various body parts from factory accidents that their destroyed minds had rendered them unable to avoid. They were covered in blood, and often bones were exposed, yet they emitted a distinct lemon scent above the unmistakable smell of death. And they were still working. They groaned a bit, but other than that the only noise in the room was the soft hum of the machines. The creatures' movements were slow and awkward, but mechanical and efficient. Then Paul moved closer, and the slaves became distracted, staring at him and trying to pull their restraints out to approach.

They must have exceptional senses of smell and hearing because no one could possibly see with those milky purple eyes, Paul had thought. The groaning increased when he grew near. Paul didn't know how he sensed it, but he knew they were hungry. And that it was time to flee.

That was when he first felt like the Grim Reaper who ushered these poor dregs to what appeared to be living death. Some of the recruits were angry when he pulled them off the streets and shoved them into the van, but many were hopeful, and those were the worst. Those were the ones who drove him back to his old home at the end of the bar.

Paul took another swig of Wild Turkey and flicked the empty rocks glass towards the bartender. His first drinks since being put behind bars were just as easy going down as they had always been. Now he needed his old liquid friend more than ever. While the bartender poured his drink, Paul looked around the bar. He didn't want to appear too anxious. The place was a dive that had become trendy in the same ironic way as Pabst Blue Ribbon and William Shatner, and the crowd reflected that, composed mostly of young, thin twenty-somethings who put forth a concerted effort to make their appearances seem effortless. Then, almost hidden behind two tall shaggy-haired indie rockers, stood an old man with a bushy white beard in a dark suit. Paul blinked, clearing his blurry eyes. *No, it couldn't be*, he thought. He blinked again and squinted to see the debonair elderly gentleman, beaming in apparently humor-filled conversation with the younger men.

Paul knew it couldn't have been him. He knew that the man with the latter-day Jerry Garcia beard and the flower pinned to his lapel, as if he was going to some geriatric prom, had met the same fate as the rest. But Paul hoped that wasn't the case. Of all the abductees, that one had been the hardest to watch as he was taken to the injection room. How he smiled and saluted and was so unaware of his impending doom. After years of living on the streets, not a tooth left in his mouth, and yet the man had still dressed to the best of his limited ability and hadn't let cynicism cleanse him of the hope that something better was coming, only to be led to that factory manned by the blind dead. Paul blinked again at the well-dressed senior at the other end of the bar and watched his white teeth sparkling as he joked with the patrons who were young enough to be his grandchildren. Paul shook his head, realizing that the booze must be making him imagine things. He did not have the same tolerance as he did prior to his prison term.

The middle-aged bartender, who looked as if she needed a drink more than most of the customers, shoved another bourbon on the rocks towards Paul. His tie was loose and his sunglasses broken. He gulped down the acrid liquor, coughed, and smiled. It was after that ninth double shot, when his cheeks were flushed and his teary eyes seemed to see more clearly, that he knew exactly what he needed to do. It was time for Paul, the man in black, the bearer of bad tidings, the abductor of the weak, the accidental statutory rapist, to be a hero.

7:53 PM

The urge to flee hit Hank suddenly.

They entered the bar in a parade of slow-moving slaves to

Sundays, passing by his stool, slight groans escaping from their gaping mouths. All their faces held the same vapid expression, a vacant look focused above the bar.

Steelers fans.

It was less than an hour until game time, so Hank quickly gulped down the rest of his whiskey and coke and slammed the glass on the bar. It was definitely time to go home. This was just the kind of motivation Hank needed. If he was constantly followed by inebriated Steelers fans, their presence would surely force Hank to leave his mundane job and get the hell out of the Male Box before he let another one of those clingy hopefuls into his life.

Several jersey-clad gents swarmed around the bar patrons, their hungry gaze moving between the pre-game commentary on the flat screen and the beer taps beneath it. He never understood the need that grown men felt to wear jerseys on game day. Did they really believe that just because Troy Polomalu's knee was sore, that the Steelers would decide to spontaneously draft a random yokel so they could save money on a uniform? Or was it some latent super hero worship? Were the James Harrison fans accountants by day and crime-fighting linebackers by night?

They seized the bar every Sunday, a throng of perennial spectators ready to shout and imbibe, win or lose. Hank didn't understand the phenomenon, but he knew that when game time approached, escape was an order.

The Yinzers—an inclusive regional group to which most native Steelers fans held lifetime memberships—were a specific breed who earned their name from an inexplicable penchant for using the term "yinz" as Pittsburgh's unfortunate answer to the South's "y'all." Blue-collar beer drinkers who worked as hard and they drank, lived for the simple pleasures and were indigenous to Western Pennsylvania. Their accents were something between a twang and a drawl with a tendency to incorporate completely fabricated expressions, like referring to bologna sandwiches as "jumbos," assholes as "jagoffs," and shopping carts as "buggies." After six years in the city, Hank still had not learned what exactly a "jaggerbush" was.

They ate fries on sandwiches and salads and seemed intent on eradicating the phrase "to be" from the English lexicon. If it were up to them, Hank thought, that famous Hamlet line would just be "or not." Their faded jeans were often covered with house paint, they weren't the strongest in dental hygiene, and they possessed the most rural accents and attitudes ever found in an urban area. They had a general code of honor, decrying the violent antics of the Philadelphia Flyers, and though they had fallen under the Pro-spell of Marshall Owens, they oddly could not be bamboozled by most politicians. And while the people of Washington, D.C., voted to memorialize Marion Barry in wax, the Yinzers found it difficult to forgive a Steelers kicker for his involvement in a drunken altercation with a paper towel dispenser. They were mostly quite harmless, happy, and honest. But the most stunning aspect was their unflappable pride in their oft-lampooned collective identity.

Hank was waiting for the day when a comedian would come on stage with "You know you're a Yinzer when..." lines. Though it would be wildly popular in the greater Pittsburgh area, Hank thought that this comic would be more of a niche phenomenon among Western Pennsylvanians who possessed an adept understanding of the obvious. Hank worked with a particularly representative member of the group: Myron the maintenance guy, a cheerful sixty-something with the volume of a Spinal Tap concert. He fit the profile perfectly. He believed a trip south of the Mason-Dixon line was exotic travel; held the same blue-collar job for ten years; was overly talkative about anything related to the Stillers, Pens, Buccos (as the locals referred to their pro sports teams) and practically the definition of office TMI; and was honest, nice, and really fucking annoying. A decent guy with a fat wife and a couple of grown kids who couldn't help but tell everyone else about what he perceived to be the most pressing issues of the century: the Steelers' offensive line, Port Authority budget cuts, and these kids today with their baggy pants. But overall, Myron was not the worst of the Yinzers that Hank had encountered since he'd migrated from the greater D.C. area six years ago.

Hank pushed his way out of the bar and into the chilly autumn street. The unpredictable Pittsburgh temperature had dropped significantly since yesterday, and it was finally starting to feel like Halloween season. Cars full of black and gold, waving Terrible Towels passed as he walked towards home. Hank stepped into the street, ready to cross Carson when a car flew past him.

"Watch it! Son of a douche," Hank shouted. He really hated drivers.

The not-so-slick black Cadillac raced down the road, only to slam on the brakes as a veritable Pittsburgh pride parade sauntered to Luigi's Bar.

After successfully crossing the street, Hank walked a block before unlocking his front door and entered his small, basement apartment. He pulled the door shut, locked it, and tried to turn the knob several times just to be sure. He'd check another five times before he went to bed. This was his fortress where he could shield himself from the inane babbling of Ben Roethlisberger enthusiasts and whatever mind-altered freaks he might encounter in the depraved South Side streets.

It was also where he kept his arsenal. In the past year, Hank had amassed an impressive, and quite unnecessary, collection of archaic weapons: a Morningstar, a flail, a mace, a bayonet, a crossbow, and several types of European swords, including a Claymore, an Estoc, a Karabela, and a Zweihänder. He kept the swords leaning against the brick walls of his living room and hung the flails from the speakers of his massive stereo system. One of the treasures was his 5-foot-tall suit of armor that guarded the kitchen doorway. The armor was thin, rusty, and far too small for his 6-foot-2 frame. Ideally, he would like to have a suit of armor that he could wear when the mood was right and there was a kingdom to defend, but this was in his price range and would have to function for now as decorative rather than utilitarian. He wasn't entirely sure why he needed his armory, but once he'd started the collection, he was unable to control his purchasing when, in fact, he found himself at a 14th-century vassal's garage sale. He'd never actually used any of the weapons, but he felt better, though not necessarily safer, about having them in his home. Who knows, there could be a time when he would have to slay those who threatened his neighborhood.

8:30 PM

Paul's dramatic race to the plant was not going so well. Had he been an actual hero, he would not have had to stop for the gaggle of Steelers fans, nor that old man bent to nearly a right angle. He would have flown right over the football enthusiasts, his cape flapping in the wind, and he would have straightened the old man's back along the way. His arrival at the Pro-Well factory would have been swift and without potholes. But Paul was not a hero, merely a drunken accidental hitman with a latent conscience. He arrived at the factory, his face flushed and his brain throbbing. The alcohol probably also contributed to the bumpy mission.

His hand clutching the work-issued gun on his hip, Paul walked through the gravel parking lot to the large factory with smoke rising from it in a reminder of Pittsburgh's old steel mill days. With all the money that Pro-Well grossed a year, he never understood why the parking lot had not been paved. Moving swiftly towards the large metal doors, Paul felt that he was regaining the dramatic edge that this magnificent rescue so desperately needed.

He slammed his free hand against the door and tripped backwards. *Damn.* He had forgotten that it was locked. He had usually been to the factory for recruiting nights, but Owens always insisted on Sundays off for religious reasons. That religion being the regional favorite: football. Second only to Mario

Lemieux, Marshall Owens was the pride of Pittsburgh, so he needed Pittsburgh to know that this pride was reciprocal. Paul reached into his pocket and retrieved his ID badge, scanned it on the panel on the wall, and entered the building. For some reason, at that instant, he fondly remembered the days of metal keys. Too often these days the artful and surreptitious act of stealing a key from a sleeping guard was now reduced to pick-pocketing a credit card.

But the night guard inside the factory was not sleeping. He was, in fact, wide-awake and waiting for the scofflaw who had entered the building after hours. Alert, the guard—disgraced priest Stan—stood on the other side of the next set of metal doors when Paul entered with his gun drawn. Stan didn't have time to move before the bullet entered his kneecap. He dropped to the ground screaming, blood seeping from the wound. He crossed himself before he raised his middle finger to Paul.

"Sorry," Paul said, and continued on towards the production room doors.

Apologies aren't very dramatic, but he was truly re-morseful, more so than Stan after he took those boys on the church retreat. Paul's quest was to save the poor captives without taking a single human life. He'd drive the guard to the hospital when he was done. But for now, he'd just take the actual keys on Stan's belt, the ones used to open actual locks that held actual chains.

He shoved his gun back into his belt. The other guards would arrive soon. He didn't have much time. Pushing through the double doors, he entered the production room and was hit immediately by that odd odor of Lemon Pledge mixed with a corpse that forgot his deodorant. The shackled captives stopped their mechanical work when they somehow sensed Paul's pres-ence, though he still was not sure how. Yet when he was out of their immediate area, they returned to work as pills and powder fell to the floor. Groaning that terrible sound with their decom-posing larynxes, the nearest workers thrashed and flailed and tried to rid themselves of their binds to push in Paul's general direction. Trying to ignore the throaty noises that could have been aborted cries for help, Paul ran towards the massive control panel about fifteen feet from the entry.

Above the circuit board, a long metal spike protruded from the warehouse ceiling. It hung down like a stalactite to about six feet above the control panel where a hook held a padlock connected to the chains that bound the enslaved recruits. Pulling a folding chair from beneath the panel, Paul leapt atop of it and reached until he grasped the lock. He yanked it down as the workers stared with their glazed eyes, their sallow, sunken, ghoulish faces (or what was left of them) vacant of expression, but somehow appearing hopeful. Or so Paul thought as he hit the button that turned the green light red, stopping the whining of the machines. Without a task, the recruits ceased their work, frozen at their posts, their lolling heads turned towards their liberator. Paul hit the switch on the left, and their handcuffs unlocked in one burst and their chains clattered to the shiny white floor.

Standing on the chair, Paul looked down on the captives. They were free now, but what did that matter when they had no powers of decision? They looked at Paul for a moment before some sort of unconscious urge took hold of them all in unison and they stepped towards the elevated man in black. The closer they came, the more the smell of death overshadowed that of lemons.

Just as the zombies bit into his ankle, Paul had an idea. It would have been a better plan just to call the cops. Or maybe even a newspaper. Or even the fucking Ghostbusters.

Yeah, he was losing a lot of blood.

He didn't even scream or cry or beg. A once black but now gray-skinned man with George Clinton hair bared his rotting teeth as he yanked Paul from the chair until the would-be hero was crowd surfing in a sea of the dead. Paul let it happen without a fight, believing that he deserved it, that this gruesome end was atonement for a selfish, wasted life. As his entrails were torn out by the horde of ravenous slaves, Paul could see the white-bearded specimen. He was looking at him with clear eyes, blue, the irises defined from the scleras, far from the weird milky pigment of the others. He was just staring. The last thing Paul saw before the zombies chewed through his throat and nearly severed his head was the old man's eyes, sparkling with the clarity of vengeance.

9:02 PM

The General watched as his fellow workers devoured that man in the suit. What had happened to these people? Did they not recall the veritable buffet that could be found in the South Oakland trash cans after the University of Pittsburgh dining hall's Supreme Pizza Days? The General had received the same injection as the rest, but he did not feel compelled to feast on human organs. He lived on the street, but he had standards! He had even known some of the strange creatures before their eyes had faded into glossy purple and their skin had turned gray. Bill, the blind man who sang opera with boom box accompaniment by the colleges, was noshing on an arm. The General looked down at his hands. They were gray and the skin was falling off, but his mind was as clear as it had been in years.

"The Detroit Red Wings are commie cyborgs."

Okay, he could still speak.

He was immune. He did not know why, but he knew that vengeance upon that scarred supervillain who chained them to this machine was definitely in order.

He had to mobilize these troops into battle.

But he should probably let them finish dinner first.

10:04 PM

Janice's, aka Annabelle Lee's, apartment was too small to appear empty. She had boxed up most of her past—peace signs from her flower child days and anarchy symbols from her time as a political punk rocker—and replaced them with upside-down pentagrams. Punk was the recent transitional period from light to dark, a subculture too angry to contemplate mortality until a heroin overdose struck. She had gone from protesting war and preaching love to throwing rocks at her old hippie friends and answering every question with a middle finger. Goth appeared to be apolitical, which was a nice break for her. Protests were tiring, as were ideological drug-induced tête-à-têtes. She didn't have the time to shift social views now that she had a real job.

Janice lit seven candles and began her nightly ritual. She prayed, tonight to Odin, that her new job would bring wealth and immortal love. She would raise enough money to afford an ornate burial in the gothic churchyard she had recently discovered across the Monongahela River in Lawrenceville. She would draw up her will because she only had a few years left. Ever since her Woodstock phase back in college, she'd had the premonition that she would die at 27. Though her flower child days were well behind her, she could never forget those words that Jimi Hendrix's ghost had told her when she was high on mushrooms during a Frisbee golf tournament. She didn't have much time, and she knew that if it were up to her parents, they would dress her in white and without the smoky black eye makeup. She also required to be buried in a cape, like Bela Lugosi. With her first paycheck, she would hire a lawyer to help draw up a will.

Adding to her sense of impending doom were the bad omens. Earlier in the evening, she'd spied a large black dog outside of her window, strolling down her alley and pausing right in her line of sight. According to the book of omens (i.e., the third book of the *Harry Potter* series) she'd purchased two days earlier, this was a sign of death. She'd better get moving on that coffin. It should be black, adorned with a silver cross and a red velvet interior.

Sitting amidst the long, tapered candles in her dark bedroom, she stared into her mirror at her burgundy lips and porcelain skin. Brushing her sleek black hair, she thought she made a far sexier princess of the night than flower child, crusty anarchist, 1950s pin-up, or Rastafarian.

Tomorrow would be the first day of the end of her life.

She would put her soul on loan to Marshall Owens and his wellness empire for as long as it took to afford the death that she'd imagined for herself since she went Goth five weeks ago. And maybe she'd even meet her own Dracula, her doomed Romeo, a tragic lover who would be with her forever in the grave. Gothic hottie seeks sensitive vampire prince to join in an eternal embrace. That's the kind of man she was looking for. Not the charming, goofy good guy, Hugh Grant (before the hooker) archetype from romantic comedies whose flaws make him endearing. No, the sullen bad boy with a blood lust from allegorical teen horror dramas. Indeed, with the recent resurgence in the popularity of the vampire, now was the time to be Goth. She was ready for a romance that would not be any fun. There would only be pain. And bloodletting.

10:35 PM

The General was growing frustrated with his troops. After they had devoured the two guards who had come to check out the work stoppage, they had just stood there, staring blankly at nothing in particular. The General seized the moment to forge his army. While the troops were distracted fighting over their dinner like kids at a piñata, he used the moment to escape to the ominous locker room where the enemy had taken his clothes. He was preparing to go into battle, and this dental hygienist look just wouldn't do. He flung the door open and raced into the clean room. He had seen that bully with the ponytail toss his uniform into the trash can when he had been clothed in the early morning hours. Pulling filthy garments from the receptacle, he tossed them on the floor until he located his iconic general's jacket and set it down while he searched for his black button-down. Retrieving it moments later, he noticed that the pin was without its signature flower. Eyes darting madly across the room, the General spied the pink carnation on the floor. He rushed to it and cradled the flower in his coarse hands. There was a distinct pattern of a boot print on its crushed little petals. Staring at the trampled carnation in his graying hands, the General felt a tear roll down his cheek.

"Snap out of it, Sergeant!" The General barked as he slapped himself in the face. "You want to cry, go join the cheerleading squad with the rest of the ladies."

There was no crying in battle. The General had a mission to accomplish. He would avenge the enslavement of all his neighbors under the Birmingham Bridge, his fellow bus riders, everyone who ever had to wear paper booties over shoes, and his pink carnation that had met a terrible end. The General stripped off the hospital scrubs and put on his black outfit and military coat and went back to the factory floor to lead his troops.

But it was not going well. He was able to lead them to the men's bathroom, but once they were corralled inside, they were a tough group to keep focused.

The fact that they appeared to be blind did not facilitate his marker-on-mirror presentation.

He had drawn a map of the factory and the Pro-Well office across the parking lot. The plan was to invade the corporate headquarters, cornering that evil Owens chap who had enslaved the General and his fellow street dwellers. If the troops had still been in possession of their brains, the invasion would have been much easier. With their vagrant lifestyle, they all should have had a deft understanding of the locations to which he referred. But he could tell that they were unable to fathom spatial relationships. So he drew a map.

The large, rather wavy rectangle on the left was the factory, and the smaller trapezoid on the right was the office building. From his many nights sleeping under the awning above the patio, he had surmised that the building had four floors and possibly a basement.

"We invade from here. You, Sergeant One Arm," the General pointed to the grizzled old man with the harelip in the torn blue scrubs who had lost his left arm at the shoulder to the vile

Pro-Well machinery. He hadn't seemed to notice. "You start to rush forward, moving into enemy turf. I assume that we will encounter aggression on their defensive line. They will try to take you down, but you must protect the rest of the troops. I will be in the middle, the quarterback, protected by a center. I will be issuing commands from my post as we move up the field. At no point will you let me get sacked!"

The General felt that he had made his point.

But the troops just continued to gurgle. Their decaying heads lolled, and their mouths gaped open, drooling blood from their recent meal.

"You, Corporal Green Hair, though you disrespected your commanding officer earlier, you are now a valuable soldier in my battalion," he shouted to the young punk who had tried to steal his fuzzy friends at the diner.

He would put their previous issues aside and focus on solidarity. But Corporal Green Hair wasn't listening. Standing in the doorway with part of a small intestine dangling from his mouth—evidently stuck on his tongue ring—he was staring intently at a roll of toilet paper.

"Private Shoeless," the General barked, with his frustration becoming increasingly evident. "You will lead the left side of the attack. Await my command, and you will rush into the end zo—"

But Shoeless was paying no attention either, as he appeared transfixed by the bathroom floor and was, in fact, facing the opposite direction of the General and his strategic drawing.

"Men! If you're not going to pay attention, I'll have to bring back the chains!"

The troops continued to groan and emit odd sloshing sounds from their throats. As the shriveled old woman he had often seen with a shopping cart adorned with signs warning about Bugs Bunny and the apocalypse wandered out of the war room, the General realized that his attack was going to be more difficult than he had thought.

Monday
8:28 AM

Hank hated taking his car to work. It seemed so despicably lazy to drive from one point to another within the same neighborhood. But he'd admittedly felt a bit uneasy when that nutjob tried to Mike Tyson his arm. He'd already made sure that the knobs of the stove he hadn't used in three days were turned to the "off" position, flicked the coffee machine back on and flicked it back off again just to remember doing so, and unplugged the microwave from the wall in case a gust of wind inexplicably entered the subterranean abode and programmed the popcorn setting, thus causing an explosion. Hank went back to the bathroom to twist the faucet handles all the way back to their "off" positions. After all, a small leak could cause a veritable tsunami inside his basement flat. Could he risk exposing his precious suit of armor to rust if it was submerged? He reached into the shower to repeat the process. *Well, this is a new one*, he thought. Hank was aware that any of these situations were about as likely as returning from the grave, but he couldn't help himself from getting devoured by his morning tasks.

He opened the door to his set of four steps that led up to the 15th Street sidewalk. He slammed the door shut behind him and locked it from the outside with his key. He shook the handle a few times to make sure, and slammed his 190-pound body against it to assure its infallibility. He twisted the handle again, all his strength pulsing through his arm. Recently, his sense of self-preservation had become rather self-destructive. His hand was red and callused in a doorknob-shaped patch of skin between his thumb and forefinger. Yet, aside from the physical discomfort, Hank found the most vexing part of his ritual to be the fact that he had the compulsive need to preserve a life that he so despised.

Hank was walking out of his apartment to the first sunny morning in a week, and if he could admit to looking forward to anything, it was to a leisurely stroll through morning rush hour, on track to arrive only fifteen minutes late for his 9 o'-

clock start time. His morning ritual caused perpetual tardiness that, had he cared more about his job, he would have alleviated with a trip to a shrink's office. Just as he stepped up to the sidewalk, that psychotic troll came ambling towards him, dressed in a white apron covered in what appeared to be marinara sauce as if he'd just gotten off work from one of the four pizza shops in the two-block radius. He was kind of limping, presumably hung over from partying too much after his shift ended. Then the creep grabbed Hank's arm and leaned in for a bite.

Hank shook free and clocked his attacker in the face. He had been craving some bad convenience store coffee and three cigarettes on his walk to the office. But after the Monday morning attack of the teeth, Hank decided that he should just drive.

The Steelers must have won last night. Or they might have lost.

Either way, there was an abundance of hungover people roaming the streets this morning. Though many had similarly shambling gaits, Hank hoped the others didn't enjoy biting as much as the one he'd encountered. As he drove down Carson Street, Pittsburghers—food service employees, convenience store staffers, and 9-to-5 stiffs like himself—were moving at the most lethargic pace, presumably dreading their arrival at their places of employment as much as he was. But Hank was moving quickly, or attempting to, as he had to make up for the time to check that every cigarette in his ashtray was completely extinguished. Not to mention that he was awakened at 4 a.m. to a blistering scream of "Motherfucker," followed by several minutes of incomprehensible, vaguely pained male shouting, and he had subsequently overslept.

He recognized several of the regular morning strollers—the artsy folk emerging from the independent coffee shop that they frequented devoutly because it was adjacent to a Starbucks, the man with his right arm gone at the shoulder who always wore a white T-shirt and carried a carton of milk, the fat women walking into the youth services center. One of these obese workers was shuffling in an almost immeasurably slow gait in front of his car. She wasn't even in the crosswalk. In some states, it would be legal to run her down. *What was Pennsylvania's stance on vigilante justice for jaywalkers?* Hank wondered. He hated pedestrians. Someday he would run them down and it would look like human bowling pins, flying in every direction, after which Hank would dance a festive jig. *Someday*, he thought, *but not today.*

"Just because you weigh as much as my car does not mean that you can overcome it in battle," Hank stated calmly, leaning his head out the window to the rotund specimen in the knee-length floral frock.

She looked up at him and growled, a strange gurgling sound emanating from her throat. Her face was a blank scowl as she glared at Hank through the windshield of his black 1998 Dodge Ram.

Then she coughed.

"I have arthritis!" she shouted at Hank, and resumed shuffling across the street.

Arthritis, Hank thought, *a new euphemism for "fat" that he hadn't heard before.* Hank hated fat people almost as much as they truly terrified him. The thought of being engulfed by a mass of blubber, of being sucked into the folds of dimpled flesh, the heavy breathing, that yeasty body odor that accompanied them like sweaty doughnuts rising. It was like Jonah and the whale. Like being eaten alive.

Shaking off a shiver, Hank waited for the gelatinous creature to pass his car, then shot off down the street to the next stoplight that was, of course, red.

It was just going to be one of those days.

8:33 AM

Marshall Owens was awakened in his lavish 32nd-floor penthouse apartment in the heart of downtown Pittsburgh with some disturbing news. There was a work stoppage at the factory. All the projects that he had rescued from a life on the street had revolted. Apparently, a living foreman was required at all times, one with electrical impulses and more motivation than an insatiable hunger for human flesh (which really wasn't all that hard to come by). Marshall Owens flailed in his 7,000-count Egyptian silver sheets for a few moments after receiving the call from his loyal assistant Harold. Composing himself, he eased out of his God-sized bed in his silk sleep tuxedo and slipped into his $5,000 leather-soled, chinchilla-fur, Armani pink bunny slippers. He shuffled across his plush bedroom carpet on the second floor of the penthouse and turned the solid-gold handle on the bathroom door.

He looked at his unpleasant visage in the diamond-rimmed mirror and shuddered. Shifting his blue-eyed gaze to Monet's Rouen Cathedral hanging above the gold toilet, he combed his deep brown hair plugs, kicked off his slippers, and hopped into the shower.

After he buffed his fingernails, put on his tailored suit, and sipped a cup of the most unfairly traded coffee he could find, he would go down to that plant of his and discipline his living employees for allowing such a travesty to occur.

That was the original plan.

But an hour and thirteen minutes later, when his chauffeured Escalade (Owens was well aware that the gas-guzzling SUV posed quite the contradiction to his environmental initiatives, but he felt that he needed a big car to complement his big lifestyle. And the Prius was kinda queer anyway) arrived at the factory, there were no employees left. No paid guards, no mutant slaves. Well, parts of the guards were still scattered on the floor, and the CEO of Pro-Well Pharmaceuticals, the savior of the South Side, the darling of local media, the most successful twelve-stepper in the history of Narcotics Anonymous, was greeted by a grisly scene of bones, blood, and security uniforms.

This was not a good way to start the day.

9:27 AM

Lillian tended to strut. She had never meant to do so, but it just came naturally. She thought she looked great, with that false sense of self-esteem that came from Botox, highlights, and near-daily trips to Ann Taylor. Lillian was not an attractive woman, but a pear-shaped 43-year-old with a protruding mole on her receding chin and an upturned nose. In the Middle Ages, she would have been considered a hag. But now her ample pay-checks bought collagen injections, control-top pantyhose, and flashy pantsuits to draw attention away from anorexic lips and slightly lopsided features.

Lillian made too much money to be a hag. Indeed, she Beadazzled herself into a Fabergé egg. Today's get-up was an opulent mélange of coral reef and Christmas tree. She pushed her jeweled spectacles atop her fluffy chestnut hair and strode through the third floor of the Pro-Well office. She thought it looked a bit empty. Good: fewer employees to protest when she completed the latest round of terminations scheduled for this morning. She was told that three would have to go. They'd better not give her trouble. She had a manicure scheduled for 2 p.m.

Once an average human resources professional, Lillian had been promoted to head of staffing relations. Now, instead of a well-intentioned mediator, she was the dreaded Management and thus reviled by most of her underlings. And recently, since incidents of sexual harassment were down and redundancy was up, she had become the Terminator. She fired people as if it was her job, which, of course, it was.

Lillian pushed open the door to her office and let out a startled yelp.

"Kelly, what are you doing here?" Lillian asked.

"Wow, you went to Ann Taylor?" Kelly gushed. "Their stuff is so nice, so classy. I just wish I could afford it, but what with the second child on the way and the fact that I've had to take unpaid leave recently because of my sub-par benefits, it's been forever since I went shopping."

Lillian gave her a scrunched smile that meant, "Shut up, you transparent nutjob!" and walked around Kelly, who was seated almost in the doorway, to her desk.

"Ooh, and you went to Talbots, too!" Kelly exclaimed. "Can I see what you bought? I bet it's super cute. Oh," she said, her tone taking a serious turn as she looked at the Tupperware of scrambled eggs that Lillian pulled from her large purse.

"Is there a problem?" Lillian asked, looking at her breakfast.

"No, it's just that I recently read a study about eggs," Kelly began, reciting yet another piece of breaking news that would be refuted in a week. "You really shouldn't be eating them. This hormone that they've been injecting into eggs has been proven to strengthen human resistance to antibiotics. It's also been linked to Type 2 diabetes and cholesterol problems."

"What do you want, Kelly?" Lillian asked irritably as she peeled open the Tupperware lid.

Every week Kelly came to her with a new fear. She had been checked for bird and swine flu, SARS, Ebola, and even bubonic plague after Adam Kaplan on the Web team convinced her that there had been a hushed-up outbreak in Brentwood. Following the shameless attempt at manipulation by flattery, it was almost too much for Lillian this morning.

"He did it again," Kelly said, suddenly serious. She tossed a small stack of papers onto Lillian's desk.

"One baby for sale. In pristine fetal condition inside the womb, just ready to be purchased. Willing to discount based on child's Mexican paternal heritage. Call 412-555-6789," Lillian read, her glasses pushed to the end of her nose. She flipped to the next page of the stack of Craig's List postings. "Missed connection: I saw you at the wedding seven years ago. You were marrying my sister, but I knew I had to have you. Call me, Manuel. I know my sister Kelly will never understand, but my love for you is undying. Please meet me at the Sleep Inn on Route 30. I will pleasure you to the sweet sounds of Telemundo. Yours forever, Carly."

Kelly leaned back in the chair, folded her arms over her protruding pregnant baby, and glared at Lillian.

"Do you have proof Adam did it?" Lillian asked.

"I don't need proof. It's always him. He harasses Pete from sales at least once a week, and he's been sending threatening messages to managers' private printers. A bunch of eyes glued onto a piece of paper that says, 'We're watching you,'" Kelly said.

"I'll have Wilbert speak to him," Lillian said.

"That's it?" Kelly asked incredulously. "He's harassing me. You didn't even look at the one where he tried to trade my house for Polordion smootdust. What the hell is Polordion smootdust?"

"I don't know, Kelly, but unless you have a better solution to this ongoing feud between you two, I'll just have Wilbert speak with him. And frankly, Adam has never come to me with a complaint about you," Lillian said.

She didn't have a real attachment to the junior Web designer, but she was inclined to defend Wilbert's team. Any shenanigans meant that Wilbert was not doing his job, and she could not have that get out. Of course, Lillian wasn't aware that Adam had the employment history of George Costanza. Nor was she aware when she hired the eclectically skilled 29-year-old six months ago, that though his portfolio was authentic, his references were as fake as Kelly's compliments.

"Well," Kelly said. "I was thinking. Why don't you move the Web team? I mean, our whole area is a jumbled mess. Hank is always whining about how we in customer service are too loud for him to concentrate. And Pete is still there while the rest of the sales team moved down to this floor months ago."

"And so you're suggesting that we rearrange the entire office?"

"Yes. We move Pete back with sales down here. Or you could just get rid of him. You know he's a terrible salesman. He's just costing the company money at this point. We put the Web team on the first floor near the call center. We leave Pete, Hank, Adam, Cameron and Gina's seats empty as an incentive to hire more customer service reps because we're really short-staffed. Have you seen the attendance here today? Half the employees don't even bother coming to work."

"Doesn't this seem like an inordinate amount of work to essentially move one employee?" Lillian asked.

"Well, you could just fire Adam. No matter where he's moved, he's going to harass someone."

"Kelly, we've talked about this several times. We have no reason to fire Adam."

"Yeah? How about this one?" Kelly yanked the papers from Lillian's hands. "Chubby Grecian goddess seeks a pair of soft feet for erotic pedi-pleasures. Race, age, gender, sexual orientation do not matter. Will be no contact above the ankles." Kelly dropped the paper to the desk in exasperation. "He even leaves my work number at the bottom!"

"Fine, Kelly," Lillian said. "I will schedule a meeting with Adam this afternoon."

"Come on, you've said that so many times, and nothing's ever been done," Kelly begged.

"Well, there is very little I can do," Lillian replied offhandedly as she began shuffling papers at her desk.

"Look," Kelly said, leaning forward as far as her engorged belly would allow, her voice taking a sinister tone. "I have certain information that I know to be true that would be very damaging to you if I let it out. Information as to why you're always protecting the worst, most disruptive team in the office. There's a company policy against what you're doing, and you don't want to lose your job for a slacker like Adam, do you?"

Lillian dropped the papers to her desk. "Are you threatening me?"

"No," Kelly said. "Just letting you know what I know."

"I'll speak with Adam this afternoon. Maybe you should leave those papers with me," Lillian said, attempting to remain calm. "It'll give me more ammunition."

"Thank you," Kelly said. She slowly rose from her seat and turned to the door. "By the way, who would I talk to about getting chili cheese dogs available in the vending machine?"

"I'll put in a request," Lillian said.

Kelly smiled and shut the door behind her. Lillian rolled her eyes and let out a sigh of relief. The woman treated each day as if it was a reality show competition, using whatever information she could find, falsify, or manipulate to bring about the professional demise of another. Donald Trump would fire her almost instantly. But she'd make it pretty far on *Love Is Blind*, Stevie Wonder's reality dating show. Terminating Adam would reflect poorly on Wilbert, but letting her secret out would be just as damaging as Kelly threatened. At 2 p.m., she'd fire Adam.

9:38 AM

"All right, a sale!" Pete Hicks was pleased when somehow his rather masochistic means of selling Pro-Well products actually paid off. Too self-deprecating to be condescending, too strange to be taken seriously, Pete was such a bad salesman that the rest of his team had forgotten him. Not that he really cared. But he always seemed genuinely ecstatic when some unwitting distributor showed interest.

"Someone actually bought your garbage?" Judy Lowitski asked.

Adam Kaplan looked on, shaking his head and smiling.

"Hell, yeah. Just gotta call this schnook back and close the sale."

Grinning, Pete punched in the phone number he had just transcribed from his voicemail. He gloated silently, leaning back in his chair with his headset on. With the arrogant air of a guilty man who'd just been acquitted on a technicality, he spun a pen between his fingers until it slipped to the floor, and he slammed the phone back on the receiver.

"Adam, you nudnik!"

Adam was giggling, a bit of a nasal laugh that gave way to massive guffaws, quite proud of this latest prank.

"You like that?" he asked, catching his breath. "Huh, you like that, buddy?"

"A mental health hotline?" Pete asked, annoyed.

"How much effort do you expend prank calling co-workers?" Hank asked, as he approached his cubicle on the second floor of the Pro-Well Pharmaceuticals headquarters.

"Well, rock me Amadeus. Look who's here!" Adam exclaimed.

"Was that Yiddish I heard, Pete?" Hank asked as he sat down.

"Yeah, I've been studying it," Pete said. "It's so foul and wonderful."

"You missed it, Hank. Earlier he cursed his computer," Adam said. "'May you find no rest even in the grave,' I believe was the expression."

"*Ruen zolstu nisht afile in keyver!*" Pete said.

"Pete, I already warned you once about that today," came Wilbert's condescending whine from the next cubicle. As the team lead, it was his job to keep the sheep in line and make them forget that there was an "I" in the entire alphabet.

"And that applies to the computer how?"

"I don't know," Pete said. "I'm still learning. But I find insults to be even more profound when the insulted don't understand them."

"Yeah, I don't think that Dell is from the Diamond District," Hank replied.

Every month, Pete experimented with a new interest. When the firings started, he was all about Stalin. A few weeks later, he spent the entire day reading Ted Kaczynski's lengthy manifesto. For a while he was quite the fan, espousing the Unabomber's neo-Luddite ideology whenever the server went down. Apparently now it was Yiddish. A philosophy major in college, Pete found himself completely unprepared for a career. He'd held a few jobs during summers off from school, but other than ponder life's eternal questions and engage in self-deprecating rants, he had no interest in anything marketable. He was a completely inept salesman but had a new pointless idea every day, like Cosmo Kramer with a job. From the hard-core Vespa biker gang to mixing one massive cocktail in a baby pool to the latest male burlesque show, he was an endless barrage of distraction.

Pete was truly a pillar of offensiveness, and he cultivated it, and it seemed only natural that he incorporate foul Yiddish phrases into his invented dialect. He was a kvetch and proud of it. Completely unqualified for just about any job, he was stuck at Pro-Well, where he announced regularly that he was the smartest person in the office.

"I want to learn some Yiddish," Adam said.

"Aren't you Jewish?" Hank asked.

"Yeah, but I dropped out of Hebrew school. Also, they didn't teach us anything fun. I know like seven different ways to say 'God,' but that's about it," Adam said.

"No talk of religion in the office," Wilbert said from his cubicle. "It makes for an uncomfortable work environment."

Pete, who had been scrawling a phrase onto a piece of yellow paper, ripped it from the legal pad and handed it to Adam in the next cube.

"Hey, Will," Adam said. "*Aroyskrikhn zoln dir di oygn fun kop.*"

"Get back to work, Adam," Wilbert said.

"What does that mean?" Adam whispered to Pete.

"May your eyes crawl out of your head," Pete replied, loud enough for the team lead to hear.

Working for Wilbert was like working for Goebbels. A really fucking annoying Goebbels who'd been to too many motivational seminars and eaten too much chicken soup for the soul. And the most offensive part to Hank was that he truly believed in his job, that menial micro-management was going to save the world. He believed that he was an essential asset to the medicine that Pro-Well marketed, that through his relatively pointless role as leader of eight people in his immediate seating area, he was making a difference. About once a month, he delivered a heartfelt tale of averted tragedy when a young girl—as that was the most innocent demographic of all innocent victims—was treated with a Pro-Well product and was able to walk again. It was a pathetic sight, particularly when Pete discovered that these so-called heroes of the everyday did not actually exist.

"Teamwork: You can reach your goals only with the help of

others" was the tagline on his emails. Hank had always thought that Charles Manson would look great above that quote.

"So Hank man," Pete said. "I was wondering, what would you think if I grew a mullet?"

"I think it would really hide those sultry eyes," Hank said with sarcasm.

"Come on, Hank, what would you think if I took on the whole mullet lifestyle?" Pete, though sardonic, was quite persistent. "You know, brought it into the mainstream."

"Well, mullets have been persecuted and marginalized for decades, relegated to monster truck rallies and Lynyrd Skynyrd tribute shows. You could be the leader—the man who united all NASCAR and WWE fans." Hank decided to play along. Planning Pete's mullet was better than work, and it was sure to irritate Judy.

"It would be a complete overhaul. I'd need a new car, or a new really old car. And a whole new wardrobe, filled with cut-off jean shorts. And I certainly couldn't work here."

"Why not? You could claim persecution," Hank said. "They can't discriminate against mullets. That's...well, that's something illegal."

"Pete and Hank, please, back to work. We have a client coming in an hour, and everything must run smoothly," Wilbert said from his cubicle.

"See, the persecution is starting already," Pete said.

9:32 AM

The recruits were officially missing. How this was possible, Owens had no idea. They were slow, grotesque, and, well, dead. Not the type that could hitch a ride out of town or could have made it very far on foot. Surely someone would have noticed three dozen corpses treating the South Side as though it was the Ponderosa buffet. The duke of drugs, the pharaoh of pharmaceuticals, the modern medicine man, Owens had a conference call and the obligation to keep up the illusion of stability.

9:36 AM

Janice, aka Mistress Jane Doe, decided that she had made the ideal choice of first-day-of-work attire. Black velvet top, long flowing black skirt, black and white striped thigh-high socks just in case she had to hold up her witch skirt when walking up stairs, black platform knee-high boots adorned with more buckles than were possibly necessary. Some longhair from sales asked her when the coven was meeting upon their introduction. *He is a very mean hippie*, she had thought. When Janice was a flower child two years ago, she was very accepting of everyone. Had she really been out of the loop that long that the entire tenets of the faith had changed?

But, as she explained to him, the look she was going for was mourning. Mourning for the loss of late nights out and the freedom that could only come with the absence of a steady paycheck.

But daily enslavement would have to do. She still had the early evening to meet her prince of darkness. And the job hadn't been too bad yet, except that a rather disproportionate number of employees seemed to be coming down with something that made them cough incessantly. Smallpox, maybe, or a spell cast by a rival pharmaceutical company. Janice had been anticipating disaster ever since that black cat had crossed her path this morning. Just an hour later, she spilled sugar (that wasn't an actual bad omen, but Janice was new to superstition that she incorrectly attributed to the Goth scene) in the kitchen while trying to sweeten her coffee and check out that hot guy she'd seen at the bars before. The one who looks like a young Pete Steele or Bruce Campbell, she thought. Janice could picture him with a chain saw attached to his arm, avenging those medieval foes who tried to stop her from being his princess.

She checked out the tattoos she could spy at his wrist, exposed when he reached for the coffee maker. The boring middle-aged women spoke of cooking shows and celebrity infidelity while waiting for the urn to fill, but he just casually moved the pot and slid his black mug under the machine to let the coffee seep in.

"No need for a third party to get involved," he explained briefly.

He didn't stay to add cream or sugar. Just black. She liked that. She also enjoyed the reactions of the office sheep: part appalled, part awed by the genius that thought of this expeditious strategy. Maybe this job wouldn't be all that bad. He had the brooding demeanor of a troubled vampire, and she could deal with daylight if he was in it.

She also found that the dreaded fluorescent lights heightened her pallor—and everyone else's. They all looked like death. They also seemed to have a lot of parties here. At 9 a.m., the accounting department was hosting an elaborate breakfast feast complete with a buffet of eggs, bacon, pancakes, sausage biscuits, and an as of yet untouched fruit tray.

She received her orientation to the data entry team from some woman who was constantly distracted by away-from-the-water-cooler talk about *Fishing with the Famous*. Clad in khaki pants that were pulled up much higher than Janice could possibly believe to be comfortable, the women—some young, some old—chattered on about fishing terminology that they had learned the week before. This was not going to help her socialize. The women then proceeded to speak of the drunk-driving troubles of certain young Hollywood socialites.

"They should all be guillotined," Janice had interjected, her first attempt at interaction with her new co-workers.

They all suddenly became silent, except a few whooping coughs. *Maybe decapitation was a bit much in the morning*, Janice thought. So she softened her approach.

"Or put in the stocks in front of Grauman's Chinese Theater and pelted with tomatoes. Waterboarded at the grotto of the Playboy Mansion."

"All drunk drivers?" asked Doug, the awkward, overweight thirty-something whom Janice had already noticed had the odd habit of plucking out his eyelashes while on the phone with clients. She didn't understand why he didn't go for his unibrow.

"No," Janice replied. "Starlets."

That had been enough first impressions for the day, she thought.

Sitting at her cubicle, she imagined the decorations she would bring from home tomorrow. A gargoyle paperweight, the guillotine pencil sharpener, her quill. Today, all she had thought to bring was her medieval letter opener, which was essentially a small sword. But how dangerous could that be?

She didn't really need a letter opener to enter statistical information into her computer. However, it was now *her* desk, and she had quite the collection of accessories that she would employ to establish herself as the office Goth. She took her small mirror out of her corset purse and checked out her stiff, black hair, which was pulled up in a bun with shorter strands almost pasted to the sides of her face. The mirror's silver stem slipped out of her hand and landed on the carpet. Sliding her chair away from her desk to retrieve it, Janice wheeled over the antique mirror and the glass splintered. *This was another sign*, she thought. But the promise of seven years of bad luck clearly offset the impending death omen she'd seen last night. Janice was a bit confused, so she looked over the first page of numbers, opened Microsoft Excel, and decided to actually start working.

9:42 AM

The General had lost some of his troops. Actually, he'd lost most of them. Something told him that his few months in the Coast Guard 35 years ago could not prepare him to lead an army of the dead. They mostly had short attention spans. In the war room—the men's bathroom of the factory—he had tried to plan their attack. But they clearly had no discipline, and now many had simply departed, following the neon lights of Carson Street. The General didn't know if the troops were leaving because they smelled all the fresh flesh in the bars or if they were merely party zombies who enjoyed the bright lights and wanted to join the fun.

The fearless leader of the dead was left with a few unfocused, undisciplined soldiers who dared to embark on the invasion. He tried yelling, but it didn't work. They were completely incapable of marching in unison, and God forbid he introduce a drum line. Clearly, his battle plan was much better in theory. But there were a loyal twelve disciples who followed, and the General knew that the flesh-eating dead were very dangerous, so he continued with his plan.

The army stood under the Hot Metal Bridge, shielded from street traffic in a position that made it very difficult for the troops to see pedestrians, let alone eat them.

"You, Private One-Eye, you stand behind me and we storm the gates of this mighty structure. If someone approaches the doors, you tackle them. Understood? You may destroy them, if you want."

The eye-patch-sporting Private One-Eye, a bearded, middle-aged, de-institutionalized nut who had become convinced that he was a pirate after losing his sight in an unfortunate eyelash trimming accident, gazed in his general direction. The General considered this a positive response.

"You, Sergeant Jawless, stand to my right and assume a fighting stance. You will serve as my safety."

"Corporal Green Hair, your youth makes you invaluable. You will sprint towards the doors as fast as you can and infiltrate the entrance."

The General knew he could rely on Corporal Green Hair. He was a true revolutionary and committed to the cause, resisting the wandering impulses of his similarly neon-coiffed friends. The other troops had much to learn from this young soldier.

"Officer formerly known as Trench Coat! Where are you going?" The General shouted amidst the plastic bags and shattered beer bottles as the tall, thin black man who usually wore a tattered flasher jacket waded through the colony of shopping carts towards several pigeons that sat near the river.

"Well, that's it! If the once and future Trench Coat is just going to wander off like that, I will strip him of his captain's rank!"

With this latest casualty to flesh-hungry curiosity, the General was down to eleven. But that would have to do, as he planned to invade the corporate headquarters of Pro-Well Pharmaceuticals within the hour.

10:02 AM

"Please, have a seat, Mr. Stanley," Lillian implored the first of her three on the chopping block.

"My last name's Gordovsky, but I guess you have the same news for Carl Stanley, so I'll just fire him myself on my way back to my desk," said Nick Gordovsky, the oft-ignored but excellent customer service rep overshadowed by his showy peers. Mid-thirties, recently married, one who would probably start itching for a raise when his new wife inevitably became pregnant. Mild-mannered and stable, one who just blended in, probably wouldn't make a scene. Lillian knew how to pick 'em.

"Well, Mr. Gordovsky, you are not being fired."

"Terminated then. Like what I'm going to have to do to my cable subscription when I don't have a job anymore."

"Your position is being eliminated." Lillian usually coaxed them to this point, but Nick's jaded attitude allowed for some modifications in the routine. "We have set up a severance package for you that includes two weeks of pay and information about extending your benefits for up to six months."

"Wow, two weeks. How generous."

"Mr. Gordovsky, the company is hemorrhaging money in this market. Even Pro-Well is feeling the recession."

"How the fuck is that possible? Everyone is on drugs."

"I understand your anger, Nick, but please know that there is nothing that we can do."

"Well, judging from those pearly white anal beads around your neck, I can see that you're really struggling." Nick rose from his seat, yanking his walking papers off her desk as Lillian fingered the opulent pearl necklace her lover had bought her over the weekend. "Thank you, and fuck you."

"Clear out your desk today. We have no need for your services anymore. At 1 p.m., security will escort you from the premises."

Nick rolled his eyes and turned suddenly, slamming his hands on Lillian's desk. He leaned down to her, his scruffy beard just inches away from her turned-up nose.

"Do I really scare you that badly?" he asked, his voice lowered, attempting to evoke fear in the pear-shaped bitch. Instead, he found himself coughing uncontrollably, a horrible hacking cough. *That freak that bit me this morning better not have given me anything*, he thought.

"Just do it, Mr. Gordovsky. You are no longer relevant."

Nick swung back around, flung open her corner office door, and slammed it behind him. Through the walls adorned with photos of herself 20 years ago, she heard Nick shouting.

"Hey, Carl, you're next. After they throw us onto the street, let's go down to Excuses and get so shit-faced we start rooting for the Flyers!"

10:24 AM

It was chilly for a bright October day, and Judy shivered as she sucked down her Newport in the Pro-Well parking lot's designated smoking area. She needed a break from her husband, Frank, and his repetitive calling. Some clown bit him— so what? She worked for the largest pharmaceutical company this side of the Mississippi, and she had an arsenal of products to treat any ill inside the house. And if she didn't, how far was the drugstore really? He was just calling because he was lazy and wanted an excuse to sit on the couch all day instead of looking for a job. They had been married for thirty-nine years, and she knew his game all too well and had just about run out of sympathy for that man.

Cigarette hanging out of her mouth, she rubbed her hands together. Was it really this cold, or was her circulatory system already shutting down? Judy was 62 and had vowed on her most recent birthday that she would age no more. That's when the makeover happened; she'd replaced the corduroys with pantsuits, the gray hair with a platinum blonde coif, and she'd even begun using mascara. Any body aches, she zapped with a Pro-Well product purchased at her employee discount.

She had never been particularly concerned with image in her youth, but now that she was almost always the oldest person in a room, she felt she needed a change. It wasn't really a midlife crisis but a pre-retirement renaissance. She was a grandmother now and just needed to feel alive. She'd been a Pro-Well employee for the past ten years, since the company's infancy, working in the same position without the higher-ups ever considering her for a promotion. She watched many employees—inappropriately attired women with skirts above their knees, men with earrings—young enough to be her children rise to the ranks of management, then depart for exciting futures. The educated youth that she never was. Before Pro-Well, Judy had spent much of her adult life working part time in convenience stores while raising three children. Today, the values were different. Now the kids went to college and slept around for years before reproducing via in vitro fertilization with donated sperm.

Judy was traditional, and there seemed to be less of that going on these days. These new hires were foul-mouthed, godless, and set on eradicating the concept of the American family.

That's why she took so kindly to Kelly, the wife of a bricklayer with her second child on the way. Good manual laborer, and Judy could overlook the husband's Mexican heritage. But the rest: Hank the homo, Adam the prankster, the completely useless Pete, that new freak in data entry who was dressed as though she was attending a funeral later in the day. Even Wilbert was having an illicit affair with a younger woman. A co-worker, in fact, who was seven years his junior. Judy knew they would all be gone in the next few years, replaced by a new batch of that lost generation. Moral transients. So if she was going to be a fixture at Pro-Well, locked in the same position until her husband stopped blowing their retirement savings at the slots, she would stay exactly the same. She had decided to remain 62. Her bathroom was stocked with anti-aging skin creams and a full pharmacy of prescription drugs so that she couldn't feel her body signaling that it wasn't on board for this revolt against time.

Judy shivered and stubbed the cigarette out in the cylindrical ashtray on the way back to the front entrance. She reached into her pocket for her ID badge, but her chilled fingers did not cooperate and the laminate slipped to the asphalt. Stooping to retrieve it, she felt her back give a spasm of pain. She'd have to take a green capsule for that when she got back to her desk. As she stood back up, she caught a glimpse of a motley procession of what appeared to be very slow-moving hospital employees approaching from the direction of the Hot Metal Bridge. She squinted, her aging eyes refusing to see clearly the shambling visitors, but the chill in the air superseded her natural curiosity and she turned back to the door, pain shooting from her hip down her right leg. She'd take a red one for that.

10:46 AM

"Sir, we have a problem," Harold said as he approached Marshall Owens's desk in the fourth-floor office. The rest of the level was vacant, as per Owens's request. He liked to conduct his affairs in private and was seldom seen by his underlings in the rest of the building.

"No shit. There's a work stoppage," Owens replied, picking up the phone receiver and beginning to dial.

"No, sir. It's worse. The recruits have left the premises."

"I know that," said an exasperated Owens as he put the phone to his ear.

"Well, we've found some. They've attacked several people on Carson Street."

"Are they dead?"

"No, sir. That's the troubling part. They appear to have become," Harold paused, working on his phrasing. "Well, infected."

He'd learned this diplomatic language from Owens when the CEO came down to the halfway house seven months ago and gave the parolees an offer none of them could refuse. But when the shit hit the fan, Harold knew he wasn't going to stay the man's Uncle Tom. He'd split heads before, and he could do it again.

Owens slammed down the phone.

"What?"

"It appears that the chemical you injected into them has caused a contagious virus."

"But they completely eviscerated their prior victims. You mean to tell me that there are minimal human remains strolling through the South Side? Large intestines slithering like worms into the Town Tavern and eating bartenders? Give me a break."

"No sir. It appears that now that they have an abundance of food, they are less gluttonous. Yes, they've fully consumed some, but others they have merely bitten," Harold explained, attempting calmness and diplomacy. This power-mad freak at the desk was going to bring the apocalypse.

"And the bitten ones are now infected?"

"Yes, sir."

"And what evidence do we have of this?"

"Sven saw one reanimate. He called it in. Then he was bitten, and well, Simon called that in."

"Did Simon eliminate the problem?"

"What do you mean, sir?"

"Did he kill Sven?"

"Yes, he put him back in the car, drove him to a vacant lot, and shot him between the eyes. That appeared to work." Harold wasn't too disappointed about Sven's untimely demise. When they were in the joint, Sven had been a member of the Aryan Brotherhood, and Harold had wanted to airhole that cocksucker for months now.

"Is Simon still out there?" Owens asked anxiously.

"Yes, sir, and he is attempting to quietly," Harold paused again, "deactivate as many as he can."

"Good. Tell him to stay on it."

"But he is only one man, sir. How can he possibly take care of this problem singlehandedly?"

What was this motherfucker doing? This was like a riot, and he'd seen what the hacks had done inside. It was all numbers. Strength in numbers and ammo. And now that he was on the other side, the one trying to quell the madness, he could see that they were seriously low on both. And what Harold knew from his days running the streets was that you can't fight people who don't give a shit about life. Harold had encountered many of them during his dealing years, but Owens had really set him straight, given him a second chance and a massive check every week for his services as loyal henchman, enforcer, and gunslinger extraordinaire. Harold was forever indebted to Owens for giving a violent ex-con a firearm, but Harold knew that the man had pushed his luck too far and that he was going to bring it all crashing down.

"He can't. Put more men on it. Then come right back here and keep watch on the door. If this becomes a full-blown epidemic, then this is the safest place to be. And Marshall Owens cannot risk being infected by a dead bum!"

"Will do, sir," Harold said and exited the room.

"Fuck, fuck, fuck, fuck, fuck!" Owens shouted from the sanctity of his penthouse of an office.

This could not be the end of everything he'd worked for. The phoenix, as he liked to think of himself, rising from the ashes of a destroyed trailer. He ran his fingers over the scars and skin grafts that covered the left side of his 42-year-old face from the ear to the cheek. Though an unpleasant sight, his nose, ears, and eyes were just as functional as they had been before the explosion. He could sense clearly, and this situation was not good.

Aside from his brilliance in pharmaceuticals, Owens was a master in the art of manipulation. When you looked like a cross between Freddy Krueger and the Phantom of the Opera, you had to have another face, a persona that would allow others to look past the disfigured mess you were forced to present to the world. But, never one to drift along with the status quo, Marshall Owens had several. There was the gentleman that he had presented to women, to attempt to manipulate them so far as to doubt the abilities of their own eyes. This was his least successful. There was the tough guy that he used when dealing with his recruits, the poker face that never divulged the pleasure he felt in cleaning up the streets. Then there was his pride: the pitiable visage of a man who was a victim of the times, one who had to work harder than anyone else for his achievements, one who gave back to the community.

His media face.

Owens knew that although he had carefully cultivated this guise of altruism (by actually becoming that which he pretended to be), a disfigured capitalist was never beyond reproach. The people of Pittsburgh, who harbored conspiracy theories covering everything from UFOs to their perennially losing baseball team, would ask questions sooner or later. It was his duty to anticipate their reaction, to never let them connect the dots. Two years ago, there had been a rash of overdoses on several of his products, including Pro-Attention (an ADD drug), Quit Pro-Quo (a nicotine urge suppressant), and the oddly named Propane (a universal pain reliever). It was the type of problem that the police would attribute to recreational use and over-prescription by lazy HMOs. Only the cops on *Law & Order* or a devoted investigative journalist would trace the outbreak back to him. Fortunately for Owens, he had the latter at his disposal.

He picked up his phone and dialed.

10:55 AM

Patrick O'Brien entered the Pro-Well offices ready to make things happen. He was on a mission from CDC Distributors to research pharmaceuticals for his firm to add to its already vast array of products. O'Brien was a buyer, in transition from years as a seller, and he had retained his smarmy demeanor even though people now kissed *his* ass. With a decade of sales experience behind him, he was quite adept at figuring out when people were lying to him. And they did that a lot in this line of work.

For the most part, it was an easy gig, traveling to different regional companies to get his hands on the cutting edge of medicinal innovation. In the eastern United States, that was mostly Pro-Well. This was his first trip to the corporate office, which was located in some sort of industrial park on the outskirts of the city's drinking district. Though he had just flown in from Baltimore this morning, he'd gotten a decent look at the South Side. Even at 9:30 this Monday morning, the street was bustling with people who looked as if they hadn't been asleep since Saturday night. *Amazing*, he thought (because his thoughts generally were not much more complex than single words), as the cab took him past a staggering girl who was having some trouble doing a walk of shame in stilettos paired with men's athletic pants and a sequined tube top. He snapped a picture of her on the Nikon that he carried everywhere as the cab drove past. He was in the city for two days, and tonight he'd hit the town. He had a pre-paid Visa card from the company that would allow him to do so, as he'd downgraded the hotel to a cheapie Holiday Inn Express.

But now it was time for work. He hit the button next to the revolving door at Pro-Well's main entrance. The parking lot was nearly desolate, save for that community of bums loitering several yards behind the doorway. A soft, feminine voice came over the intercom, asking the purpose of his visit.

"Patrick O'Brien. CDC Distributors," he said, smirking as he heard the revolving door unlock.

Just as he entered the threshold, an abrupt thud against the door made him turn around. One of the parking lot bums, a particularly gnarly-looking specimen with a bushy beard and black dreadlocks that were peppered with gray pushed against the door behind him. O'Brien jumped forward, avoiding the vagrant who nearly crashed into him. Though the bum looked as if he hadn't bathed since Mel Gibson was sane, he was wearing lavender hospital scrubs, and when he thumped past him, O'Brien got an odd whiff of lemons.

"I think you gotta get tighter security, sugar," O'Brien said, approaching the babe with the sweet rack behind the front desk.

"Sorry about that, sir," she said, her eyes on the disheveled intruder. "Could you please check your cell phone here with me? Company policy."

"No prob," O'Brien said, beaming as he tossed his cell phone on the desk.

No ring, O'Brien observed. Not that marriage had ever bothered him before. On the road, he'd done a few married chicks, but mostly just the bridesmaids at bachelorette parties. He had quite a way with the drunk and depressed. Maybe he'd ask the receptionist to accompany him to that tiki bar he'd seen by the hotel. Seemed like a place where bikinis may be the uniform. But he'd check out the ladies in the rest of the place first. No sense blowing it all on the first one he saw. And she seemed pretty distracted with the lemon-scented vagabond who'd just infiltrated the premises.

The bum was making his way towards the restrooms and the receptionist ran from behind the desk to push him back in the direction of the door to the parking lot from whence he came. O'Brien figured he'd better get to work. Get the job done quick, then booze, broads, and, well, bars. He really should make that last entry more creative if he was going to start using that line.

"Wilbert Sarducci. What floor's he on?" he shouted to the receptionist, who had her hands on the derelict's shoulder blades as she tried to move his short, stocky frame closer to the revolving door. He kept turning his head to her hands and snapping his teeth together as if he was either trying to bite her or he'd forgotten how to talk.

"Level three. Walk straight out of the elevator and make a left. He sits near the Web and customer service teams," she said.

"Thanks, babe," O'Brien said, walking to the elevators. He turned slightly and gave her a wink. "I'll see YOU later."

But she wasn't listening. In fact, she was wincing in pain as the bum sank his teeth into her ringless hand.

10:56 AM

A successful invasion, the General thought. Now we just need more people who can speak well enough to be granted permission to the building, and, one by one, we will arrive. It will be slow, he surmised, but effective nonetheless, and once inside, the employees will be given no choice but to present his troops with an executive feast.

10:58 AM

David Straub sat at his cluttered desk in the center of the *Pittsburgh Daily Dispatch* newsroom. His modest work area was covered in stacks of papers for his current investigation into the Public Works Department's sketchy street-cleaning practices that really seemed just an excuse to ticket the taxpayers. He didn't have a full cubicle or shelves to display his accomplishments, so he had to mount his three Golden Quill award plaques on the wide support column next to his chair. He leaned back, running his fingers through his short, curly brown hair. The story was going nowhere. Unable to reach the director of Public Works or anyone at the Parking Authority, he was beginning to think that the piece would have to wait, to sit on the back burner while he pursued other projects. But what other projects? David had been at a loss recently, which did not help to maintain his image as the brilliant young journalist that his awards indicated. And with the spate of layoffs in his office and the industry in general, this was not the time to have writer's block.

He was pushing his unneeded glasses down to the end of his nose so he could more clearly ogle his plaques when his phone rang.

"David Straub at the *Pittsburgh Daily Dispatch*," he answered.

"David, it's Marshall."

"Oh, Mr. Owens, how have you been? How's things down at Pro-Well?" he asked loudly enough that his co-workers would envy the 32-year-old's personal connection with the king of Pittsburgh industry, the reason for two of his Golden Quills. Sandy Baker, the middle-aged reporter on the crime beat who sat across from him, rolled her eyes and turned up the volume of her police scanner.

"I've got a situation here, David," Owens said with an urgency that the award-winning journalist had heard him use only once before.

"Anything like the last time?" David asked.

"I'm not sure yet, but it looks that way. Have you heard anything about attacks in the South Side?"

"Just bits and pieces on the police scanner. Sandusky on the beat went down to check it out. Why?"

"Make sure it doesn't get back to me," Owens said. "Steer this Sandusky character far, far away from my direction. Steer him towards Mexico if you have to. Also, next week we'll be unveiling a pill that has helped control borderline personality disorder in laboratory rats. Your exclusive. We'll fight sociopaths together."

"Sounds good, Marshall, but I'll just need some more details," David said smugly, pushing his glasses up his nose.

"You'll know when I do," Owens said and hung up the phone.

David put his phone back on the receiver and smiled to himself. Who knew that Marshall Owens had also found a cure for writer's block?

10:57 AM

Will had a nasty habit that was apparent to just about everyone but himself. Peering over Hank's shoulder to monitor his progress on a Web page was obnoxious, but his tendency to stand so close that his crotch nearly brushed Hank's shoulder was an outright abomination. Did he not realize that he had grown wider in recent years? This may have been vaguely inappropriate for a thinner man, but Will's bloated front side put him far too close to Hank. Will's cropped brown hair, glasses, tucked shirts, and rotund physique made him look a lot like Peter Griffin. Today he munched on one of his token butter-on-white-bread sandwiches, licking the lard off his lips while critiquing Hank's latest copy.

Hank tried to ignore him and focus on work. It was too early in the week for a full-blown confrontation, although a debacle always made the job more interesting. Lately Hank had found himself hoping for a paper jam whenever he used the printer in order to present himself with a distraction, a simple problem for which he could execute a simple solution that would break up the monotony of the day. Hank could hear Myron the janitor taking about last night's Steelers game from across the room. When launching on a diatribe about anything local, Myron's amps went up to 11.

Hank had no good reason to hate Myron and actually felt quite bad for his profoundly negative feelings towards the janitor. But Hank could not tolerate the man's excruciatingly irritating habit of narrating his life. Every banal action had verbal accompaniment.

"I'm just going to walk around your desk right over here and empty out this trash can," he'd say, or, "I'll be walkin' into this here bathroom right about now to 'vacuate these here bowels, then clean the sinks." And as unnecessarily detailed as his explanations were, they did not contain deep-seated emotions about the metaphoric content of cleaning the bathroom, using the act of wiping down the windows as an allegory for his pitiful existence. Scrubbing grout did not trigger a haunting memory of his first love whose death was still shrouded in mystery to this day. He was not on his knees, rubbing a toothbrush between the tiles while he ran through the facts of the thirty-year-old case again and again. *With each sweep of the floor, he remembered Anna, her lifeless body swept away by the ocean tide. He didn't know why, but three decades after her drowning death that police had ruled an accident, the memories were suddenly flooding back like the water in his beloved's lungs.*

But he did not have guilt that crippled him to abandon his dreams for an anonymous existence in menial labor. In fact, Myron married the first woman he felt that he could live with, and no debilitating feelings of culpability were to blame for Myron's lowly fate. Hank thought that would have been fascinating. What an intriguing hobby—to narrate one's life as though it was a work of literature, to provide insight into actions with the distinct voice of a character. This would actually be quite easy—that is, if the narrator had something to say. Myron, tragically, did not have anything close to a unique perspective on the world, so he recited his actions with all the personality of a narrator in an instructional video on how to build a bird feeder.

Hank listened to Maria Cortez giggle at Myron, finding his uneducated Pittsburgh naiveté amusing, endearing even. He often wished that he could delight in such meaningless distractions, but he was completely incapable of abandoning his disdain to allow himself to momentarily betray the tenets of his invented faith in the only thing he knew these days: his anger.

"I can smell the booze on you," Will observed.

"You're so close to me I'd imagine you're smelling it directly from my liver." Hank heard Adam stifle a laugh.

"I'm reading your copy, Hank," Will retorted. "When Mr. O'Brien arrives, please stay away from him. Whiskey is not a professional scent."

Lauren Abrahms from sales was handling the CDC account but had been a no-show this morning, so John McAvee, the head of the sales team, had asked Will to personally look after Mr. O'Brien until she returned so that another rep would not steal the lead. And verbal rim jobs were Will's specialty.

"Neither's sweat," Hank replied, shoving his rolling chair back until he bashed Will in the legs. "I'll email this to you. I'm going out for a smoke."

"We have a deadline, Hank," Will said to Hank's back.

"So do I. I always try to smoke at least five cigarettes by noon, and this will only be my fourth so far. I've got catching up to do," Hank said, pulling his leather jacket from the post affixed to his cubicle wall.

"Wilby, my man!" came a voice from the elevator.

Hank turned and got a look at a tall, lean man in a cheap suit with a playing card-themed necktie. His brown hair was slicked back with too much gel, and he wore a used-car salesman's smile with a toothpick jutting from his teeth. His arms were raised in celebration, and he was yelling to no one in particular. Will turned abruptly, shoving the remains of his I-can't-believe-it's-a-butter-sandwich into his pant pocket, and walked towards the man.

"Yo, I'm Patrick O'Brien, CDC Distribution and Technology," O'Brien said, handing Will a shiny black business card emblazoned with his smirking portrait. "Sorry, took me a while to get here, just checkin' out the nightlife on the street. Flew in this morning from Baltimore—only a forty-five-minute plane ride—can you believe that? Then the cab took an hour to get me to my hotel, then I had to check out that sweet drinking district you got down there. Tried to count the bars, but got to sixty and then just gave up. Banks converted into bars? What a world."

Hank was amazed at how little this fast-talking sleazeball needed to breathe.

"Well, it's good to meet you, Mr. O'Brien. I'm Wilbert Sarducci—," Will said, attempting to get a word in. He wiped his butter-covered hand on the side of his khaki pants and extended it to the visiting client. O'Brien high-fived him instead.

"Call me Rick. So drugs, eh? Oh, sorry, gotta be politically correct. Meds. So what's the deal with that new one, Probalsis? You know, I was thinking about that. Shouldn't it be Pro-Cocksis 'cause you know, that's what it's really for, got it?" O'Brien paused for a second to laugh at himself, then continued quickly. "Not that I need any of that for personal use. Speaking of, who is that slice you got working at reception downstairs? She kept me entertained and could for much longer than just signing in, you know what I mean?"

"Yes, Sandra is a charming girl."

"Yeah, she could charm the flames off my Camaro." He winked. "So let's get to this. Sorry if I'm a little talkative." He quieted his voice a little bit so only the nearest eight people could hear. "Got some real bad ADD. Never take my Rits, though, when I go on the road. Like to sample the wares, see which comp's got the best ones. Think we could get started with some of that. Then, I figured, hit the factory. See how these meds get made." He clapped his hands together in a grandiose, swooping motion.

"Well, Rick, since you just got in, I was thinking you could relax a little bit," Will said.

He had received direct orders from Mr. Owens not to take O'Brien to the factory. Apparently there had been some sort of work stoppage: broken equipment or something like that. Owens had assured him that it was merely a minor setback and would all be mended by tomorrow. But for now, Will was to keep the visiting pharmaceutical distributor busy at the corporate office and with any other distractions that he appeared to enjoy. And judging thus far, O'Brien was a man easily distracted. Strip clubs and sports bars seemed about right. Will's woman would be upset, but she of all people would understand the sacrifices one must make for the greater good of the company.

"I was thinking I could take you on a tour of the office, let you sit down with some of our specialists and I'd take you to lunch and let you see our fair city," Will said. "I know a gentleman's club downtown with a fantastic lunch buffet."

Hank's face contorted, and he looked over at Pete, who was stifling laughter into his coffee mug.

"Oh, dude, sounds great, man. I can't eat on an empty stomach, so I'm gonna hit the snack machines, then we'll check out some of those," he paused, "specialists you were talking about." His inflection made "specialists" a double-entendre. "Then I'm all about that men's club. They got fried chicken there, man?"

"Of course they do, Rick," Will lied. His woman had very strict rules about even glancing at other ladies, and Will had not been to a strip club in years. "Let me take you over to Angela in quality assurance."

"I like the sound of that," O'Brien said, grinning.

He pulled a small comb out of his lapel pocket and ran it through his short hair. Will put his chubby hand on O'Brien's right shoulder and shuffled him to the other side of the floor to QA. O'Brien, toothpick in mouth, indiscreetly ran his eyes over Eileen Carson from customer service as she walked past. He nudged Will in the arm, and they kept walking.

"All right, show's over," Hank mumbled as he got up from his desk.

He walked to the stairs, passing the women waiting for the elevators to transport them one floor down to the lobby. He jogged down the stairs and out the back door to the parking lot. Would it be a Megadeth or an Armored Saint break? Loud metal and cool nicotine, that's what Hank needed right now. He turned left out the door towards his car. If he had turned right, he would have seen a group of ten gray homeless corpses forming something like an offensive line near the building's main entrance.

11:07 AM

Nick was typing quickly in his cramped corner cubicle, sending emails to clients. Officially letting the poor Pro-Well customers know that he would no longer be around to provide them with that outstanding customer service that was apparently still never good enough to make the Wall of Fame that honored those who dazzle with their remote assistance.

"Dear Rocci," he typed, his neck aching, his throat swelling, sweat pouring from his pale brow. "I regret to inform you that as of this afternoon, I will no longer be handling your account at Pro-Well. Please direct all further inquiries to Claire Harrington. She will ahandke yrour account untilllllllllllllllllll-llllllllllllllll"

Nick's head smacked down on his mouse, sending the email to distributor Rocci Dawson. His death was quick. Just the stoppage of his heart unexpectedly after what seemed to be no more than an ailment easily treated by Pro-Nose. Well, the bite on his wrist had appeared to be getting infected. But it wasn't really that painful. Deep in the bowels of Pro-Well Pharmaceuticals, his death, much like his hard work, went completely unnoticed.

For now.

11:08 AM

Peace, Hank thought. Peace that can only occur alone exhaling a Marlboro Red in a beat-up, black '98 Dodge Ram to the soundtrack of Dave Mustaine singing about his darkest hour. Hank closed his eyes and let the moment take over. No office gossip he couldn't give a shit less about, no computer, no Will Sar-*douche*-i. He'd have to reenter the corporate abyss in a few minutes, but for now, it was too serene.

Recently, the repetition in his life had been growing more evident. He hated how complacent he'd become, a slave to the system he had once tried so hard to avoid. He'd even started obeying company policy by leaving his cell phone in his car every day. Awake at the same time each morning to sit in the same box and write the same technical drivel: He needed a break. Hank had begun to feel that if he didn't make a drastic change, his life would be nothing but a long string of monotony. Evenings spent drowning in whiskey at the Male Box and the Bat Cave had once provided a respite from the ennui, but now they had also become repetitive. Yet Hank could not shake the temporary ease that the booze provided, so he was locked into the routine and felt that not even Harry Houdini could free himself from this restraint.

Monotony was Hank's greatest fear. Life would be so much easier if it was goblins. They were physical, tangible, and he had the home arsenal to fend off an attack. But boredom was ever encroaching. A real sneaky bastard that crept up on him, dragging him deeper and deeper into his rut. Hank had armed himself in case of any possible anachronistic threat—he could take on the flying monkeys from *The Wizard of Oz* if need be—but no amount of heavy artillery could combat the notion that his life was slipping away into the chasm of the oppressively mundane.

So Hank cherished the moments that were his and his alone. The simple pleasures derived from smoking a cigarette in his car or lifting a barbell at the gym. He knew that if he didn't chop off the head of that Goliath boredom, it would swallow him slowly until he was trapped forever in a life dictated by the demands of the utility companies.

11:10 AM

If Nick's brain had still been intact, he would have been pleased that his usually indifferent co-workers noticed his re-animation. After about three minutes of death, he rose from his cubicle, his chiseled face gray and rotten, his eyes as glazed as a Krispy Kreme doughnut. Slowly, he ambled the three steps to Monica's desk. When the petite blonde saw the remains of her co-worker approach, she screamed.

Nick did what came naturally and tore the flesh from her shoulder with his teeth. Needless to say, this garnered quite a bit of attention from the rest of the drones. They knocked him to the ground, attempting to subdue him, but Nick was now merely a mass of flesh-hungry human remains. There was no reasoning with a zombie, and he did not hear their pleas for mercy, their attempts to calm him by stating that they were sure he could find another job, that there was no need to panic.

All he could hear was his gut.

And it was hungry.

11:12 AM

Eileen Carson was ravaged next to the elevator. What was left of her intestines spilled onto the blue carpet in a sanguinary disaster. She had thought that James and Linda Schenn had looked a bit ill when they approached her. They walked slowly and awkwardly as though they had just learned how. Eileen had stopped to ask her recently married co-workers if they were all right when they lunged. Tackling her to the floor, their teeth bared, the newlyweds ripped at her throat. She couldn't even scream when they opened up her stomach and began to feast on her vital organs one at a time. They would have finished, had they not been interrupted by Tom Finnegan. He was still alive, and apparently fresher than the disemboweled administrative assistant.

11:16 AM

"Sir, they're inside the building," Harold reported.

"The recruits?" Owens asked.

He was sweating; his empire was crumbling. Cleaning up the city streets, donating employees' money to charity, medicating the people on the cheap. The veneer was fading, quickly becoming more translucent until eventually the citizens of Pittsburgh would see right through. His fans in the press would make him into the monster that women in pickup joints thought he was when he bared his terrible smile to let them know who bought their drinks.

"No. They're stationed outside the front door. There seems to be an outbreak among the office staff."

"Stand guard at my door. Do not let anyone onto this floor," Owens commanded.

"But sir, I could at least neutralize some of them. I am armed," Harold pleaded.

He really wanted to whack someone. The rest of the men in black were able to indulge in their violent urges all day. But Harold was not allowed such freedom of expression. Owens had taken quite a liking to the former crack, pot, and heroin dealer, and the two had forged a bond over their shared experiences in the drug world. They were both trying to change their lives but could never shake their roots. Though he'd amassed quite the personal fortune, Owens spent his money as one would expect from a man reared in a trailer park. His gold-plated, diamond-encrusted lifestyle reeked of the *nouveau riche*.

Harold hid his violent urges well behind a mask of eloquence and "yes, sirs," unlike some of the others who had absolutely no self-control. Rapists were still rapists even in a room filled with the dead, and there had been a few incidents of certain henchmen being caught violating the recently deceased female recruits.

But being Owens's right-hand man was currently advantageous. He appeared to be the only one remaining, as he had been unable to reach any of the others in the field. When he called Michael five minutes ago, the phone was answered by a guttural gurgle that Harold could not take as anything but bad news. He needed to do something, to stop whatever that scarred madman had started in the factory. Harold was beginning to feel that if he survived this, he would be tried at Nuremburg. Just by following the orders of the man who wrote his ample checks, he felt like a war criminal.

"They can take care of themselves. Stay at your post," Owens barked. He felt as if the hair plugs were popping out of his scalp.

"Yes, sir," Harold replied.

He'd ride this thing out for a while with a .45 in his pocket. Above all else, Harold had a keen sense of self-preservation. He'd learned it the hard way, from an angry absentee father who only showed up only when he needed money, and who put Harold on the streets at the ripe old age of 11 to sling crack to neighborhood addicts. Pop said it was to "earn his keep," but most of his earnings went to things that Harold didn't want. At 11, he had no interest in six-day benders with drug-addicted strippers or high-stakes poker games. Harold wanted kid stuff—video games and a baseball glove. But instead he was busted at 13 and sent away to juvie where he honed his survival skills in a jail for truly disturbed children.

Harold excelled at the detention center and was even released after only six months for good behavior. He was rational and exercised self-control, and if the warden was suspicious of any illicit activity among the inmates, Harold was the first boy he'd ask. Of course, selling out his fellow prisoners did not make him popular. Not two days after his release, the first attempt on his life was made.

He was in the midst of an intense game of one-on-one at a local court when a shot rang out from the bleachers. Sitting with the teenage girls who thought basketball was sexy and the teenage boys who'd put money on the match, there was a hooded youth aiming a .38 at Harold's head. When they heard the gunshot, the girls scattered. But the boys, well, the boys knew that they lived in a part of the city where the police didn't respond to emergencies. To them, the cops were the enemy and in order to keep themselves safe, they had to be their own law and order. The seven boys on the bleachers tackled the hooded adolescent to the ground and beat him mercilessly.

Harold and his friendly opponent ran from the court to the grass and watched the boys kick the stranger's head until blood streamed from every existing facial orifice and the new ones that they'd made. Harold reached into the grass and picked up the .38. Pointing the gun at his intended assassin, he stared at the boy's mangled face. Harold had never seen him before, didn't know who this adolescent was or who had paid him for the hit, but he knew what had to be done. If there were people who wanted to kill him, young Harold would have to send a message. Aiming the gun at the boy's forehead, Harold pulled the trigger.

The boys dragged the corpse to the river and threw it in. They never heard about the incident again. Not in the newspapers, not on television. No cops even came sniffing around about the dead teenager in the Ohio River with a hole in his head. The boys never spoke of it again, but it shaped Harold for the rest of his life.

Now at the age of 34, after two stints in prison and a failed marriage that ended in a restraining order, Harold still thought of that 14-year-old boy and the decision he had made that day on the basketball courts.

Kill or be killed.

11:18 AM

Serenity later, Hank thought as he closed the door of his car. He hit the lock button on the remote control, waited until he saw the headlights blink in recognition, checked each door handle to be sure that he could not open any of them, pushed in the already closed gas tank cover, then hit the lock button and watched the lights flash again. He paced slowly towards the office building, taking one last drag before stomping out his cigarette by someone else's car. If somehow his precious vehicle of unrepentant masculinity had developed a gas leak on the way to work, he couldn't risk it catching on fire.

Scanning the bar code of his ID badge, he swung open the back door and entered. Hank avoided the front entrance so he'd never have to smile back at Sandra, the overly made-up receptionist with the platinum blonde *Karate Kid*-era Elizabeth Shue haircut. People who smile at you when you barely know them: That was something Hank truly despised.

He moved swiftly up the steps to the second floor to the cubicles of the damned where, like Sisyphus, they worked every day to accomplish nothing.

The office housed about seventy people on each of the second and third floors, forty on the first, and, from what everyone could tell, no one on the fourth except for His Majesty Marshall Owens. Hank understood why the CEO would want to be sequestered. That face must have been twice as frightening in person as it was on the 6 o'clock news. But it seemed truly unnecessary to cram the rest of the staff into tiny pods in an egg carton. Each was a mere five-foot-by-five-foot box with an open wall that allowed nosy employees, like Kelly and Judy, free peeping privileges. Hank simply didn't care what his coworkers were doing in their walled cages and could not fathom why anyone would wonder about his menial day-to-day actions. No matter how much time Kelly wasted by reading the side effects of every Pro-Well product at her desk, Hank knew that reporting her to management would not alleviate the helplessness he felt day after day.

He pulled open the glass door to the second-floor office space and slipped into the men's room adjacent to the stairwell.

Entering the rather spacious room, Hank was struck by a rancid smell, like no other bathroom odor he had ever experienced, and Hank had been to seedy gay bars in New Orleans. No, this was far more intense than anything he had ever encountered. Like rotting meat, bad cheese, and sulfur all mixed together in the olfactory equivalent of drinking a gasoline and V8 cocktail poured over egg salad. It got worse as he approached the row of urinals and the motionless man Hank vaguely recognized from customer service—Vince, maybe?—

in a striped polo shirt who was standing at one. He was slowly tilting forward, his hands frozen in the process of unzipping his pants, until his head smacked the restroom's tiled wall.

"Holy shit," Hank exclaimed. "Are you okay, man?" he asked, pulling the *possible*-Vince's shoulder.

The man lifted his head and peered up. Hank jolted back as he saw the gray skin and glassy eyes. The man opened his mouth, exposing rotting teeth and retracted gums, and bit the air where Hank's arm had been just a moment before. He leaned towards Hank, taking his hand out of his pants and reaching for Hank's face.

"Well, fuck you, dude," Hank said, punching the mutant in the head. He remained for a second to watch the thing in the golf outfit fall to the floor before turning his back to it and running to the door.

Outside of the men's room, the office was nearly vacant, save for the three blood-soaked employees noshing on what appeared to be a woman lying on the long table from this morning's breakfast party in customer service. Then he spotted Maria Cortez, a pretty customer service rep who always wore her button-down shirts with minimal buttoning, at her desk with the phone to her ear. *How could she be so oblivious to whatever it is that is going on?* Hank wondered. He approached her desk and saw that she was punching numbers in on her phone, but unless she was trying to dial one of the moons of Saturn, there could not possibly be that many digits needed.

Carefully, he walked to the cubicle opposite hers, learning from the bathroom incident not to get too close. The partition that separated the two came only to Hank's chest, leaving him a clear view of Maria's dead face and the vapid expression as she continued to punch numbers in the phone.

Keeping his eyes on her, Hank stepped backwards slowly when suddenly he was being pulled backwards into the conference room.

11:19 AM

It took David Straub only twenty minutes to travel from the *Pittsburgh Daily Dispatch* building downtown to the Pro-Well parking lot in the South Side. He heard over the police scanner he kept in his car that there had been more reports of mayhem in the area, and not the drunk and disorderly type usually associated with East Carson Street. These were attacks—random vicious attacks that seemed to be occurring for no reason. David didn't know how, but they had something to do with Pro-Well, and this time, he was going to do something about it.

After graduating from journalism school ten years ago, David had found that in the real world, newspapers had no use for people who want to plagiarize *The New Yorker*. After two years of waiting tables in Manhattan, trying to editorialize his way into the press, David was finally offered a position at the *Pittsburgh Daily Dispatch*. It wasn't the most revered publication but a standard mid-market newspaper, and it would be a good launching point to become the 21st-century Bob Woodward. Unfortunately, he pontificated himself right into city council meetings and dull charitable events. But it was at one of these galas, a fundraiser for sickle cell anemia, that he made the acquaintance of one Marshall Owens, a rising star in the medicine industry. The CEO had taken quite a liking to David's educated naiveté and had courted him with exclusive stories about Pro-Well's latest innovations in exchange for his help covering up some of the less popular aspects of the business. And it had been working. David had the awards and the prestige and the immunity from layoffs, and Marshall stayed out of prison.

But recently, the Faustian bargain had begun to haunt the young journalist. While packing up to move into a newly purchased townhouse in the trendy Mexican War Streets in the North Side, he found one of his old ethics books from college. Forgetting that he was racking up quite the rental fee for the U-Haul parked outside, David began reading the book, his eyes brimming with tears when he finally admitted the fraud that he had become. So when Marshall Owens called this morning asking for yet another favor, David decided to eschew his duties as a shill and actually investigate.

He parked his Jetta in the rear of the Pro-Well lot and stepped out of the car. Nothing appeared out of the ordinary. The parking lot was filled with the modest cars of the employees, and he could make out the shadows of people working in the office. He pulled his small digital tape recorder out of the pocket of his tan suede jacket.

"Pro-Well corporate headquarters. October 11, 2010. Appears to be business as usual here."

Maintaining his focus on the windows of the office, David began to walk around the building to the front door. Besides the car passing on the nearby on-ramp to the parkway, the only sound was the crackling of the gravel beneath his feet. *They really have to get this paved*, he thought. He reached the front entrance of the office and gazed into the floor-to-ceiling glass window to the right of the revolving door. He ripped his decorative thick-rimmed glasses from his face and stared at the scene of carnage in the lobby.

What appeared to have recently been a blonde woman with a dated haircut was lying on the floor, her nose and eyes the only part of her face intact. A stump of a large intestine protruded from the empty pit that was once her midsection. Her clothes were torn away, and pieces of business casual attire were strewn in what could only have been the aftermath of a deluge of blood. At least three other bodies lay behind her near the elevators in the same state of mutilation. Blood dripped from the inside of the revolving door that housed what was once a man, his left hand still intact, raised, and pressed against the glass as a warning to ye who enter here.

David blinked in disbelief as he pulled the tape recorder from his jacket pocket.

"Disregard earlier note. Pro-Well lobby is a scene of carnage. There are what appear to have been several employees savagely maimed on the floor. I cannot see any sign of their as-

sailant, but the corpse stuck in the revolving door leads me to
believe that he or she or, fuck, *they* escaped through a different
exit. There is blood everywhere, and the people are barely rec-
ognizable. This is—shit—this is more brutal than Manson!"

David stopped to regain his composure. If this panned out,
it could be his *In Cold Blood*. Fuck Woodward and Bernstein,
he thought. This could turn him into Capote.

He hit the record button on his tape recorder and lifted it to
his mouth. He inhaled, ready to unleash more gruesome adjec-
tives to most accurately capture this scene of bloody carnage
for his rapt future readers. He was about to tell the digital
recorder that this damage looked more like something inflicted
by animals than humans when a set of sharp, jagged teeth sank
into his neck, ripping a piece from his plaid collar. He tried to
scream, but only a gurgle came out as his attacker drove him
to the ground. His eyes were open wide with the curiosity that
is innate in all those who have ever aspired to break a story. He
lay on his back, writhing in pain, while his gray assailant in
hospital scrubs started ripping pieces of flesh from his shoulder.
Tape recorder still in hand, he smashed it into his attacker's
face, and the thing tumbled to the gravel. Though seemingly
unscathed, it struggled to sit back up like an infant whose motor
skills had barely progressed enough to master the mystical art
of walking.

David held his right hand against his neck to try to quell
the copious bleeding while he lifted himself to his feet. He
kicked the freak in the head, further impeding its labored efforts
to regain balance. As it fell back to the ground, David stumbled
back the way he had come, leaving a trail of blood that gushed
from the gaping hole in his throat. Pain coursing from his neck
and shoulder to seemingly everywhere in his body, David tried
to push through the lot back in the direction of his red Jetta.
Blood poured through the gaps between his fingers and ran
down the front of his jacket as he felt more and more as if his
skull was being filled with air. David tried to fight the light-
headedness, pushing his hand down harder into his neck, but

to no avail. He could no longer feel his legs as they carried him towards the Jetta. He shoved his right hand into the pocket of his khaki pants, pulling out his keys.

Approaching the Jetta, he fingered the bundle of keys until he came upon the remote control. As he tumbled to the ground, he hit the unlock button. His face hit the gravel, leaving his last living moment a painful one.

11:27 AM

"Shit, piss, fuck, cunt, cocksucker, motherfucker, tits!" Owens shouted in his office as he watched his media lackey fall to the ground in an ocean of blood.

He didn't usually quote George Carlin, but he felt the seven dirty words were the best way to describe this moment. David had no reason to come here except betrayal, to turn his bene-factor's misfortune into his own personal gain. His allies were turning against him. Was this his Valkyrie? Was there no one in his inner circle that he could still trust? He thought about the news that Harold had given him earlier. All his men were dead, either at the hands of the recruits or of one another. His loose ends were either dead or mostly dead and unable to speak anyway.

Except for one.

Owens peered through the peephole on his door and saw Harold pacing in front of his office. Just one left, one who could definitively tie him to this outbreak. Owens returned to his desk and sat down in his chair. Only one left, a potential star witness for the prosecution had he not been the very one who had en-gineered this entire catastrophe. One ex-con, a violent drug dealer whom Owens had tried to rehabilitate, whom he had trusted with his empire, his life. One deranged thug who had been blackmailing the vulnerable Marshall Owens into silence for months. A greedy hood who was ungrateful for the sacri-fices that the CEO had made to try to help him change his life.

A moral to the story. Not every one is as capable of redemption as Marshall Owens, the selfless, disfigured victim of a lifelong criminal's machinations.

Or that's what everyone would believe.

Owens clicked his computer out of sleep mode and began typing.

11:29 AM

"Rock me like a fucking hurricane, Hank! Why did you come back?" Adam asked as Hank stood up from the floor of the conference room.

"What are you talking about? I went out for a cigarette, I come back, and it's a goddamn war zone! What the hell are you guys doing in the conference room?"

"Somebody decided that we needed to be here," Pete said sarcastically.

"As safety officer of the floor, I am in charge," Will said.

"You locked us in a damn conference room," Pete countered.

"In the event of an outbreak of workplace violence, employees will seek refuge in the nearest conference room. Pro-Well Emergency Procedures Manual, Section 12.8. The glass," he tapped on the window, "is bulletproof."

"All right, Joe Friday. Did it say anything about what to do if the employees start eating one another?" Hank asked.

Will hung his head in silence. Hank surveyed the crowd in the conference room. He was pleased to see Pete and Adam, but Will, Judy, Kelly, that sleaze from Baltimore, and the chubby weirdo from customer service made the vibe a bit less pleasant. He almost neglected to notice Myron, who was standing uncharacteristically silent in the corner. And there was that weird Goth chick who smiled at him at the Bat Cave. What in the Pro-Hell was she doing here?

"We saw two freaks eating that babe by the elevators, and we got the hell in here," said O'Brien, toothpick still hanging out of his mouth, his suit jacket slung over his shoulder to reveal the full disco-ball quality of his silver shirt that was buttoned to only about halfway up his chest. "I don't know what's going on, but there are some majorly mental employees," he added.

"They ate Jonah from the call center," Kelly said, clutching her swollen belly as she sat cross-legged on the floor. Though she was in no hurry to join the blood-spattered scene of mutilation in the cubicles, she couldn't help but wonder how long they'd be trapped in this room with the most edible thing being the ficus in the corner. She couldn't eat people the way her co-workers were outside the conference room. At least not yet. There was seemingly no end to the pregnant cravings. She might not be able to hold out as long as the Donner party did.

"Actually, Amy and Doris from accounting ate him," Judy added, always the busybody. She was clutching her left wrist and holding her sweater sleeve in place over it.

"It's…" Janice began as Pete cut her off.

"Don't say it again, Elvira."

"Well how can it not be? There are what appear to be corpses walking around eating people. It's obviously a *zombie* apocalypse!" Janice finished, stressing the zombie part.

"I suppose you were hoping for vampires," Pete retorted.

"Both of you idiots shut up! What is sure is that some sort of virus has gotten into our co-workers and we have to do something before Tom from quality assurance makes us his personal buffet," Wilbert exclaimed, pointing towards the row of five windows that looked out at their ravaged second-floor cubicles.

There was Tom, all six-and-a-half feet and 270 pounds of him lurking, staring into the room with glazed eyes, his usually shiny bald head now chipped with a matte gray finish, half his green tie ripped off, his white button-down shit stained with blood. He looked like the ghost of post-apocalyptic Christmas future.

"Close the blinds," Hank said, reaching for the Venetians' string. "They seem to be pretty stupid. I mean, it appears that

Tom has forgotten how to use a doorknob. Maybe if they don't see us, we don't exist."

Pete followed and helped him with the rest of the cheap, white Venetians that were normally used to conceal what Hank thought to be management's nefarious plots. Now they had a bunker.

"Why don't we stay here for now, pool our knowledge of what we've seen of them so far to formulate something resembling an attack strategy, and get the fuck out of this office." Hank paused, recalling the pizza shop worker earlier and his affinity for biting. "Oh, shit."

"What?" Janice said, enraptured by his every word. Too bad she was not feeling more articulate, but her co-workers were eating one another and she thought he would understand.

"I think there's some out there, too. The goddamn biting fetish—I saw that this morning. Some rabid dickbrain tried to bite me when I left my house this morning. I knocked him out," Hank said.

"How did they become like… that?" Kelly asked, blinking back tears.

"The bites," Janice said in a patronizing tone. Everyone turned to look at her, except for Doug, who was busy trying to remove chunks of hair from his head. "Just like in *Night of the Living Dead.*"

"You are aware that George Romero is not a documentary filmmaker?" Pete asked, thoroughly irritated with this new hire.

"I know that 2012 isn't till next year, but I think we have an apocalypse on our hands," Janice said.

Hank watched as the employees nodded and bowed their heads almost in unison, as if they were about to surrender to these decaying gray monsters. They looked almost reverent for a moment.

"I wish we had flying broomsticks," Janice said, breaking the silence.

Was she insane? Hank asked himself. Judging by the expressions of Pete, Adam, and Kelly, they concurred.

"All right," Hank said, exasperated and waving his arms wildly. "We've gotta get the fuck out of here."

"But you said they were outside, too," pleaded Judy.

"Yeah, but if I'm gonna die today, it's gonna be at a bar with twelve goddamn shots of Jack in my stomach," Hank said.

"Hank, I'd probably go for getting a blow job, not giving one," Adam said, laughing at himself, hand in the air, waiting for a high-five that was never going to come.

"Fuck it, I'm out of here!" Hank said, turning towards the door. His co-workers were becoming vastly more irritating than the cannibals' moans on the other side of the wall.

Hank swung the conference room door open and was greeted by Tom's massive frame parked right in the doorway. He stared straight ahead, his mouth gaping open to display what appeared to be part of a pancreas hanging out of it. Hank slammed the door shut and turned back to the others.

"I think we need a plan," he said. Relieved that he still had his cigarettes in his pocket, Hank took out the pack and lit one.

"Hank, put that out. You can't smoke in the office!" Will commanded.

"I don't think we're allowed to murder our co-workers either," Hank said, exhaling a cloud of smoke from his nose.

"They are not murderers," Will said. "They are valued members of our Pro-Well family. You cannot judge them all by the actions of a few."

"Bullshit," Pete said. "I saw Lawrence Jacobs tear out Carol Thomas's vocal cords. I'm pretty sure that killed her."

Will was quiet, hanging his head and mumbling something about judging thy neighbor.

Janice, who had grabbed her corset purse from her desk before sprinting to the conference room, pulled out a metal case and removed a clove cigarette from it. Putting it to her lips, she lit it with a crucifix lighter.

"Now that's just offensive," Judy said, staring at the flaming cross.

"Hank, can I bum one?" Pete asked. Hank tossed him a cigarette. Janice, who was seated next to Pete in a wheeled chair at the long conference table, lit it for him with her incendiary device.

"Please, put that out. I'm not supposed to be around smoke with the baby," Kelly pleaded.

The smokers continued to puff away, ignoring the pleas of the dissenting few. O'Brien removed a flask from his jacket pocket. It was in the shape of a voluptuous female torso, and he massaged the breasts with his thumb before taking a swig. Reaching into a knee-level pocket of his khaki cargo pants, Doug pulled out a small baggie and a short straw and snorted a hit of the white powder inside.

Now that's surprising, Hank thought.

"People!" Will exclaimed, attempting to assert control over a group of white-collar drones who were completely and certifiably freaking out. "Compose yourselves! This behavior is completely illegal! You are employees of Pro-Well Pharmaceuticals! Please show some respect!"

O'Brien belched loudly. "I'm not," he said.

"Yes, I know, Rick. And I will do everything in my power to ensure your comfort during this mishap," Will said, amazingly still focused on client relations.

"I think this is a little more than a mishap," Janice said.

"I'm sure this will all blow over soon," Will said, shuffling over to the file cabinets at the windowless side of the room. Pulling one open, he continued, "Now, Rick, I believe we have promotional materials in here somewhere that you may peruse at your leisure."

Will pulled out a shiny folder emblazoned with the Pro-Well logo—simply a stick figure with a bandage on his head lying in a hospital bed contained inside a circle with a red line through it—and continued his verbal assault. "We really have been doing some fantastic work with comfort for herpes outbreaks. Also, since Pro-Well's introduction of Pro-Citrusade in 2002, scurvy has been at an all-time low."

"Dude, no offense, but this is the first pharm comp I've

seen that has turned their employees into flesh-eating freaks," O'Brien said. "Thanks, but I think I'm cool here."

"Well, I really hope you change your mind, but for the time being, is there anything I can get you? I know I had planned that lunch at the strip club, but seeing how we're trapped in this room, I think we'll have to hold off on that," Will said, his voice cracking as it reached an abnormally high pitch. He was going to lose it any minute. Hank stabbed his cigarette out in a coffee cup that someone had left on the table.

"Ah...strippers... Yeah, that'd be nice," O'Brien said, closing his eyes to let his imagination take hold.

"Okay, I'll head over to the snack machines and get you some food, and you, new girl, please give our guest a lap dance," Will said, pointing to Janice.

"Are you out of your mind?" she asked.

"Wilbert man, really, it's okay. I'm not hungry: no need to leave the room," O'Brien said, calming Will. For the moment at least. The room went silent, and the gurgling groans from the office floor were more audible.

"So," Hank began, "is there anyone else in this office who is still, you know, normal? Or is it just us?"

The employees at the conference table shook their heads, except for Myron, who was slumped in the corner with his chin resting on his chest. He was helpless as he had always been. Indeed, for his whole life, mediocrity had always eluded him. He was a janitor and a Pittsburgher and nothing else. He had no interests outside of local sports franchises and no skill other than the ability to operate a mop wringer. He wasn't even in charge of infrastructure, just cleaning. Always below the mean, Myron had given up striving for average when he was cut from Little League in the fourth grade. Since then, he had assumed the role of professional spectator, watching the achievements of others from the nosebleed section.

In his younger years, he had held a job at Three Rivers Stadium, cleaning the peanuts and beer cans from the stands after his beloved Steelers played. He had once shaken the hand of

Franco Harris, and this proved to be the highlight of his life that he managed to incorporate into conversation with everyone he met. Pittsburgh and all its achievements constituted Myron's existence and made him feel that his underachievement was balanced by Pittsburgh's now annual recognition as one of the nation's most livable cities. He took it as a personal commendation when an issue of *National Geographic* that featured a two-page spread of a Primanti's sandwich (a local phenomenon that contained French fries, coleslaw, and tomatoes, along with the standard meat and cheeses between two pieces of Italian bread) hit the stands. Just a few years ago, when most locals were inconvenienced and annoyed by Pittsburgh's hosting of the G-20 convention, Myron was ecstatic that foreign dignitaries would see his fair city, which he loved so much. The mere fact that the president had heard of Pittsburgh gave Myron an overwhelming sense of undeserved pride.

He felt honored to work at Pro-Well, as it was proving to be a formidable influence in a market that, although he could neither understand it nor afford its wares, was important nonetheless. Marshall Owens's face was all over the news these days, and Myron could brag to his cronies at the bar on Saturday mornings that he was part of the organization. He followed Owens's civic initiatives religiously, pledging wholeheartedly his support of even the more absurd anti-pollution acts that his boss proposed.

Myron had never actually met Marshall Owens, but he saw Owens's electronic signature on his meager paychecks every two weeks, and that was enough for him. His job, the Steelers, the city: That was his life. It was all he knew. And now it was all on the brink of devastation. To Myron, there was nowhere else to go—the world ended at the West Virginia border. The idea that it could all soon be destroyed was proving far too much for a simple man like Myron to handle. His mind was fragmenting to the point where he could not formulate thoughts that could reach his mouth. So he sat in silence, intensely debating how the Penguins power play could be used to repair the dry wall in his kitchen.

"Lillian," Will said suddenly. "I haven't seen Lillian yet."

"Forget her," Pete said in his rural twang. "She's a schmuck."

"Do not speak of her like that," Will said, his mood growing weirder every second.

"Why the hell not? I'm not risking my life for that *machashaifeh*," Pete countered.

Lillian was the most despised member of the Pro-Well staff. A chubby hag who disguised her flabby unpleasantness under designer clothes and ornate jewelry. Hank longed for those days when hags were hags. Before Ann Taylor, Talbots, Chico's, and Liz Claiborne allowed them to be incorporated into mainstream society. She should have worn a cloak and rung a bell when she approached, like a leper, Hank thought. And everyone *should* be warned when Lillian is approaching. If she came to talk to you personally, you knew you were fired. She was the grim reaper of office jobs.

"Because he's sleeping with her," Judy declared.

"That's disgusting," Adam said, shivering.

"Do you really think she's alive?" Doug asked, raising his head up to reveal a new bald spot at his hairline.

"She's tough, a survivor," Will said.

"And she's got a corner office," Kelly added.

"She'll never get out by herself," Will said. "I think we need... I think we need to save her." Suddenly, manic Wilbert took over again. "I'm going," he shouted, making a beeline for the door.

Doug leapt from his seat, and, with Hank, grabbed Will and dragged him from the door. But the fat man was feisty, and it took Adam's and Pete's involvement to get him settled down in a chair.

"I have to get her," Will said, breathing more heavily than usual.

"Is she hot?" O'Brien asked, spinning in his chair at the head of the table.

"No fucking way," Pete said.

"Sorry, man, but I'm not going after any girl right now unless she's hot. I don't want my last chick to be a butterface or anything. No offense, ladies. I mean, you're pretty cute and all," he said, looking at Janice, "but I'm not into the whole dead thing."

"Well, I'm not into the whole douche thing," Janice retorted.

"Do you ever go out in the sun?" O'Brien asked.

"No," Janice replied curtly.

"I'm actually with Wednesday Addams on this one," Hank said. "No need to be orange."

"Wow, that was gay," Adam observed.

"I know a lot of chicks that tan that aren't orange," O'Brien said. "They just go to cover their stretch marks for work."

"Strippers," Pete said.

"That may be the sleaziest thing I've ever heard," Janice said.

"Well, I don't think I've gotta worry about that when I do my striptease," Adam said, laughing.

"If you're still around to do it," Pete said.

"Come on, Pete. You know you're doing it with me," Adam urged.

"I would not pay to see either of you strip," Kelly said.

"It's not stripping. It's a burlesque show," Adam explained.

"It's not your dream guys, but the ones you settle for," Pete added.

"That's awesome!" O'Brien exclaimed. "Can I join? Just wanna give back to the community and all."

"Why the hell not?" Pete said.

During this exchange, Hank had been thinking. While the others fretted and freaked and panicked and started to mourn everything they had to lose, a strange calm had come over Hank. There was a problem, and its milky eyes were staring him right in the face, teeth bared, ready to eat him alive. Unlike his everyday life and confusion and paranoia and the sense that boredom was invading like a fog with shackles, here was something real, tangible, and dangerous. Hank looked at the abandoned coffee mug and the stream of smoke that was emanating from it and realized that he had not stabbed his cigarette out in its entirety. His fear of burning down his apartment led him to compulsively destroy all chances for cigarettes to reignite, even testing them on his fingertips to ensure that the cherry was officially extinguished.

Gazing at the coffee mug that sat between Pete and the Goth chick, Hank realized that he was not the threat that would accidentally burn or flood his residence. With the moans and gurgles on the other side of the wall growing in intensity every minute, Hank finally felt in control, and he suddenly knew exactly what he needed to do.

"Sar-douchebag," Hank said suddenly, awakening from his trance. "We can save Lillian."

Will gazed up at him hopefully without even correcting his name. "Really?" he asked, his eyes brimming with tears. The team lead had just gone through every emotion in the span of three minutes. Hank wasn't surprised by the tears.

"What, are you nuts, man? They just said she's not hot," O'Brien said, spitting the flask contents onto his silver shirt.

"It's not about her," Hank said. "Really I don't care if that odious bitch lives or dies. I find her to be a contemptible shrew, but that is not what this is about. It's not about anyone here. I don't care if they bring you back to whatever bowling alley you were conceived in."

"It was in the theater bathroom during intermission of *Deep Throat: The Musical*," O'Brien said.

"Even better," Hank said.

"Wouldn't it be hard for the female leads to sing?" Pete asked.

Hank ignored him. "The point is that there is an enemy out there. A common enemy. And we cannot let our petty differences get in the way. This is about control. Controlling a situation for once. It's been too long since I felt I had any control over my life. Too long that I've felt like the square root of a prime number, a 22nd birthday, a maxed-out credit card," Hank said. From their expressions, he could see that he was losing his audience. But he was on to something, so he continued, "Ineffectual. Pointless. But now, with those legions of ghouls just steps outside that door, I know how to save us. We need to assert ourselves over these beasts, become the power that we were supposed to be, grasp our destinies. I'm going to save that money-grubbing hag because it's us against them."

"Hank, you are officially my weirdest friend," Pete said.

Hank thought of the rush he got from helping the General escape those homeless kids over the weekend. He thought of how long his deep contempt for just about everyone he met manifested itself as debilitating loneliness and a numbing sensation, like Novocain for the soul, that stemmed from a notion of helplessness, that his life was out of his control. He still hated these people, particularly Will, but for the first time in years, Hank felt something. This would be his day. He would seize the day, along with all its assets, and make it his bitch.

"I'm doing this because it will make me feel alive. I spend all day staring at a screen, then all night drowning in booze and meaningless sex," Hank continued. Janice perked up at this last part. "I've been on the verge for a while, people. And I would really love to hurt someone right now. I figure we can start with them."

Hank pulled the string, and the blinds popped open, revealing a gore-filled scene of office mayhem. Several of those corpse-looking things were approaching the conference room while others were perfectly content to eat large intestines and others still appeared engaged in menial desk tasks. Karla Winthrop was standing by the printer at the end of a row of cubicles, waiting for a sheet of paper that she already held in her hands. Jason Stewart was still on speakerphone with a client who had long since hung up, blasting the dial tone around the floor. And the fat ladies from the customer service department were not going to let death put an end to a good brunch, so they continued to stuff their rotting faces with the unrecognizable remains of the co-worker on the table.

Kelly vomited on her gorged belly. Not too much, just a mixture of pregnancy ills and a reaction spit to the truly grotesque scene at her place of employment. No one commented as she wiped the sick off with the back of her hand and onto the carpet.

"I know what you're saying, man," O'Brien said, unexpectedly. "Sometimes I feel like a breast implant that a chick has removed after she gets pregnant and her boobs get bigger on their own. Just the distributor of this crap that probably doesn't really do anything anyway. I mean, people are still just as fucked up as ever, even though they're all on Prozac. I'm in. I'll help save the ugly chick."

"She's not ugly," Will said. "She's an amazing woman."

"Yeah, I'll believe that when I see it," said O'Brien.

"I'll go," Will said, breaking free from Adam's and Pete's restraints as he rose from the chair.

"Yeah, I figured that," Hank said.

"Count me in," Doug said, his left eyebrow almost halfway gone.

11:30 AM

Lillian had been cowering under her desk for about twenty minutes, re-enacting the bomb-scare drills of her youth, listening to the moaning. Where was Wilbert? Hadn't he promised to protect her if any of her many terminations went awry? This was far worse than she could have ever expected. Unless... Unless he had been... No, she couldn't let herself think like that. *Stay optimistic*, that's what Wilbert would say. *We'll get married sometime, but right now let's keep it discreet, as our jobs are so important to us.* He said that, too. Maybe he wasn't coming. Maybe he really didn't care. She'd been frantically dialing his cell phone for the past half-hour. But Wilbert was so rule abiding, so devoted to the Pro-Well lifestyle, that he almost always left his phone in his Volvo station wagon.

Her office line had been disconnected since she called Harold right after Nick from customer service first appeared at her door with blood dripping from his lips. Harold put her on hold when she asked to speak to Mr. Owens. Calmly, Harold had asked what was wrong.

"The employees have gone mad," she had cried into the receiver. "They're killing one another and eating some while they are still alive and screaming!"

"Remain calm, and stay in your office," Harold had said. "I will speak to Mr. Owens."

Then the line went dead, and, unlike her co-workers, it never came back to life. She tried dialing over and over, but there was no sound. Had Owens himself been killed? No, she mustn't think that either. If that man could be killed, then what chance did a middle-aged woman in middle management have? Probably the same chance that Wilbert had. *Oh, please get here soon*, she prayed. She was far too glamorous to be eaten alive. This couldn't be the end.

She crawled out from under her desk and accessed her Microsoft Outlook account again. She hit "send" on the email to the police that she had attempted to mail a several minutes earlier, but the same message popped up on the screen warning her that she had no Internet connection.

Please, she prayed. *Please, Wilbert, don't be dead. Or a rabid corpse.*

11:32 AM

After several moments of panic, Marshall Owens now had a plan. Alone in his luxurious office on the fourth floor of Pro-Well, he was hiding from the veritable monster that was born in his lab. And he was not going to let all that he'd worked for go to waste.

Born into a family of scumbags in Connellsville, about an hour south of the city, Marshall had been the toast of the trailer park for as long as he could remember. His parents depended on his experiments for a ticket out of Dodge. Marshall had been the local prodigy since he started mixing household chemicals together at the ripe old age of seven. A yearly winner of science fairs, Marshall was the brilliant mind inexplicably born to an unemployed French and Indian War re-enactor and a truck stop waitress. Marshall was on the fast track out of the white trash ghetto, and his parents invested all their meager funds into grooming him for a life of success, which he was always told would be for the express purpose of taking care of the people who had taken care of him. With all their attention bestowed upon Marshall, the elder Owenses virtually ignored their daughter, Susan, until she gave birth to her first child at age fourteen and subsequent children on a nearly bi-annual basis for the next six years.

Young Marshall was on the road to greatness when Dad launched a cannonball through a neighbor's window in a dispute over a pygmy goat. When Dad went off to jail, Marshall's college funds went with him. Dear Ol' Dad was killed in prison almost instantly in an altercation over his French sympathies, and 17-year-old Marshall was left in charge of Mommy Dearest and Sweet Sister Susan and her four little bundles of terror. That's when he fell into the lucrative meth market, renting a trailer that he turned into a lab for crystal creation and experiments in other unnatural party chemicals. Quickly, he became the supplier of his rural town, turning heroin-addicted high school dropouts into Sarigon (his own creation) freaks.

As fast as money was rolling in, his family spent it on the finest Wal-Mart fashions and the shiniest rims for the wheels of the trailer. But Marshall managed to save enough over his seven-year run to develop an entirely new fatal poison, undetectable to Connellsville law enforcement's limited resources, and he disposed of Mom, Susan, and the kids. His first experience sacrificing the dregs. He thought he'd have some sort of sentimental attachment to them, like relics from his childhood, but he found the grieving process easily imitable, like every other emotion he'd learned from observation. Now he was free to hoard as much money as possible, and he harbored dreams of penthouse life in the city, of tan women in his hot tub, solid gold jewelry, and a butler, far away from manic blue-collar drug addicts. Brewing what proved to be his final batch before fleeing to Pittsburgh, a test tube shattered, allowing noxious gases to escape and cause an explosive chemical reaction.

Moments later, Marshall crawled through the ashes of his trailer, the left half of his body in flames. He realized that he had to sacrifice the dream of the groupies, but leaving the hospital disfigured and grafted with some new skin, he decided that he would have everything else. He gathered his prototypes from his storage unit and departed for the city. Within a year, Pro-Well Pharmaceuticals was born. First a modest venture, the company quickly grew into the region's largest manufacturer of medicine, and Marshall cultivated his new public image as a charitable entrepreneur and the poster child for second chances.

He hired ex-cons and put them on the straight and narrow as factory employees, he gave back to the community, he kept the people pumped full of chemical solutions to all their woes. But it was never enough. And after a male enhancement drug backfired and turned the lab rats into obedient slaves that could still function without a heartbeat, he realized that he could create a manner of mass production that would humiliate Henry Ford and every sweatshop proprietor. He gave the ex-cons a new assignment: to procure workers for the factory, degenerates that no one would miss. Their paychecks increased, and all these thugs had to do was keep their mouths shut. And up until the escape last night, the system had been a smashing success. Production had never been higher, and his costs had never been lower. But now, for reasons he didn't entirely comprehend, his empire was crumbling and the façade was becoming a window with curtains slowly tugging back. He would not lose it all today.

He had ordered Harold to shut off the phone lines and Internet connections in the office, so there would be no outgoing

911 calls that could tie this absurd outbreak to him. The nearest cell phone tower collapsed courtesy of an infected civilian who dropped dead at the wheel and ran his SUV into the structure, killing cell reception in the building. Right now he was safe, knowing that the dead couldn't speak to implicate him in this epidemic that had relatively reasonable Pittsburghers eating one another in the streets. And the only one who could still speak would never be believed when Owens was finished drafting his email.

"To all of my friends," the message on his computer screen read. "These may be the last words that I ever write, so I am choosing them carefully. I blame no one but myself for this disaster that has claimed countless sacred lives in the beautiful city that has been so good to me. Unfortunately, the goodwill that I have striven to foster through my work in the community has been exploited for greed and destruction. As you may know, eight months ago I took it upon myself to employ several parolees from a local halfway house, to try to help them reclaim their lives just as I had reclaimed my own. I tried to lead each one from the life of crime that had sucked me in during my youth. But I have realized now that redemption is not for the weak.

"A certain ex-con showed such promise, a former drug dealer who was anxious to leave behind the criminal life and better serve his community. Through his hard work and seeming sincerity, he quickly moved up the ranks to become my most valued employee and friend, my personal assistant. But three months ago, I learned that he did not deserve the trust I had so generously bestowed upon him. He had found an experimental drug that I had developed to ease the pain of erectile dysfunction that I had discarded because it turned the laboratory rats into flesh-eating monsters. He then took it upon himself to experiment on humans, something so reprehensible and unethical that I could not comprehend it. He abducted unfortunates and injected them with the serum. When I discovered his vile actions, he blackmailed me, exploiting my passion for my company by claiming that if I did not go along with his diabolical plan, he would implicate me, as this all had happened on my property.

"Please, my valued peers, find Harold Johnson and make him face the consequences of his actions. Your friend, Marshall Owens."

The CEO read through the email. It was perfect. He hit the send button.

"Harold," he shouted in the general direction of the door. No response. "Harold!" he shouted at a more disruptive volume.

Owens heard the key turn in the lock, and his trusted assistant/bodyguard/latest fall guy entered the room.

"You needed something, sir?" Harold asked.

"Yeah, I was thinking we should probably get rid of Lillian Glabicki," Owens said. "I know she promised to keep everything quiet, and she has, but I just don't trust, you know, female hysteria and all that. I think that if she lives through this, she could make things very bad for us."

"You want me to take her out?"

"Yeah, just shoot her, quickly. We have more important things ahead of us."

"Will do, sir," Harold said as he turned abruptly and left the room.

Owens didn't know how many employees were still alive in the office, and he didn't care. He would remain sequestered in his office with every potential leak plugged. After witnessing Straub's brutal end in the parking lot, the CEO did not anticipate the return of his loyal pawn. He didn't really need Lillian Glabicki dead, though the weak HR rep probably was already. It was merely a suicide mission. And if Harold did manage to whack Lillian, the bullet in her head would match his gun. It covered every angle. For the first time all day, Marshall Owens felt a tinge of what it would be to relax again. The infected did not have a long life span, so he figured he'd be out and back at his penthouse in the next day or so.

11:34 AM

Corporal Green Hair had been quite effective at tight end, but, aside from the lone dreadlocked intelligence officer, the General and his nine troops were still unable to breach the impenetrable corporate fortress. The General stood in the parking lot, growing more and more frustrated while the troops stared at nothing in particular. The General looked at his watch: 6:46, it read. It was much earlier than he thought, as the sun had been up for what felt like several hours. Damn, it would take forever until the mass lunch exodus.

Lieutenant Trash Bag Cape walked into the revolving door, attempting to enter the building, apparently to sample the already picked-over corpses on the lobby floor. However, the officer was lacking the appropriate credentials, and the receptionist was dead, so he continued to walk in place as if he was on a sadistic treadmill, smashing his body against the glass that refused to budge. The General had fitted the hobo with his regular attire by emptying a refuse tin onto the gravel. He felt that his troops would be more motivated within their comfort zone, and to the man he once knew as Brother Sam, the newly christened lieutenant, nothing was more natural than a trash bag worn as a cape.

The enemy was ready, the General thought. His army did not know how to engage in subterfuge, and his ranks continued to diminish. Colonel Napkin Man, named so for his penchant for sucking a napkin over his mouth at all times, had dropped to the ground for no reason and stayed there, motionless, dead. The General surmised that his troops were hungry. No one edible had entered or exited the fortress in quite some time.

The General looked around the parking lot for a sign of life. His blue-eyed gaze drifted over the arachnid-like Hot Metal Bridge, and his spirits brightened. A group of people were staggering slowly over the bridge, some on the pedestrian walkway, others in the middle of the road. *Mercenaries*, the General thought. At the rate they were moving, they would be there in an hour. But the army could wait for reinforcements before launching their attack. Their ranks depleted, they did not have much of a choice. So they'd wait.

11:35 AM

"Okay, the mission is simple," Hank said, huddling with Doug, O'Brien, and Will at the end of the conference table. "We get Lillian, and we get supplies, and we get the Hell back here as soon as possible."

"Supplies?" Doug asked. "Why don't we just get her?"

"I realize that the cocaine makes you think this is some sort of an awesome mosh pit, but the rest of us want to get out of here," Hank said.

"This isn't cocaine," Doug defended himself, pulling out the little baggie of white powder. "It's Pro-caine, Pro-Well's legal dietary supplement."

"Dude, can I try some?" O'Brien asked.

"Mine," Doug said authoritatively.

"Focus, people!" Hank said. "Our first order of business is to fashion weapons out of whatever we have in here. Pete, what have you put together?"

"I've got the wooden pointer for the dry-erase board. A harpoon, if you will," Pete said, picking up each item from the opposite end of the conference table and presenting the pieces like evidence at a trial. "A telephone that has been inexplicably disconnected," he said, holding up the heavy, multi-line phone.

"Pete, leaving the cord hooked into it, would you hand me the receiver?" Hank asked as Pete unplugged the receiver from its massive base.

Hank held it up for his audience.

"We will use this as a flail," Hank stated, as he stood up from his chair and began to swing the phone over his head.

The receiver flew off the wire and hit the wall. Janice scurried from where she was leaning against the wall, retrieved it from the floor, and handed it back to Hank.

"That was bound to happen," Hank said. "But we know that there is no shortage of phones in this office. So if this happens to you, just grab another from a desk."

"You are destroying Pro-Well property," Will said, attempting to be condescending while completely defeated.

Pete ignored him and presented the next item: a plastic-wrapped stack of printer paper.

"A bludgeon," Hank explained. "Next."

Pete raised the large, almost obelisk-shaped glass flower vase that until recently had sat in the center of the table.

"Another bludgeon," Hank said.

Pete raised the laptop that had been abandoned earlier by someone who was now probably eating a co-worker.

"Yet another bludgeon," Hank said. "Questions?"

"What exactly is the plan?" Will asked.

"Bludgeoning," Hank replied.

"My specialty. You know, aside from extensive management training and a degree in business administration, I also have a bachelor's in bludgeoning," Will said with sarcasm. He was the team lead, he was supposed to be in charge, and now this deranged writer with a penchant for extreme tardiness was drafting a certifiable suicide mission. *They may as well be armed with dental floss*, he thought.

"I think it'll work, but I want the spear," O'Brien said, jumping from his seat and grabbing the wooden pointer from the table. He held it in the air and posed, right hand on his hip. "Hey, can you get a photo of me with this thing?" He asked, handing his camera to Kelly. "I've gotta get souvenirs from this."

"But it just looks like you're making a presentation in a conference room," Kelly said, handing the small Nikon back to O'Brien.

"Well, you've gotta get one when I come back then, when I'm all covered in blood. Man, that'll be a sweet screensaver," O'Brien said.

"All right," Hank said. "Men, grab your weapons, and we go get that butter-mint-dressed broad. Pete, hold the fort here."

"Will do," Pete said, then he paused. "Is Myron dead?" he asked, looking over at the skinny, balding janitor who was silent, almost forgotten in the corner.

"No, I ain't," from the floor came the unmistakable drawl of someone fluent in Pittsburghese. Everyone looked over and stared at the old man as he finally lifted his head. "Yinz are all concerned about yinzselves. Yinz seen what's goin' on out there. If this is what it like in tha rest o' tha 'Burgh, we ain't got nothin' left here. Imagine what they doin' ta PNC Park."

"Whatever," Janice said. "I just want to warn you guys before you go out there, you should shoot them—," she stopped herself. "Er, hit them in the head. I don't know if you can destroy their brains with a stack of paper, but you can try."

"Once again, this is not a zombie flick," Pete said.

"I intend to hit them in any way that I can," Hank assured her. "All right, men, are we ready to beat the shit out of our co-workers?"

"Can you bring me back something to eat?" Kelly asked. Although her cravings dictated that a chili cheese dog was necessary, she felt she could live with something simple out of the vending machine to hold her while they were locked in this room.

"Not until we're all famished," Hank replied.

"I have some Doritos in my desk," Kelly pushed. "If you're in the neighborhood."

Hank waved her off. "Ready?"

"I'm gonna go Pro-Well. It'll make going postal look like a kindergarten brawl," Doug said.

He was pumped. Ever since the divorce, he'd been trying to better himself in preparation for the lengthy custody battle he was about to endure. The first order of business was to lose weight. Well, that wasn't for the judge or child services, but seeing him back in his 36-inch waist slacks would sure make the wife jealous. If she found him irresistible, there would be no need to fight for his seven-year-old daughter in the first place.

So he started taking Pro-Caine, a unique dietary supplement meant to be ingested in pill form three times a day. It was supposed to control his appetite, but Doug often found himself grinding his teeth, engaged in long conversations with total strangers about the meaning of life, and listening to his old Motley Crüe records from his teenage years. The pill form proved too intense for mid-mannered Doug, so he ground the capsules into a white powder so that he could control his dosage. The drug was perfectly legal for test subjects like him, but it had not yet been granted FDA approval. The side effects of intense heartbeats and yanking his hair out by the roots would probably be ameliorated when the drug was perfected.

Right now, Pro-Caine was serving its purpose. Doug had lost thirteen pounds in the past week and felt intensely motivated at work and much more outgoing in social situations. He felt like he could accomplish anything.

Doug stood up and pounded his chest, exploding the Pro-Caine in his lapel pocket. It floated into the air in a cloud, then the tiny particles dispersed onto the carpet.

"That's probably a good thing," Hank remarked. "Now everyone else: When we return, let us back in immediately."

"How are we going to know that it's you guys?" Judy asked, ending her question with a series of coughs.

"Because we'll be speaking English," Will said. For a man whose main career objective appeared to be motivating others to achieve mediocrity, Will was truly beginning to lose his edge. He was becoming more cynical by the minute. He'd feel better when he knew that Lillian was safe, he reassured himself. He stood up, regaining his composure. "We can do this. We're a team, defenders of wellness."

"We're not calling ourselves that," Hank said.

11:52 AM

Lillian's office was only one floor above the conference room where the employees were stranded, but it looked to be an arduous journey just to the stairwell. So Hank, Will, Doug, and Rick O'Brien opted to take the elevator, which was located just around the side of the conference room. Hank had been unwilling at first to allow himself to be confined to an even smaller space, but after stepping outside the conference room they ascertained that the petite Claire Harrington from customer service was to the stairwell what Cerberus was to Hades. She was standing directly in front of the door, her lavender button-down top soaked in blood. O'Brien stared at her as if it was some sort of macabre wet T-shirt contest while Claire chewed on Terry Hawthorne's optic nerve like a living person would eat beef jerky. His dead body was lying on the floor in front of her, an empty eye socket staring up at them. Claudia from the call center was busy tearing chunks of flesh from Hawthorne's back, her Flo Jo nails that severely impeded her ability to type finally finding their purpose. Andy from IT was trapped inside the stairwell, repeatedly walking into the door and bouncing back, then doing it all again.

Staring through the clear walls that encased the stairwell, Hank and the others watched the strange behavior of the ponytailed tech geek with the Hobbit-adorned cubicle and an apparent inability to feel pain. This newfound imperviousness to physical trauma would have been quite useful if the IT professional was ever engaged in a serious battle with Orcs. But right now, his coworkers were his enemies, and they were not created by an evil wizard with Dr. Frankenstein ambitions, and full-body armor did not fit into the business casual dress code. And although Andy looked more like one of the suspendered nerds from a board game shop than a dangerous adversary, the living employees thought the elevator was becoming more appealing by the second.

Will turned first to lead the others around the corner to the elevator fifteen feet away. They had not yet made it out of the doorway.

"Aaah!" Will shrieked as he bumped into Tom's massive stomach. He screamed, not like the 50-year-old man that he was but like the babysitter hiding in the attic after she realized that the calls were coming from inside the house.

Wilbert jumped back, his short, rotund frame knocking O'Brien on the floor and the wooden conference room harpoon from his hand. Quickly, Hank picked it up and in one smooth motion, stabbed it into Tom's ample gut. Bouncing back without even tearing his shirt, Hank stabbed him again. And again. They really should have sharpened the pointer before bringing it into battle. Right now it was like trying to impale someone with a pool cue.

Looking up into Tom's gray, lifeless face Hank held the pointer like a javelin and stabbed it through Tom's gaping mouth. The pointer broke through the back of his skull, and Hank drew it back quickly while Tom slowly tumbled forward. Hank jumped to the left as Tom's massive frame landed on O'Brien and Will, who had not been able to get up from their fall yet.

"Please, get this dead guy off me," O'Brien pleaded.

11:55 AM

"He's amazing," Janice, aka Mistress of the Moonlight, gushed as she peered through the blinds to watch Hank stab the large zombie in the head.

"Yes, Tom from accounting, you will be missed," Adam said.

"Not him," Janice said. "Hank."

Adam laughed, joined by Pete.

"So you've got a thing for Hank?" Judy asked, somehow managing to grin with disapproval while tilting her head back to attempt to stop her nose that had just started bleeding for no discernible reason.

"Do you think I have a chance?" Janice asked.

"I think you've got more of a chance with Tom out there," Pete said.

"What do you mean by that?" Janice asked, confused.

"It means he's gay," Kelly said.

"You're kidding," Janice said, smiling. "There's no way that man is gay."

"Of course he is," Kelly said. "Good looking, in good shape, doesn't want to have sex with your friends after he marries you. He's gay."

"Come on, you're fucking with me. You're all fucking with me," Janice said.

"Now dear, listen to me. I have some amazing pranks that I've pulled at work. Why recently I sent Kelly's husband an erotic email, pretending to be her sister and requesting that he meet me at the Sleep Inn on Route 30," Adam said.

"Aha!" Kelly leapt from her chair, pointing at the culprit.

"But really, my best ventures are always solo outings, and do you actually think that this group would collaborate on anything?" Adam continued, putting his arm around Janice's narrow shoulders. She immediately shook him off.

"He's an ass-tronaut," Adam added, bursting into uncontrollable giggles.

Pete smirked, catching Adam's glance and his need for validation.

"You like that, dude?" he asked. "I just came up with it."

"It was quite brilliant," Pete said as he reluctantly gave Adam a high-five.

Judy let out a series of five massive emphysema coughs.

"He's really gay?" Janice asked. The rest of the room nodded, except for Myron, who had resumed his 1950s bomb scare pose on the floor. "How gay?"

"What do you mean, how gay?" Pete asked.

"Yes, either he's gay like Hank or he loves the ladies like me," Adam said, going into a knee-jerk "last day on Earth" mode. He winked at Janice.

"Well, he may not be entirely gay," Janice said. "I mean even Elton John was married to a woman for a while."

"I think Elton John is about as gay as they come," Pete said.

"Okay, bad analogy, but you know what I mean," she said.

"So you're telling me that you would actually fuck a gay guy?" Pete asked, growing amused by this exchange.

"Well, if I fucked him, he wouldn't really be gay, would he?" Janice asked.

"Point taken," Pete said.

"But what if he just turned to you because he knew that he was probably going to die today and just wanted to have sex one last time and didn't care who it was with. They just had to be, you know, not dead. Wouldn't you want your last time to be with someone who really wanted it with a woman?" Adam pleaded.

Janice turned away from him and rolled her eyes. Maybe she would have liked Adam in her hipster days, but she'd evolved way past that. He was a prankster, the antithesis of the dark, brooding type that she had come to so desire.

"Could you all just shut up?" Judy shouted, her voice strained and cracking. "My head is killing me, my nose is bleeding, and you people and your blasphemous talk are driving me insane."

"What's wrong with you?" Janice asked, trying to be sympathetic but choosing the wrong words.

"I'm fine. I just left all my medications in my desk, and I'm really not in the mood to go back and get them," Judy snapped.

"Did you get bitten?" Janice asked.

"As a matter of fact, yes," Judy said. "And this conference room doesn't have any Kills-Germs-Dead, so I'm trying to stave off infection with my immune system that, let's face it, is not as good as it once was."

"I see," Janice said. She was prepared for this.

"What are you implying?" Pete asked, growing wearing of Janice's zombie conspiracy theories.

"Nothing," Janice said.

When Judy became a zombie in the near future, she'd really show them. *So it begins*, she thought.

12:02 PM

The elevator ride up one floor was not as bad as Hank expected. He always hated the people who take the elevator in this four-story building—only three of which had occupants—but desperate times, et cetera. After peeling Will and O'Brien off the floor, they were back on the move. Of course, after O'Brien demanded that Doug snap a photo of him with the now completely deceased Tom. The flask-drinking pharmaceutical distributor gave a thumbs-up and feigned an expression of shock for the camera, and they were back off to rescue the Terminator, as the disgruntled staff referred to Lillian.

They slinked slowly down the wide hallway, their bodies close to the wall. O'Brien had relinquished the pointer to Hank, who had proven his superior skill with the weapon. Will was armed with the telephone receiver, Doug the ream of paper, and O'Brien the flower vase.

"This is ridiculous," O'Brien said, staring at his new, translucent purple bludgeon.

"You'll get a new weapon when we get to the supply room," Hank whispered to him as they crept towards the elevators.

Doug, who refused to slow down no matter how much the rest urged him, reached the elevators first and pressed the down button. Almost instantly, the doors opened and revealed Omar Davis from data entry, his dark skin now appearing as if it had been bleached. His mouth was open wide as he stood motionless in the center of the elevator car. In one sudden motion, Doug leapt through the doors and smashed Omar in the face with the paper.

Blood spattered against the wall of the elevator, and at least one of Omar's bright white teeth fell to the floor. He lay on the ground, his arms flailing slowly in a swimming motion.

"This is pathetic. Finish him off," Will said. He was growing increasingly anxious. With every moment wasted on debating whether to kill these swine, there was the greater chance that one had had its way with his woman.

Doug leaned over and smashed Omar in the head with the paper, the blood spurting from the data entry clerk making the elevator look like a Bates Motel bathtub. His face contorted into a deranged grimace, Doug continued to clobber Omar until his skull was smashed and the plastic tore and sheets of letter-sized printer paper flew from Doug's blood-soaked hands.

A flash erupted in the elevator as O'Brien whispered, "Awesome."

"I think he's had enough," Hank observed, wiping the dead man's blood from his neck.

Hank entered the elevator, followed by the others, and pressed 3, leaving a bloody fingerprint on the button. Five seconds later, they stepped out on the third floor, greeted by a scene of utter devastation.

"Ugh," Will said, looking away from the remains of a corpse that lay just in front of the elevator doors.

They could tell by what was left of the calf-length T-shirt dress and stretched canvas slip-ons with their treads worn away almost completely that this had to be Edith O'Conner. Customer service from the very beginning and fattest woman that Hank had ever seen. He was relieved that she had been eviscerated. He shivered just thinking about her massive bulk coming towards him, mouth agape, bottomless belly aching for human meat. Besides boredom, the morbidly obese were the only things that scared Hank. Claire Harrington had looked pretty grotesque, but blubbery, jiggling flesh—whether infected or not—was too much for Hank to handle. And now they didn't even use cutlery.

Hank shivered. He thought that Edith had smelled bad in life. He'd heard women warning new hires to never go to the bathroom within ten minutes after she'd been there. Now, her insides—or what was left of them—were spilling onto the floor, revealing a rainbow of partially digested foodstuff where most of her stomach used to be. Hank leapt over her, trying not to breathe the stench of death, gas, bowels, and a processed meat and grease cocktail. This was an olfactory nightmare. If the Hell's Angels had engaged in a crank-fueled orgy with farm animals and members of the Occupy movement in a frat house the day after a mixer with the bulimic sorority, the lingering smell would actually have been nothing like the odor at the Pro-Well elevator bank. But it may have been comparably unpleasant. O'Brien leapt over the corpse, and Will ran around her massive frame in quick baby steps, followed by Doug. There was no one else in sight.

Hank led his co-workers around the corner into the main floor, so that they were directly above the conference room where the others were waiting. On this floor, a large kitchen and an adjacent supply room occupied the equivalent space. Passing the kitchen doorway, they caught a glimpse of Jamie Landers from HR. Her blouse was ripped open, exposing her lace bra that covered her 27-year-old breasts that would have been perfect had they not been gray and rotting. She was leaning over the counter, holding a femur like it was a turkey leg, gratuitously sucking the meat from the bone.

"That's a shame," O'Brien said, snapping a photo as they passed the kitchen.

The group entered the supply room to find an armory full of mundane office supplies.

"Grab as much of this shit as you can," Hank said. "Anything that looks like it could be used to bust some heads."

Hank managed to stuff three staplers in his pockets; *decent projectiles*, he thought. He picked up another ream of paper and looked around the cramped room. The shelves were filled with printer cartridges, boxes of pens and paper clips, and more reams of paper. He grabbed a few rolls of packing tape and put them on his wrists like bracelets.

"Check this out!" O'Brien exclaimed, holding the sharpened arm of a paper cutter like a machete.

"Careful! You're gonna kill *me* with that thing," Will pleaded as O'Brien swung the arm around like a Samurai in a very bad martial arts movie.

In Doug's experience, office supplies could be quite dangerous. He'd sustained several blood blisters on his fingers from the staple remover, his hands were covered in paper cuts, and once he'd even stapled his thumb. He'd rolled over his toes with his desk chair, smashed his hand in the copier, and burned himself while attempting to clear a paper jam. Recently, he'd even managed to injure himself with a chipped coffee mug. He was truly terrified of the damage this hyperactive slimeball could do with a paper cutter.

"This is a bust," Hank said, turning to his cohorts. Will was holding a pair of scissors in front of his face, proud to have found them.

"Well, those are pretty decent, but there's really not that much in here," Hank said, gazing out the door to the row upon row of cubicles on the office floor.

His eyes rested on a cane-length umbrella with a somewhat sharp metal point at the end. It was white with what appeared to be a pink design, but it would have to do. And it would be much more effective than the myriad of Post-its in the stock room.

"Forget this," Hank said. "We're looting the desks."

Hank headed out the door, grasping the pointer, keeping the bloody end at a distance, and swooped down upon the cubicle. He hooked the curved handle into his belt and began ransacking.

"You can't do that," Will yelled after him. "That belongs to Marcia Tomlinson!"

"Well, now it's mine," Hank said, yanking her phone receiver out and tying the cord to his belt loop.

O'Brien rushed to the next cubicle and frantically yanked open the desk drawers.

"Jackpot," he said, grinning as he held up a bottle of bottom-shelf rum. "In case we need to light anyone on fire."

"Good thinking," Doug said, tearing through the contents of Keisha Randall's purse. He pulled out a home pregnancy test and switchblade.

"You guys've got some seriously fucked-up employees," O'Brien observed as he removed a monthly calendar of scantily clad first lady lookalikes from Anderson Spacek's desk drawer. He checked out a coy photograph of a Betty Ford impersonator seductively drinking from a whiskey bottle in the Oval Office, shook his head, and placed the calendar back in the drawer.

It was at this point that Will took action and broke into a goofy fat man's sprint past seven rows of cubicles to the west side of the floor to Lillian Glablicki's office.

"Oh fuck," Hank said as he yanked Marcia's keyboard from the cables connecting it to her desktop computer and sprinted after his immediate supervisor. O'Brien tore Marty Tresori's Terrible Towel from the thumbtacks that held it to the cubicle wall and followed while Doug continued to remove bottles of nail polish and tampons from Keisha's purse.

If they were not in such a hurry, they would have noticed twelve of their hungriest co-workers emerging from the restrooms.

12:10 PM

Judy's condition was visibly deteriorating. She was lying on the floor, her head in Kelly's lap as the younger woman ran her hand through her processed blonde locks. Janice did not take her eyes off of them as she sat at the conference table, smoking a clove. Pete was pacing around the room while Adam stood watch by the window.

"I made a promise to myself to stay at sixty-two," Judy croaked from the floor.

Jesus, she's only sixty-two, Janice thought, *she looks ninety.*

"I think I'm going to keep that promise," Judy said.

"You're gonna be okay," Kelly coaxed, practicing those maternal instincts that she didn't really have, but, being a mother, thought she needed.

"I'm not. Look at my arm," Judy insisted, raising her wrist to Kelly's face. The area around the bite mark was all colors of decay, a festering mess of a gangrenous infection that appeared to be getting worse by the second. Kelly winced. "I don't think I have long left."

Janice kept her hand steady on the base of the receptionist-caliber, multi-lined telephone. Judy's face was even whiter than it had been earlier, leaving almost no contrast with her light blonde hair, except for the bluish hue that was creeping into her cheeks like the veins were on the brink of a Chernobyl-caliber explosion.

"Where the fuck are they? I'm about to raid Hank's desk for his emergency cigarette stash," Pete said in the midst of his forty-fifth lap around the conference table.

"You can have one of mine," Janice offered, opening her silver case of cloves.

"This isn't gonna turn me into a vampire, is it?" Pete asked, pulling a clove from the pack.

"If only it were that easy," Janice mused as she lit his cigarette with the crucifix.

Pete took a hit of the clove, and his face contorted.

"What is this hippie shit? This is terrible," he said as he took another puff.

"It's a Goth thing," Janice said. At least that's what Wikipedia had told her.

Pete coughed.

"I think my lungs are broken," he said. "I've sprung a leak."

Clove in hand, Pete resumed his pacing. Myron kept his head on the table while Judy reflected on the end.

She thought of the past thirty-five years of domestic ennui, of her two sons she trained to never love another woman as much as they loved her and the Lord. She thought of the high times as she raked in the money bagging groceries while her husband bet on the horse races. Then she thought of losing it all when his gambling spun out of control after he got into the fledgling pigeon triathlon scene. She thought of his years of drunken depression and bouncing from job to job while she grew older and older and her choices kept slipping away. She thought of her ecstasy when she landed this job at Pro-Well that paid her four full dollars more per hour than that last gas station gig. And she realized that the job that had saved her life was going to kill her.

Then everything went dark. She didn't see a white light, but a black hole. She couldn't be going to Hell, she thought, not after thirty-five years of faithful matrimony and life as a good Christian woman. Silently, she cursed God for being a godless liar for a few seconds before her mind went dark, too.

As Judy's eyes rolled back in her head, Kelly put her fingers on her neck and felt nothing. Kelly screamed so loudly that even Myron awoke.

"Oh, my God! Get her off of me! Get her off me! She's dead! Get this dead bitch off me!" Kelly shrieked.

Adam ran from the window and callously knocked Judy's corpse off Kelly's lap. With the strength that pregnant women everywhere dream of, Kelly jumped up and started doing a manic tap dance, waving her hands like they had no joints to rid herself of the air of death that Judy had breathed onto her.

"Oh my God! Oh my God! That's disgusting!" she cried.

Adam knelt down and grasped Judy's good wrist. Clamping his thumb down on the vein, he checked her pulse.

"Yeah, she's dead," he said, dropping the arm to the floor with a thud.

"We should say something," Janice said as she rose from her chair.

"Like what?" Pete asked. "Of all the people here, I'm not really all that sorry *she's* the one who's dead."

"We should still say something, like a prayer. It would be good for our souls," Janice said. She kept the phone in her hand as she walked towards the body.

"Who knows any prayers?" Pete asked.

"I'll start," Adam offered.

He walked to the shelf in the corner of the room and pulled a Kleenex from the box and sat it atop his head. The tissue yarmulke fell from his nearly shaved scalp twice during his ten-foot walk back to the corpse. Placing it back on, he stood over the body and carefully tilted his head down in reverence.

"Barukh atah Adonai, Eloheinu, melekh ha'olam," Adam sang slowly. "Asher kidishanu b'mitz'votav v'tzivanu. L'had'lik neir shel Chanukah."

"That's the blessing for Chanukah," Pete said.

"Well sweet child o' mine, that's the only one I know. There's one for dead people, but I get it mixed up with the blessing for wine," Adam said.

"Why don't you try one of them?" Kelly suggested, patronizingly.

"I don't know either," Adam stated.

"Well, I know Judy was a lifelong Steelers fan," Myron said as he finally picked himself up from the corner.

"No, she wasn't," Kelly said, but Myron didn't listen. He continued to walk towards the body and began to sing.

"Here we go Steelers, here we go. Here we go Steelers, here we go. Pittsburgh's going to the Super Bowl," the custodian sang, clapping his callused hands at the pauses in his rendition of the Steelers Fight Song.

"Okay, please stop," Pete said.

"Cheer the Steelers, black and the gold. It's time for Pittsburgh's heart and soul. Steeler Nation's got the best fans. We're for Pittsburgh, six-time Super Bowl champs," Myron continued.

"This is so wrong on every level," Kelly said beneath the old man's crazed song. "Myron, please."

"It's like watching different stages of madness," Pete said, moderately amused.

"Roethlisberger will let the ball soar. Here we go, cause he's got Mendenhall, Sanders, and Ward. Here we go, Wallace, Heath, and Brown will make a touchdown. And if you get in their way, they're gonna knock you around," Myron sang, doing an impromptu jig over Judy's corpse.

"I never knew there were so many words to this song," Janice remarked.

"Now the offense is ready to score. Here We Go, and there's one thing we know for sure. Here We Go, if we don't get it in the end zone, we'll get three points off of Suisham's toe,"

Myron said, the dance escalating to a combination of con-vulsing, skipping, and solo tango.

"This really should stop," Kelly said. "This is completely inappropriate."

Myron grabbed Kelly's arms and pulled the pregnant woman around in a resistant waltz.

"All right, dude. It's time to knock it off," Pete said, ap-proaching the reluctant dancing couple. Hopping over Judy, Myron pulled Kelly to dance away as Pete chased them to around the conference table.

Janice kept her eyes on Judy. The dead woman was twitching.

"We've got Keisel and Farrior. Here We Go, Polamalu, Woodley, and Harrison. Here We Go, the other team won't get any ground. 'Cause the defense is gonna bring the steel curtain down," Myron shouted as Judy sat up.

"Oh shit!" Adam yelled.

Judy was crawling to her feet, her skin gray and her eyes a glazed, bleached eggplant swirl. She looked much older than sixty-two. If she could see her own reflection in the glass window and her eyes were still sending signals to her brain, she would have been horrified. The amply applied ivory foun-dation did not make a decent death mask. Her skin was cracking beneath the makeup, and her gums had retracted during the three minutes that she had been in the state that is, on every other day, considered dead. As terrifying as Adam al-ways thought her aging *Bride of Chucky* look was, this was far worse. It was like the Cryptkeeper got Rogaine and a perm.

Adam kicked her as she gurgled and groaned. Judy's corpse caught him in one of his kicks and pulled him to the ground. As his thin frame thumped to the floor, Judy bared her yellow teeth and leaned down to his leg. Adam kicked her in the chest with his free foot, but she kept coming, her teeth growing ever closer to his ankle.

Janice leapt from her chair, phone in hand. Quickly swooping down, she slammed the phone into Judy's flesh-hungry face and the corpse fell back, releasing Adam's leg. He jumped up and grabbed a ream of paper from the shelf while Janice took another whack at Judy's head. Blood spattered on the white wall of the conference room, and Judy lay motionless on the floor for a second time.

Janice stood up and dropped the phone onto the forever sixty-two-year-old corpse. There was blood dripping from her face and chest, but she looked triumphant.

"I told you to hit them in the head," she said.

12:13 PM

Rose Polaski was in search of some entertainment. The old folks home where her selfish shrew of a daughter had put her was becoming oppressively boring. That was just like her, she thought, finding the first place that would hold her mother hostage and writing a blank check. The ungrateful cow. Maybe one day her children would put *her* in such a place, one where they made the residents sleep on racks and other medieval torture, or chiropractic, devices. That would be the most delightful revenge. Of course, Rose wouldn't be around for that. In fact, she wouldn't be around much longer with the cancer, a very slow and deliberate cancer of the lung that was a death sentence with no chance of appeal.

She wouldn't go out in a blaze of glory, but by wasting away in a hospital bed if the nurses at that terrible place where her ungrateful daughter had put her would even take her to the hospital. Maybe they'd just put a pillow over her face in the middle of the night. She wouldn't even wake up. Then when the place gets raided a couple months later and the staff is discovered to be angels of death, her wretched daughter would become overwhelmed with guilt and take her own life. Well, Rose could always hope. Right now, she was on her way to the newsstand to pick up some reading material to alleviate the torture of the home with the rest of the invalids. She was also picking up some cigarettes because, as she saw it, if she was dying, why not speed up the process? At least for now she could still walk. Soon she'd need a wheelchair, and that would be a real hoot, having servants push her around all day. She thought of how much fun it would be to soil herself while Nurse Sally was changing her diaper.

Rose walked down Carson Street, smiling at the passersby. She grinned eerily, eliciting smiles from younger folks who couldn't help their lips from curling upward when they saw what appeared to be a shrinking old blue hair on the brink of dementia. They smiled and some even waved while Rose giggled gleefully, plotting their respective demises. Fully cognizant of her malicious wishes, her sadistic gaze rested upon each passerby. The young man with the paint-spattered jeans— she imagined him later that day falling from the ladder he carried over his shoulder. She pictured that young woman in the tight skirt and stiletto heels electrocuting herself while drying her perfectly straight, highlighted blond hair. Rose's terrible thoughts kept her spry through the boredom that was supposed to be her golden years.

She took solace in her magazines. Tabloids. Porn for the elderly. She loved the bad news. Maybe a deranged sexual deviant would escape from the psych ward and begin exposing himself in the nearest Build-a-Bear Workshop. Maybe the Doctors Without Borders would start taking liberties with the rape patients in Uganda. Maybe tornadoes would decimate the Red Cross tents. Or vampires would crash a blood drive. Well, here's to wishful thinking.

Rose weakly pushed open the door of the newsstand and shuffled in. The chubby teenage girl with the purple hair wasn't working today. She was always here on Mondays. Rose wondered what happened. Maybe she'd been abducted by a recently paroled kiddie rapist who now had her in a dungeon, using her as his own personal sex slave. Maybe some adolescents had cyber-bullied her to suicide or at least a severe eating disorder that required hospitalization. Ah, the things Rose missed about youth.

In her salmon pants and flowered top, Rose walked meekly towards the magazine rack that housed her favorite reading materials. The news had been slow recently, but Rose had high hopes. Maybe another priest had molested deaf altar boys. That would be interesting reading. Maybe an ice cream man was abducting children and keeping their frozen corpses right next to the Fudgesicles. Maybe a meteor had hit the Make a Wish Foundation. That would be her last request, if the charity honored the dreams of *les anciens*. Kids were lucky to die young, she thought, before they experienced the tyranny of their own ungrateful children, evil nurses, doctors who do nothing but lie and steal your money, and the general public that assumes you are senile just because you smile at no one in particular. But you can't help it because you are imagining the whole place blowing up and shrapnel blinding all the ones who stare.

Suddenly, Rose heard a thud against the window. She usually would just ignore the South Side noises, preferring her own twisted wishful fantasies to the bleak, boring reality of the everyday, but this time was different. The thud was followed by a scream, a tortured, pained scream of true agony. Rose dropped *The National Enquirer* back on the shelf and scurried to the windowed storefront. On the other side of the glass, a young woman's face was smashed against the dirty window. Blood oozed from where her ear used to be, and behind her, a gruesomely disfigured corpse of a man was biting fiercely into her neck.

Rose hopped back from the window and hurried to the door. She pushed it open, triggering a bell, and stepped back onto the sidewalk. Across the street, women were screaming and men were on their cell phones, presumably with police. Rose took a step towards the young woman who was slowly falling to the ground while the gray man tore chunks of flesh from her ample back. Rose moved closer to him as he looked up from what was now the corpse of the young woman. Rose was fascinated by this live enactment of something even more exciting than what she could read in the tabloids.

From around the corner of 16th Street, a man turned the corner onto Carson, stumbling a little but seemingly indifferent to the bloody mess on the sidewalk. As he moved closer to the carnage, Rose noticed that he too was a gray, flaking disaster of a human being. She saw that his black and white striped polo shirt was spattered with blood and part of his left cheekbone was exposed. He shuffled past the corpse on the ground and Rose approached him. She waved her arms in the air, trying to catch the attention of his blind eyes. She was eager, screeching, "Pick me, pick me," like the scrawny fifth grader anxious to be chosen as a part of somebody's—anybody's—kickball team.

The cheekless man moved towards Rose as she spread her arms wide and waited patiently because, though zombies move slowly, they are still quicker than lung cancer. This would show her daughter for letting her spend so much time alone. Let this be a lesson; you put your mother in a home and she winds up getting eaten by the living dead. Rose closed her eyes until she felt the sharp, broken teeth rip into her chest.

Then she felt that it was time to scream.

12:18 PM

"Lillian, Lillian. Open up!" Will shouted as he banged his fat fist on Lillian Glablicki's corner office door. There were no windows in her office, as a view of her clandestine meetings with very angry employees would compromise Pro-Well's peaceful image.

"Wilbert? Is that you?" a meek voice came through the door.

"Yes, it is. Please unlock this, and I'll take you somewhere safe!"

The door swung open, and Will swooped down over his lover who was cowering next to the desk. He crouched on the floor and cradled her small head against his flabby chest.

"Dudes, get the hell up!" O'Brien said, holding the paper

cutter blade at his side as he fidgeted in Lillian's doorway. "They're coming."

"Who?" Will asked, momentarily forgetting that they were under siege by the predatory dead.

"Them," O'Brien said as he raised the blade and pointed to seven office workers in various stages of decomposition who were approaching from their cubicles. Though moving slowly, they were closing in from all angles as if they could sense the presence of warm, tasty flesh.

Brandishing the pointer in one hand and the umbrella in the other, Hank faced the enemy. He was ready. Unfortunately, Will was not and Lillian was screaming.

"Oh, shut up," Hank said.

Will pulled Lillian to her feet, keeping his arms around her puny upper body as Hank and O'Brien prepared for battle. The visiting distributor struck the most fearsome pose he could imagine, his face a grimace, clutching the blade in both hands, his front foot on a pivot. As a child, he'd always fantasized about being at the plate at Wrigley Field, but this was much better. The batting stance helped him add an element of familiarity in an increasingly unfamiliar situation. Suddenly, Doug came flying past the desks, fully loaded on Pro-Caine, snow globe in hand, barreling towards the enemy with a loud, wailing battle call.

He smashed Allen Reynolds from QA in the head with the Christmas-themed glass orb and it shattered, Santa's sleigh flying into accountant Valerie Atkins's face. Allen went down, but Valerie didn't flinch. She kept stumbling along until she was within a few feet of Lillian's office. Then, without sufficient warning, O'Brien wound up and swung the paper cutter blade back and Hank jumped just far enough away to avoid a slice to the jugular. Shifting his feet and stepping forward, O'Brien twisted his hips, and the blade connected with Valerie's throat, the sharp force sending her head off her neck.

O'Brien threw his arms into the air and stepped to the side like he was taking off to first base. Luckily, he forgot to put down the bat. Valerie's headless body fell to the ground with a thud.

"O'Brien knocks it out of the park!" he shouted, though the swift drop of the accountant's head to the floor looked more like a sacrifice bunt.

Lillian continued shrieking and cowered in Will's pillowy chest. O'Brien walked towards the zombies, now assuming the persona of a Western gunslinger. He wanted to say, "Make my day," but it seemed redundant and futile. Meanwhile, Allen Reynolds was regaining his composure and lifting himself from the floor by climbing up Doug's leg. The manic customer service rep tried to shake Allen from his ankle while engaging in valiant battle with the others by flailing attempts to beat them all with a three-hole hole punch. He was getting a few good whacks in when Hank threw one of his staplers, hitting Carl Kovalesk in the head, momentarily knocking him off balance.

Like a grenade, Hank thought, *ideal for clearing his way into battle if, in fact, the stapler had exploded.*

But it would have to do. Hank stepped in on behalf of the overly energized customer service rep, stabbing administrative assistant Yolanda Cornelius in the neck with the pointy end of the umbrella. Yet, she didn't fall. He stabbed again while O'Brien whacked at Allen's hand, which was relentlessly clutching Doug's ankle. With a few snaps of the weapon, the QA rep's hand fell off at the wrist, but Doug dropped to the ground as the blade sliced into his Achilles tendon.

"Owwwwww!" Doug screamed, reeling in pain on the floor, blood gushing from his ankle.

"Sorry, man," O'Brien said. "I really did not mean to do that."

"I told you to be careful with that thing," Will said from the doorway where he was still holding Lillian tightly, blocking her view of the ultra-violence occurring just outside of her corner office.

Planting his wrist stump into the millimeter-thick carpet, Allen dragged himself the few inches to where Doug sat, the zombie's loss of an appendage having seemingly no effect on his mobility. With the hole punch disregarded on the floor, and his hands busy stopping the flow of blood above his left heel, Doug was defenseless as Allen sank his yellow teeth into the bleeding man's good leg, tearing the flesh from the muscle and the muscle from the bone. Doug screamed again in pain while Hank and O'Brien—now a bit more conservative with his makeshift katana/baseball bat—fended off the advances of two dead administrative assistants and Leslie Gonzalez, the bilingual interpreter.

These gray, moaning creatures had a strange fighting style. They didn't really do anything, but continued to stumble forward, chomping their rotting teeth wildly at the air. It wasn't all that difficult to fight them, Hank thought. Just stay on your feet, keep them out of biting distance, and, apparently, stab them in the head. Nothing else seemed to stop them. Their Teflon skin did give them an advantage, but Hank wasn't having that much trouble. And aside from slicing his ally, neither was O'Brien. But Doug was down for the count. After Hank broke the pointer in half when he delivered a particular whopper of a hit to Leslie, she fell to the floor and was thus fully fixated on sinking her teeth into Doug's chest.

He wailed for as long as he could while O'Brien slammed his blade right into call center rep James Hartnell's skull. At that moment, Hank got the eerie sensation that he'd seen something very similar in a movie before. And on posters and T-shirts. Fuck, he thought, *Dawn of the Dead*, the machete zom—. He didn't even want to think the word. Morticia better not have been right.

12:21 PM

The General was ecstatic. He hadn't even sent out a formal invitation, but so many people kept arriving at his parking lot party. In just the past hour, his ranks had swelled from nine to around thirty. He stood by the front entrance with his legions behind him, sporadically gazing at the Hot Metal Bridge to see more allies approaching. He didn't know why they were drawn here, but each of them seemed to know that this is where it started. And this is where it would end.

Unfortunately, there had yet to be a response from inside the building. The General looked up at the windows but could not see a single sign of life. Maybe if he checked the other sides, he would catch someone and deliver a threatening message.

"Troops!" he shouted to the groaning dead. "I am embarking on a reconnaissance mission for which I will circumnavigate the fortress. I will require backup because we never know what kind of sharpshooters they have on the other side of the fifty-yard line."

He waited. But no response came. They'd follow, he thought, just as they had before.

12:23 PM

Now that Myron was in the manic portion of his newly acquired bipolar condition, it was Kelly's turn to hold her head in her hands. The janitor was babbling incoherently about the Steelers, his unemployed brother with a cyst on his neck, and the Sham-Wow. There was some racist stuff here and there, but everyone pretty much ignored him anyway. Janice, aka the Lost Love Named Lenore (*was that too long?* she wondered), had pulled the dry-erase board from the wall and rested it in her lap as she drafted a set of clearly defined principles that she would present when the others returned. If they ever did. She was growing increasingly worried. She could deal with losing the grim reaper of lonely women at last call and the fat men, but not Hank. He was their default leader, and, no matter what his buddies said to destroy her dreams, he was hot.

She liked to think that she traveled from scene to scene to keep her life interesting, to explore her options and find her true identity. But the moves were usually spurred by the simple fact that she'd exhausted all her options. Quite plainly, she'd fucked all the guys, thereby screwing all the girls. She knew that she needed to put a stop to this tendency, but her usual entrance to subcultures was through the bedroom of a male member. But Goth had the star-crossed lovers, the immortal passion, and she decided to find it before she slept her way out of yet another fringe movement. Though she hadn't given the scene much of a try yet, she had settled on Hank, whose non-Gothicness she knowingly overlooked. She scolded herself for thinking about sex at a time like this, but extreme circumstances bring people together, right? She had an apocalypse vibe going.

Janice pulled out the small antique compact mirror from her purse and patted her stiff hair against her cheeks. She reapplied her dark lipstick and started to wipe Judy's blood from her forehead with her lace sleeve. Then she decided against it. *The blood was kinda sexy,* she thought, *in a* Carrie *sort of way.*

Pete was busy surveying the scene outside the conference room window. It was looking pretty quiet for now. *He could make a break for it,* he thought as he scanned the laptop on the table, the last viable weapon aside from a few reams of paper. Then, thud! Amelia from—well, he didn't really know what she did—crashed against the glass, one of her eyes falling from her face, held on only by a nerve. Pete let go of the blinds that he was holding open with his thumb as Adam let out a stifled guffaw.

The other employees looked over at him. Adam sat in the one rolling chair with armrests, his feet firmly planted on the edge of the conference table. He held his cell phone to his ear and was apparently listening to something quite humorous while the others feared for their lives.

"What are you doing?" Pete asked.

Adam held up his finger to hush him and continued to giggle.

"What the hell, Adam?" Kelly said from her seat at the conference table.

"It's these messages from my buddy. This real estate guy I know. I posted an ad on Craig's List this morning, claiming that he was giving away a drop ceiling," Adam said between chuckles. "He's gotten like forty calls already and he says he's gonna kill me. This is his third message. He gets angrier in each one. You wanna hear it?" He held his phone up, and Pete swiped it from his hand.

"No, I don't want to hear it, you stupid ganef," Pete glared at Adam. "But I'm curious, when were you going to tell us that you had a working cell phone?"

"I didn't know. I shut it off earlier 'cause he kept calling me."

"But your phone is working?" Kelly asked incredulously.

"I guess so," Adam said. He paused. "Oh."

"Yeah. Oh. Meathead," Pete said, pressing 911 on the cell phone keys. He turned to Adam. "And get out of my ass groove."

"We've been here for like an hour," Adam protested. "How can you already have an ass groove?"

"You mean to tell me you don't know how quickly an ass groove can be established? Get up," Pete said as he was connected with emergency services.

"911, what's your city and state?" the dispatcher asked.

"Pittsburgh, Pennsylvania," Pete replied, sliding into the chair that Adam had just vacated.

"If you're calling about whatever the ruckus is in the South Side, all the available officers are dispatched," she replied.

"Everyone?" Pete asked. "Because we're trapped in an office, and we haven't seen anyone outside and no one's come to get us."

"Boy, I said everyone. You guys got EMTs, fire trucks, cops, I think even a volunteer local militia is out there helpin'. There ain't nothin' else I can do. Just sit in your office and pass the time like you always would. It's not five yet. Get back to work."

"But all the employees are eating each other," Pete said to empty air. The operator had hung up. "Muter fucker."

"What?" Kelly asked.

"Well, apparently the emergency operator finds whatever is going on here to be a massive inconvenience. And they've got everyone out already. And, oh yeah, it's all over the area. So we're fucked."

"Let me call my husband," Kelly said, scrambling from the chair.

Pete tossed her the phone, and she frantically pressed several buttons. Putting the phone up to her ear with the first semblance of hope in the past hour, she listened to dead air until the busy signal came on. She looked at the phone screen. "All circuits are busy," it read. She hit the call button again and waited, for the same result. After three more tries, she slammed the phone onto the conference table.

"Well, don't break it," Adam said, reclaiming his cell from the table.

"What's wrong with you?" Pete asked Adam. "Why didn't you tell us you had a working phone?"

"I forgot about it," Adam said. "It was off, and I was distracted."

"No shit. We're all distracted. But I want to get out of here."

"Some of us have families," Kelly said.

Suddenly, a knock came on the door and Adam was relieved that it drew the scrutiny away from him. He wasn't known for being particularly honest, but he had truly forgotten that he had his phone on him. And it didn't help anyway, so what were they so mad about?

"Let us in!" came O'Brien's voice from the other side of the glass. Pete ran to open the door.

"Holy mother of Pearl Jam!" Adam said as Hank, O'Brien, Will, and that creepy Lillian woman pushed into the conference room.

The fact that they were all soaked in blood was Adam's first impression. Hank didn't show it as much as the rest because his maroon button-down shirt, though torn, just looked a bit wet. O'Brien was carrying a rather large blade that looked vaguely familiar, and Hank held an umbrella and was armed with an arsenal of desk supplies, some shoved into his pockets and others, like staplers, attached to his belt. Lillian had either sat in blood or had a really explosive period, Adam surmised, and Will's glasses had been cracked, but he was still wearing them.

"What took you so long?" Kelly asked.

Hank thought for a moment. In flashbacks, the scene would have gone something like this: Doug gets eaten while he and O'Brien momentarily clear a path of incapacitated decomposing co-workers, Will attempts to carry Lillian away from the carnage and drops her to the ground. He picks her up, and she screams, probably because her Talbots skirt is irreparably stained. It would look like a good snapshot reel in end credits of a movie. And they even had the pictures because that idiot O'Brien had documented everything that had happened. The photos actually might be decent proof as a defense when they were all inevitably brought up on charges for decapitating three co-workers. *But you see, Your Honor, we were battling flesh-hungry corpses. Look what they did to Doug here. It was us or them. Please take pity, Your Honor. We had no idea how deadly a paperweight could be.*

"What happened to her?" Hank asked, pointing to Judy's corpse with the shattered skull that they had "buried" under the conference table.

"She did it," Kelly pointed to Janice.

"Well, it worked," Janice defended herself. "She died, woke up, and tried to eat Adam. I whacked her in the head like I knew I had to."

"You know, she's right," Hank said.

Janice's eyes sparkled, "I know," she said, coyly. No, now was not the time to play the femme fatale.

"It's true," O'Brien said. "I was out there, kicking ass and taking names. I was stabbing all of them." He demonstrated by stabbing the paper cutter blade in the air in front of him as Kelly wheeled her chair away from him. "And they just wouldn't fall. I mean, no matter how many times I got them, they just wouldn't fall." He got back into his batting stance and swung blade. "I was like Mark McGwire out there, chopping their heads off and sending them over the wall in left field."

"What's wrong with you?" Janice asked. "Did you kill Doug for his Pro-Caine or something?"

"No, that was an accident," O'Brien said. Janice, Pete, Adam, and Kelly looked at one another in confusion. "I'm just post-battle high!"

"I think that's called post-traumatic stress disorder," Pete said.

"What happened to Doug anyway?" Kelly asked. "And did you bring any food?"

"He got eaten," O'Brien said. "But it wasn't totally my fault. It was heat of the moment, man."

"Okay, so you killed Doug," Pete said. "Any idea how we get the hell out of here?"

"I do," Janice said, presenting the dry-erase board.

12:29 PM

Finally, some excitement, Harold thought. He had been standing guard outside of Marshall Owens's door for what felt like hours, and there did not appear to be anything to guard the boss from. Without a key, no one could access this floor. The elevator required a combination, and the ID scanner at the stairwell entrance only accepted his, Owens's, and the maintenance crew's badges. And he knew for damn sure that none of those corpses were locksmiths.

Guarding Rashard James, the Crips leader who headed up the drug trade inside, had been his function in prison. Harold had been his loyal servant, too, but it had not been nearly as boring there. If someone got shanked, it was right in front of him. Although Harold mostly stayed out of the action for reasons of self-preservation, it was like watching porn to him. Now he could only imagine what fun the employees were having slicing each other up downstairs. He had really wanted to join the festivities. So, naturally, he was overjoyed when offered a reprieve, a mission.

Realizing quite astutely that the main elevators would probably be infested by dead cannibal employees, Harold decided that the freight elevator, which was only accessible by keyed entry, would provide the path of least resistance.

So he opted to take the stairs.

He wasn't actually concerned about saving any living office workers, but decided that those dead freaks definitely had to go. They would do him no good. He opened the dead-bolted door from the main area of the fourth floor and entered the stairwell.

"Fuck-ass shit," he muttered, scanning the scene of carnage that awaited him.

Blood soaked the steps, creating what was sure to be a safety hazard if he had to run. Three eviscerated corpses lay at the bottom of the stairwell, minuscule remains of business casual attire peeking out from exploded organs and torn ligaments. But the most disturbing sight was inches away from his feet on the landing. The corpse of a man in a light blue shirt, gray trousers, and a navy striped tie was sprawled out on the floor. His body possessed more of its original form than the three at the bottom of the steps, but his head was dangling onto the top step, attached only by a few nerves. Harold fingered the gun in his belt holster. Having dealt with these creatures on a daily basis for the past few months, Harold was confident that he would need the gun only in an emergency and had not packed any additional bullets to reload. There was no fucking way in Hell he was using his piece on Lillian Glabicki, wasting ammo when he could just break her neck in less than a minute.

Harold took his first step down the stairs, carefully placing his foot flatly in the pool of blood that enveloped most of the stairway. At that moment, the corpse of a man shambled onto the third-floor landing, his ripped button-down shirt exposing three broken ribs that protruded from his torn, gray flesh. He looked up at Harold, the vacant eyes and blank expression Harold knew all too well to be that insatiable hunger. The creature shuffled right into one of the corpses on the floor. He stopped, kicked, and continued to attempt to walk forward without deducing that the dead body was a hindrance. His feet barely leaving the floor when he walked, he trod forward, mere inches at a time, pushing the corpse as he stared at his prey on the landing above. He kicked and shuffled until he reached another barrier, the stubborn staircase, an obstacle that was unmovable to even the most determined zombie. His feet pushed the corpse into the step, and the dead man finally fell, his face smashing against the right angle of the fifth step.

"For fuck's sake," Harold said as he carefully strode down the steps.

Unfazed by his latest debacle, the zombie flailed his arms until something innate told him to prop himself up with the use of his hands. As the dead man pushed himself back from his face-plant, Harold stomped his foot down on the creature's head, smashing the thing down so its gaping mouth effectively ate the fifth step. There was a crunch, and that was it. Harold had curb-stomped a punk or two in his dealing days, but this was an entirely different sensation. You didn't hear the distinct sound of a skull cracking and the teeth shattering. It was almost like this thing's skeleton was already soft and rotten.

Harold continued down the steps to the third-floor landing. He pushed open the door and entered the office. The place looked like it had seen a riot. Desks had been ransacked, papers were strewn everywhere, and employees lay dead on the floor. He turned right and strode towards Lillian's corner office. The door was wide open, and a pool of blood served as a terribly macabre welcome mat. Two severed heads sat on the floor, along with a disembodied hand. Harold quickly located the remains of the owners of these parts, one of whom was covered in sparkles, presumably from the smashed snow globe that was on the floor. He peered inside Lillian's vacant office, seeing a room that appeared just as it should on a weekend.

Harold turned around and walked back to the stairwell. Well, she was gone. Probably dead. Her Ann Taylor jacket was still hanging from the coat rack in the corner of the room, indicating that she had left, or been taken, in a hurry. Though she was missing for only a short period of time, she was presumed dead. That's what he'd report to Marshall Owens.

12:31 PM

"What we are dealing with is a full-on zombie attack," Janice, aka Madame Malevolent, said as she unveiled her dry-erase board presentation. She paced back and forth in front of the board like she remembered her college professors doing. It made them look official, she thought.

"Don't say that," Will said from the end of the table where he cuddled with Lillian in a monstrous middle-management embrace.

"Excuse me?" Janice asked.

"Zombies. I find that offensive. These are our friends, members of the Pro-Well team. I think we can come up with something with fewer derogatory connotations," Will proclaimed.

"How 'bout ghouls?" Pete asked. "Rotting parasites. Flesh-eating douchebags at work."

"Cannibal corpses," Hank suggested.

"Nice, man," Adam said, raising his hand to give Hank a high-five. Hank accepted, cigarette between his fingers.

"You people are missing the point. I was thinking more along the lines of *living impaired*," Will said.

"But that would imply that these creatures are dead, which they definitely do not appear to be," Kelly chimed in.

"Exactly," Janice said. "The living impaired are not staggering around trying to eat us for lunch; they're six feet under in coffins. Oh, beautiful coffins with deep scarlet lining and a rich mahogany finish." Janice let herself drift into her fantasy for a moment before continuing her educational lecture.

Opening her eyes from the dark subterrain of her imagination, she saw everyone in the room—even that completely unhinged custodian—giving her cockeyed "That bitch is crazy!" looks.

"Anyway, this is what we know," she continued, using half of Hank's wooden pointer to display the enumerated articles on the left side of the board. "One: The enemy is impervious to feeling pain. Two: Their sole vulnerability is their heads. Three: They do not seem to have any senses except the notion of hunger. Four: They want to eat us. Five: They are walking dead. But how did they become this way? you may be asking yourselves. A good question, for which I have no answer at the moment."

"I believe that—" Lillian was cut off by the suddenly vocal janitor.

"It's our sins as people. This new way of life. I seen it. There's no good people no more. Satan has released his hounds, and they're devourin' us one by one until we're all his slaves," Myron proclaimed.

"I thought Judy was dead," Adam said.

"Yeah. Right. When there's no more room in Hell, the dead will go to work," Hank said sarcastically.

"You guys ever heard of the Gay Bomb?" Adam asked. "Well, the government actually worked on this thing in the early '80s. If you set it off, it would make the enemy gay and they would just start humping and we'd be able to kill them real easy."

"Is that what happened to you, Hank?" Pete asked, smirking.

"Pete, that is inappropriate," Will said. He was back on his politically correct game as he sat in a chair with his arm around Lillian.

"Yeah, when I was a Green Beret," Hank responded sarcastically, ignoring Will.

"Anyway, well this has gotta be a cannibal bomb or something, set off to get the whole population to kill itself," Adam explained.

"So you think it's terrorism?" Kelly asked.

"Yeah, al Qaeda," Adam said.

"Okay, that's actually not a bad explanation," Hank said. "Except for the gay bomb analogy."

"I think it's intergalactic warfare," O'Brien said. "See, all these aliens, they hate us because they don't have the Internet. And since they don't have the Internet, porn is not easily accessible. They're all pent up out there, a bunch of puritans. They've just gotta unleash a big angry dump on us 'cause we're the party planet. Shoving a big dildo up the ass of the awesome planet Earth is what they're doing."

"Ah, the old sexually-repressed-extra-terrestrials-unleash-their-plan-9-to-steal-our-smut ploy," Hank mused. "Though I have yet to see an anal probe."

"Where is the ass of the planet?" Adam asked.

"Cleveland," Hank replied.

"How do you know they don't have the Internet?" Pete asked with sarcasm. He was beginning to have fun with the visiting client. "I mean, they've probably hacked into ours from light-years away just to check out the Paris Hilton sex tape."

"No, that doesn't make any sense," O'Brien explained with certainty. Even Hank had to admit that he was a pretty decent salesman, if for no other reason than unflappable confidence. "If they were going to pirate our celebrity sex tapes, they'd go for one with Pamela Anderson. And they can't. They wouldn't be able to get a wireless signal."

"All right, stop!" Janice commanded, throwing her hands over her pale face in frustration. "Right now it doesn't matter how they got here, but they are here, and we have to get out of this conference room at some point. So that brings me to the next lesson. How to fight them. There is really only one rule: Hit them in the head, and destroy the brain."

"That's right, bitches!" O'Brien exclaimed, rising from his chair and thrusting the paper cutter blade in the air.

"I'm confiscating that for now," Pete said as he pulled the blade from O'Brien's grasp and placed it at his feet.

12:35 PM

The phone rang. Anxiously, Owens picked it up after one ring. "Hello?" he answered in feigned fear.

"Marshall, it's Bill. Are you okay?" City Controller Bill Callahan's voice came through the phone.

"For now," Owens said. "But I don't know for how long."

"What's going on there?" Bill asked urgently, his concern genuine. "I just got your email. What the hell did you get yourself into?"

"Trust, Bill, too much trust. Redemption. My dreams all gone wrong. Bestowed upon the wrong people."

"Yeah, man. What were you thinking hiring criminals?"

"The wellness of the world depends on it, Bill," Owens said, assuming the persona of a man who has seen the error of his ways. "But now I see that it has cost the lives of many."

"This isn't your fault, Marshall," Bill said. "A man of your stature is always going to be a target of greedy bottom-feeders. We can get the details later, but right now we've gotta get you out of there."

"Nonsense. I deserve this. It's penance for my mistakes," Owens said weepily.

"Marshall, listen to me. I've called the police and told them to get down to Pro-Well right away. This thug who's behind this, what does he look like? I'll get his mug up on all the channels and make sure he doesn't get out of town. This thing has affected so many people now, I doubt it'll be a citizen's arrest that nabs him."

"Harold, he's black. About six-foot-four, give or take an inch. He shaves his head. Has a goatee. Muscular. He's wearing a black suit. He left for now, but I don't know when he's coming back. Harold Lawrence Johnson. I'm sure you can find one of his numerous mug shots in records somewhere. Please, you must stop him before he destroys anything else!"

12:37 PM

Harold had just pulled his fist back to deliver a strong rap on Marshall Owens's office door when he heard his name mentioned. He dropped his hand, stepped closer to the door and listened.

"Son of a motherfucker," he said under his breath, listening to his boss dictate his ticket back to prison.

Harold didn't survive a childhood in the ghetto and three stints inside by failing to read his enemies, but Owens had fooled him this time. Maybe it was difficult to decipher the expressions beneath such severe burns. Or maybe Marshall Owens was the most worthy opponent that Harold had come across. Whatever the reason, Harold was not going to be hoodwinked or bamboozled anymore. He had forged his skills in manipulation and double-crossing in veritable brimstone.

12:51 AM

The Pro-Well employees were starting to get a bit tense. With the demises of Doug and Judy, it had finally dawned on them that they might also meet their ends today. And at work of all places. Seated around the conference table, the employees were more subdued than before.

"I pretended to be in the volunteer club in high school so I could put it on my reésumé," Janice said. "I only went to the meeting when they were taking the photo for the yearbook, so by all accounts, I was in the club."

"I never had Hydroproxybeciloma," Kelly said. "I made it up because *General Hospital* was getting really interesting and I didn't want to miss it that week."

"Really? Hydro-Plaxico-Burress isn't a real disease?" Pete asked.

"I once touched a stripper during a lap dance and the bouncer beat me up and threw me out of the club," O'Brien contributed, reclined in his chair with his feet resting on the table.

"So you were punished for that?" Janice asked.

"Yeah, the bouncer was huge."

"Then you paid for your sin. We're talking about all the awful shit we've done that we've gotten away with."

"Oh," O'Brien said, finally comprehending the conversation. "Well, I've always gotten caught."

"I was at this amusement park when I was fifteen," Pete said. "And you know that game that no one ever wins, where you have to toss a metal ring around a glass Coke bottle?"

Janice, Adam, and O'Brien nodded. That seemed to be enough for Pete to continue.

"Well, there was this retarded guy working the game," Pete began to explain.

"Pete!" Will scolded. "That's offensive. It's special needs." Will was desperately clinging to the familiar, to old habits that persist when everyone around you has died. It gave him the feeling of having some degree of control, even if it was just over words.

"No, not special needs. This guy was a total tard," Pete continued. Will rolled his eyes and looked defeated. "Anyway, this mongoloid had his back turned and I reached over and placed the ring on the bottle, then acted all surprised like it was really difficult and I couldn't believe I'd won."

"What did you win?" O'Brien asked.

"A giant, plushy pink flamingo," Pete muttered, ashamed.

"You know, these don't really seem like egregious offenses that would warrant this kind of punishment," Hank observed, ashing his cigarette into the abandoned coffee mug.

"I shot a man in Reno," Myron said as he rose from his seat.

"No, you didn't," Pete countered.

"Just to watch him die," Myron continued and sat back down.

"All right, we've officially lost Myron," Kelly said.

"When I hear the whistle blowing, I hang my head and cry." Myron continued to quote Johnny Cash's "Folsom Prison Blues."

"I think this is actually an improvement," Hank said.

"I once convinced a girl that I was being deported to Israel so she'd have sex with me," Adam said. "It worked, but I was discovered in the morning when I wasn't too worried about missing my imaginary flight."

"That's brilliant, dude!" O'Brien said as he leaned over the desk to high-five Adam.

As their hands slapped, a deafening boom echoed in the room.

"Guns. That's just what we need," Kelly said sarcastically.

"Actually it is. I'd rather have a .45 than a fucking ream of paper," Hank said.

He rose from his chair, along with Janice, Adam, Pete, and Will, and they rushed to the window. Hank pulled up one set of blinds and saw a tall black man in an immaculately tailored suit, aiming a revolver at Jordan Palmer from customer service who was lying on the floor with part of his skull shattered, pieces of his brains splattered on the carpet. The man looked up from his prey and spotted several normal flesh-colored faces peering out the conference room window. He ran the twenty paces towards them and stood directly in front of them with his gun pointed at Adam's nose.

"Let me in the fucking room!" he commanded.

Pete rushed to the door and unlocked it, and Harold entered. Kelly looked him up and down.

"You don't work in the office," she said.

"No shit. I work for Marshall Owens," Harold said, heading for the table. "Why you got a dead lady covered in paper under the table?"

"We didn't have a shovel," Hank replied.

"You work directly for Owens?" Kelly asked, always dying for the inside scoop. "What do you do?"

"I'm his personal bodyguard," Harold said shortly without looking up from Judy's lifeless form. He seemed oddly intrigued.

"Well, we're trying to get the fuck out of here," Hank said. "Got any suggestions?"

"Not a good idea, man," Harold said, finally looking up at Hank. "There's a whole shitload of those motherfuckers standing outside the doors. You wanna make it through that, you gotta get yourself equipped. I'm talking heavy artillery, and I doubt any of you white-collar folks brought a firearm with you to the office."

"I wish I could turn into a bat," Janice mused.

Harold stared at her, perplexed.

"We have weapons," Pete offered, pointing to the assortment of makeshift flails and bludgeoning devices on the end of the conference table.

Harold laughed. "Well, what was I thinking? Shit, you guys've got a laptop. You could just sabotage its Facebook page and it'd all go away."

"Internet's down," Adam said.

"Actually this paper cutter blade is pretty sweet," O'Brien said, holding up the bloody blade. Pete rushed over and yanked it from his hands.

Harold surveyed the carnage from both the dead and the living that covered the blade, then looked around the room at the blood-spattered employees.

"You guys've been busy," he observed.

"Yeah, and we really want to get out of here, but these zombies are at every exit," O'Brien said.

"That's what you've been calling them? Zombies?" Harold asked.

"That's the name we decided on. It seemed most appropriate," Hank explained.

"You guys got a plan?" Harold asked, intrigued by this vigilante sect of white-collar drones.

"We need more weapons," Janice said. "We can't really do all that much with the reams of paper."

"I told you, the blade is awesome," O'Brien insisted.

"To slice up who?" Janice asked, irritated. "From what I heard, you used it to chop Doug's foot off."

"Hey, that was an accident!" O'Brien shouted, rising from

his seat at the table. "I decapitated a shitload of those dead freaks with it!"

"Yo, shut the fuck up," Harold said. "I'm gonna get outta here, and it'd be a lot easier in an armed group. I say we round up whatever we can use and get the fuck outta this place."

"What about Mr. Owens?" Kelly said.

"Fuck Marshall Owens," Harold replied. "That motherfucker's goin' down, and I'm not bailing him out this time."

"All right, I'm ready," Adam said.

"Wait, what did you mean by that?" Hank asked Harold. "What does Owens have to do with this?"

"Nothin', man," Harold said, covering himself with all the phony, awkward, forced sincerity that a thug could muster. "I misspoke."

"No, I don't think so," Hank said, moving closer to Harold, the bloody pointer in his hand.

"I didn't say shit," Harold said.

"What does Owens have to do with this? Did he cause this?" Hank asked, inching closer.

"Man, I don't gotta tell you shit," Harold said.

"What did Owens do?" O'Brien yelled, brandishing the blade that he had stolen back from Pete. "Who's Owens?" he asked as an afterthought.

Harold raised his gun and pointed it at O'Brien's face. "Get that thing away from me."

At that moment Will—in a rare moment of decisive action, the type of swift movement that was only made by those who were totally sure of themselves and highly motivated—jumped from his chair. After years of affirmations that he could do whatever he set his mind to, that he was "worth it," Will leapt onto Harold's back, grabbing his left arm, which held the gun. With the fat man on his spine, Harold fell to the floor, his strong hand still grasping the handle, his finger on the trigger. Lillian joined the fracas, motivated by the motivation of her strong lover. She grabbed at the gun, and suddenly, BANG.

12:56 PM

Kyle Kennison had just awakened from a mighty slumber if there ever was one. Apparently band practice was canceled because his guitarist Mike's imaginary medieval fiefdom was about to overthrow the powerful imaginary kingdom of Livankia in the Mount Lebanon High School parking lot. Kyle had never witnessed one of these epic battles, but they sounded pretty metal to him. Swords and wars, Satan's Fist should write a song about it, if they ever played a gig.

At thirty-one years old, Kyle was still living the rock star dream. A three-million-dollar trust fund from his hotelier parents effectively kept him out of the job market and just about everything else that his father had wanted for him, but Kyle had been honing his singing abilities by shouting along to Accept and Iron Maiden records for years. Unfortunately the rest of Satan's Fist—that to date had played one full gig of Metallica covers at a kegger in a friend's basement—was not as committed to his rock n' roll dream. Dave and Tim had jobs, and Mike had the fiefdom of Norgeland. Kyle's worry-free financial situation allowed him to live the rock star lifestyle to the nth degree. Getting a new tattoo of a different girl who broke his heart every couple of weeks, sleeping until the bars opened, and being more metal than you—that was Kyle's life, even though his name was Kyle.

Since band practice had been canceled, he didn't have much to do, so Kyle pulled his black jeans out of the hamper that had been wasting away by the washer for three weeks, threw his tattered Judas Priest T-shirt over his skinny chest and pulled his leather jacket from the hook by the giant coffee tin filled with cigarette butts in the entry way of his Mt. Washington home. He ran his hand through his long, dyed black hair and pretended not to feel the bald spot that was ever expanding on the back of his head. Kyle's skin was as pale as a vampire's because he made a habit of sleeping through the sunlight. This was actually kind of an early day for him. He pulled on the leather biker jacket that would have perfectly complemented the bike he might one day own if he ever passed the damn licensing test, and walked out the door to the brusque, sunny October afternoon.

Kyle pushed his cheap wraparound sunglasses onto his nose, blinded by the sun. He'd head down to the Bat Cave, grab a sandwich and some beers, and wait until everyone else showed up to tell them about the party he was attempting to plan for whatever holiday was up next. *Did people get off for Columbus Day in this state?* he wondered as he walked down the quiet residential street towards the incline to the South Side. He wasn't averse to walking down the steep hill, but he and that heavyset chick with the leopard print skirt and catlike eye makeup had broken his futon last night and Kyle was feeling kind of worn out.

He approached the rather antiquated ticketing booth at the end of the funicular and tossed two crumpled dollar bills and seventy-five cents in a combination of nickels and pennies under the clear bulletproof window and the clerk pushed his ticket out at him. Kyle picked it up, shoved it in his pocket, and walked to the boarding area. The car was on its way up, approaching him slowly, but Kyle felt that he could sneak in a quick smoke. He pulled his beat-up pack of Pall Malls out of his pocket and lit a broken cigarette. The car was about thirty feet away from him now, so he reached back into his pocket for his just-purchased ticket. He pulled out a receipt for a gyro, a ticket stub for a Midnight Mania show at the Rex Theater, a condom, a phone number scrawled on a bar napkin for someone named Jill, and another napkin with his own number written on it. Where was his Incline pass? Kyle scoured his pockets as the car pulled up at the Mount Washington station. The doors opened as he pulled out his ticket and smiled expectantly at the car.

But when the passengers began to disembark, his glee melted into confusion. He didn't remember seeing any flyers for a South Side zombie walk today. Kyle was a regular staple of the festive parades down Carson Street, armed with a water gun to kill his heavily made-up friends and acquaintances as they stumbled from bar to bar. But the organized zombie crawls were never violent, so Kyle was quite confused by the scene of utter carnage inside the funicular car.

He took another hit of his cigarette as he recognized Bella, one of his favorite strippers, as she disembarked. She stared at him, her eyes glazed and blood dripping from her stained teeth.

"Hey, Bella, why didn't you tell me you guys were doing this today?" Kyle asked, "You know I like to be the zombie slayer."

Bella just continued to glare at him, and a groaning noise emanated from her purple lips.

"Shit, you're really in character today. I'll run back home and grab my Super Soaker," Kyle said.

But as he turned away from Bella, he walked straight into Jen, the petite redhead who had quit the pole-dancing scene when she got married a year ago.

"What's up, Jen?" Kyle said. "I'll be right back. Gotta get my weapon."

Jen clamped her teeth at her friend, spattering blood as she chomped at the air. Kyle quickly pushed her aside and skipped away from the Incline station.

"I'll see ya guys down there," he shouted back.

Slowly, with the groaning noises they'd practiced during three years of zombie walks assuming a much more natural tone that they hadn't been able to muster while they were alive, Jen and Bella slowly ambled in the direction that Kyle had run.

1:02 PM

With both hands, Lillian pried the firearm from Harold's grip. Hank gazed at the hole in the wall across the room while Will rose from the floor. In her small, manicured hands, Lillian kept the gun pointed at Harold as he picked himself up from the carpet.

"Congratulations," he said. "You just wasted a bullet."

"Look, we just want to know what's going on," Hank said calmly. "If Owens has something to do with it, then I think we can assume that this whole disaster is centered on Pro-Well, which means that we are much safer outside of this office. So start talking."

So, with the squat, coral reef-attired HR manager who was in love with a fat middle manager who owned a veritable library of self-help books pointing a gun at his face, the ex-Crip started talking. He relayed the diabolical tale of recruiting the homeless and killing them instantly with injections into their veins that revived them moments later to a semi-conscious state that made them ideal workers but also flesh-eating ghouls. He described the slave conditions in the factory and the street dwellers they had procured who, due to physical disability, were not fit for labor and were thereby used as food. It was all going so well: Profits were up, and Harold and the other men in black received hefty paychecks for their efforts.

"Until they escaped last night," Harold said. "They ate the night guard and destroyed the whole fuckin' place."

"They unionized," Hank observed.

"Yeah, and now they're out there eating people," Harold said.

"But the zombies in here, they're not homeless," Kelly said. "Unless... That would explain so much."

"Well, I don't know what to tell you about that," Harold replied. "I guess the shit's contagious."

"So Owens developed this virus?" Janice asked. "I knew zombie powder was real. Has he been to Haiti recently?"

"Look, I don't know how he comes up with this shit. Far's I know, he does everything on the fourth floor. What about you, Glabicki? You know where anything else goes on?"

"Wait, you know him?" Will asked.

"Well, yes," Lillian said meekly, as if she had been apprehended for a murder for which she'd framed the butler.

Harold said, "You haven't told them."

"What Lil-a-Bye?" Will said. "What haven't you told us?"

Lillian looked into his wide, wet eyes. "I'm sorry, Sweetie. I just couldn't."

"Lil-a-Bye?" Adam asked, part amused, part repulsed.

So Lillian told her story.

"My husband had just lost his license to practice law. He'd been disbarred for taking bribes to provide shoddy defense to his clients, but Owens didn't know that. He had just moved to town and was looking for some start-up capital. He was so young, so earnest, so naïve. Marshall had seen my husband, Bernie, on TV. My husband was cleaning out his office, terrified of what would happen next, disgraced, the pariah of local law, when, like a savior, in walks Marshall Owens, the burns not yet fully healed, with a business proposition. Bernie saw an opportunity to invest in this young scarred man and his vision to heal the world. And with it he saw a way to heal his own reputation.

"Instead of exploiting his accused clients, he would help a reformed criminal. Or at least that was what it would look like to the outside world. I should have known that Bernie would never change. I should have known that he saw a swindle, an easy way to take the money and run. And he tried. After five years of helping Marshall build the company, of investing money that he didn't have, Bernie tried to take back what he had never given. Of course Marshall noticed. He was prone to micromanaging and always kept a close eye on his finances, always taking all his papers to multiple accountants to get a second opinion. And that's when he caught him. Bernie had just emptied out his bank account and was back at home packing when Marshall arrived. He said he could take the evidence to the police, along with all the sordid details gathered by the P.I. he'd employed when his suspicion was first aroused.

"Or he could take Bernie back to the lab with him. He had a special experiment he wanted him to be a part of. He said that now it was Bernie's turn to keep a secret, that they must trust

one another implicitly now that each knew the truth. At first
Bernie was confused. That is, until Marshall opened the door
to a back room in the lab upstairs. There was a girl on the table,
couldn't have been older than sixteen. She had been sliced open
from her chest down to her pelvis and what Bernie later learned
to be her appendix was removed. She was alive, for the time
being, with an IV hooked into her arm.

"'I'm learning anatomy,' Marshall said.

"Bernie stared at him, repulsed, finding Marshall's mangled
face even more repugnant than the sight of his victim on the
table. Finally, he was able to say, 'You have to let her go.'

"'That's it?' Marshall responded. 'Bernie, you're so short-
sighted. I know that you're just a common crook and could
never fully comprehend, but you must understand what we're
doing here is for the greater good.'

"'What *we're* doing here?' Bernie quivered. 'Marshall, I
had nothing to do with *this*.'

"'You financed this,' Marshall said. 'Well, I guess it wasn't
actually your money, but your name is all over it.'

"'But she's just a child,' Bernie pleaded.

"'She's a whore,' Marshall said. 'I picked her up hitch-
hiking outside of the jail, right after she'd been released. See,
she's still wearing her bracelet. She offered to blow me for a
ride. Course I let her. I don't see that much action anymore, for
obvious reasons. She was all too anxious to let me take her
wherever I wanted.'

"'You don't have the right to torture her,' Bernie said,
pacing around the operating table, his eyes never leaving Marshall's gleaming gaze. Bernie was never a brave man. Too
scared to rob a bank, too crooked to work an honest day, he
was content to take what wasn't his quietly, to prey on those
when they were at their most vulnerable. But clearly he had un-
derestimated Marshall Owens. And his jubilance, his righteous-
ness, his lack of remorse, and the way he just didn't seem
bothered by the eviscerated girl on the table, it all truly terrified
Bernie.

"'And you didn't have the right to steal,' Marshall countered, his increasing confidence driving Bernie further into timidity. 'But now, from the body of this crackwhore, we now have the specimens for experimentation. Don't you want to rid the world of varicose veins? Look at her perfect legs.' He pointed to the exposed limbs of the presumably comatose teenager. 'I picked up an old woman the other day. Calves practically looked like a fucking road map. I'm studying the difference to eradicate that problem once and for all.'

"'What do you want from me?' Bernie asked. He didn't want to know any more about the experiments and just how many bodies were hidden in his place of business.

"'Same thing you've been doing. I want nothing to change,' he said, 'But I want your help once in a while. Clearly, you have proven that you cannot be trusted with money, but I don't think that you'll have any trouble helping with the acquisition and disposal of the specimens.'

"And that's how it started. Bernie was blackmailed into being an accomplice. He didn't tell me about what he was doing—he didn't tell me much of anything—and I didn't ask. I had no idea about his plan to run off with the money, as I was here at work while he started to pack a few belongings from our home. By the time I returned, nothing was out of place except for Bernie. He was passed out on the couch with a bottle of bourbon spilled across his chest."

"All right, all right, that's enough," Pete said. "Your ex is a blackmailed victim who oddly enough made his living blackmailing his own victims? Save it. You knew. You didn't tell us. You suck. End of fucking story."

"Exactly," Hank said. "Unless it ends with a lynch mob, witness protection, or hanging out of a helicopter, I don't want to hear anymore."

"Mental institution," Lillian said.

"Perfect," Hank said. "Let's move on."

"You really should have told us," Will said.

"Why?" Pete asked. "It really wasn't all that relevant."

"Because then we'd know who was responsible," Kelly said.

"Yeah, but it doesn't help us get out of this building," Hank countered. "Jesus, Lily Munster over there gave us better advice."

Janice smiled. She wasn't sure if that was a compliment, but she liked hearing him refer to her nonetheless.

"I just wish I had known all along," Will said, a note of melancholy in his voice. His lover had been involved with some unsavory characters.

Suddenly Myron stood from his chair in the corner of the room. He took a few steps towards the rest of the refugees at the table, waving his finger wildly at Lillian.

"I cross-check thee," he proclaimed. "Let the wrath of the Tanger be felt upon yinz."

"What's wrong with him?" Harold said.

"Oh he's been merging the Bible and the Penguins blue line for a while now," Adam said.

"I summon the Geno to ice you, harlot swine."

"He's on the offense, Myron. Yessh," Adam said, wagging his thumb at the janitor. "These old guys never get hockey."

"Well, I say we leave that scarred nutjob in his fortress of solitude and get the hell out of here," Pete said.

"I'm with you on that, dude," O'Brien said. "Can I have my sword back?"

"No," Pete retorted.

"So far all I've seen's the blade," Harold said. "What else you guys got?"

1:38 PM

Adam thought the scene would have made an amazing montage. His blood-spattered co-workers were working diligently in the conference room to craft weapons out of mundane office supplies. They were preparing for battle, fashioning an anachronistic medieval arsenal. Well, some were hard at work.

O'Brien was snapping photos of everyone else's efforts, constantly mumbling about the vast fortune he would amass from his inside look at the chaos when it was all over and how women would be clamoring for their own inside look at the man who'd shown such audacity when surrounded by the walking dead that had been scaring movie-goers for decades. Adam was busy whispering the names of entrees and watching the famished Kelly twitch.

"Stuffed peppers," he said. "Chicken pot pie."

Cigarette hanging from his lips, Hank was taping Keisha Randall's switchblade to the side of the conference room's disconnected phone base.

"See, you can use the phone as a shield while you simultaneously bludgeon and stab your attacker," he explained to Pete at the end of the conference table.

"That's awesome, man," Pete replied. "You've definitely redeemed some of the gayness you exhibited earlier."

Hank ignored him. "Now you do the same with the ream of paper and the scissors."

His hair falling in front of his face, Pete unrolled a length of tape and began securing the scissors to the unlikely bludgeoning device. While Pete was occupied, Hank reached to his side to grab one of the three umbrellas he had nabbed from the cubicles. Raising the pink umbrella above his head, his middle finger slipped and hit the button, causing it to burst open, revealing a several images of Hannah Montana surrounded by a pink polka dot pattern.

"I spoke too soon," Pete said.

"What are you doing?" Janice yelled from across the table.

"This faggy abomination will function as a lance in case we need to joust," Hank explained calmly.

"You can't open an umbrella inside!" Janice shrieked. "It's bad luck!"

"Really?" Pete asked. "You're concerned with superstition right now?"

Janice, aka the Duchess of Dusk (she was beginning to run

out of ideas and her potential Goth titles were starting to sound more like alliterative Babe Ruth nicknames) took the hint and dropped the issue.

"Please, don't say faggy," Will said.

"Sorry, I never meant to offend myself," Hank replied.

Kelly sat at the table, drawing a map of every door and hallway that she could remember in the office. As she prided herself on being the eyes, ears, and nasal cavity of the company, her rendering was actually quite accurate. O'Brien huddled over her shoulder, pointing to the locations where he had seen zombies. According to the former salesman, they were everywhere, including the women's restroom.

"So somehow, on your trip to the second floor, you encountered zombies in the mailroom and the call center, which are on the ground level?" Kelly asked dubiously.

"Ah, no, I dunno. I don't think we were there," O'Brien covered. "But I'm sure they're down there."

Kelly rolled her eyes and pushed the paper across the table. "Whatever," she said.

Adam walked behind her and whispered, "Chimichanga."

This scene should have music, he thought. Real montage music like "Eye of the Tiger." He started to imagine the fast-paced, somewhat cheesy '80s rock soundtrack that would provide a backdrop for the scene, so he took it upon himself to rock out from time to time. Pete caught him playing a quick air guitar interlude and whacked him on the side of the head, bringing Adam back to the mission at hand.

Get laid.

That was the plan. There was Kelly, his chubby, pregnant nemesis, and the end of the world didn't feel soon enough for him to take a stab at that. When she wasn't scribbling the building's blueprint, she was studying the every move of each of the trapped co-workers. Admittedly, he had done things, but he knew that he would never be that desperate.

"Arby's big beef and cheddar," Adam said quietly.

Lillian had twenty years on him and was occupied cuddling

with his boss and they were whispering into each other's ears. Not to mention the fact that she was holding a gun. And then there was the new girl. Amidst all the chaos, he had caught the name Janice. Thin, petite, and actually kinda cute underneath all the black eye makeup, she was currently fashioning an ominous sign written in some sort of improvised Olde English print on a manila file folder.

"Beware Ye Who Enter Here," it read. Quickly, she spun her chair around to Harold, who was dragging Judy's body from beneath the conference table. Her paper burial dirt fell to the floor as the muscular bodyguard pulled her by her once white Reeboks.

"Wait a second," Janice said as she slid to the floor.

She placed the sign on Judy's chest and, with two thumbtacks that Hank had lifted from the supply room, pushed them into the upper corners of the manila folder into the dead woman's chest.

"What is that for?" Harold snapped.

"It's a warning," she said.

"To who?" Harold asked. "Those freaks can't read."

"Ye who enter here," Janice explained.

"Is that really necessary?" Hank asked.

"Yes, they seem to retain some primal urges, like eating and being part of a group," Janice explained. "Maybe they still have some need for self-preservation. If they see this, they'll know we're a force to be reckoned with."

"I'm for it," Pete said. "It's not every day a dead lady gets holes in her tits."

"You motherfuckers are sick," Harold said.

"Prop her up against the wall out there. Then they'll get the full effect," Janice said.

As Harold dragged the body towards the door, Adam decided to make his move.

"Bacon Egg McMuffin," he whispered as he walked past Kelly.

1:43 PM

The General was ecstatic. Never in his life had he thrown a soiree like this and it wasn't even soir yet. He was so happy about his newfound popularity that he forgot that he was launching a rebellion. He was too busy socializing, or trying to, as his new friends did not seem too talkative. But the General paid that no mind. He was just happy that there were so many seemingly like-minded individuals. He couldn't even get Rabbit, Ladle, and Bob to accompany him to Mario Lemieux's house. And he'd even drafted invitations on discarded receipts he'd found outside the gas station. He had carefully scrawled the time and place for their pilgrimage on the slips of paper and dropped them off in the shopping carts under the Birmingham Bridge. No responses. Not even for a mission of that caliber of excitement. When he lived in a stairwell at the side of a bank parking lot in Oakland, he couldn't even convince Sombrero Man to attend a lecture on the basics of space flight.

But now they were all flocking to him. Most were strangers, but there were some familiar faces in the crowd. He recognized Johnny, the chubby Gulf War vet who lived off disability benefits and hung out in area drugstores. He tended to purchase an unnecessary amount of birthday balloons and was currently carrying a bundle of them to the parking lot party. Johnny staggered into the parking lot, his rigor mortis kicking in to clutch the strings of seven Mylar balloons. He was wearing a tight T-shirt that read, "If you're hot, I'm single."

The General reconsidered his plan for an immediate invasion. He wanted to mingle with all of his old and new friends who'd arrived at his party.

"Johnny!" the General shouted as the limping war vet approached. "Welcome to the invasion. May I, may I offer you a place in my army?"

Johnny just kept walking, clutching the balloons, seemingly unaware of the General. He staggered past his old buddy and crashed right into the side mirror of a parked car. Knocking the mirror off its hinge, Johnny stumbled into the side of the car and lost his balance. The General watched his friend fall to the ground, landing first on his knees, then smashing his face against the asphalt, as if he had forgotten how to use his hands to break a fall. He just didn't have that instinct anymore. Johnny peeled himself up from the sidewalk slowly. Opening his hands to press them against the ground, he released the balloons from his grasp.

The General watched as the shiny silver birthday wishes rose into the sky until they escaped from view.

This was going to be a very long day.

1:56 PM

Janice knew exactly what she wanted. Even if she wanted it for a very short period of time (which she usually did), she made every effort to get it (which she usually didn't). At this moment, she wanted Hank. Unfortunately, his attention was devoted solely to taping a phone cord to the ends of two halves that he had broken from the already broken wooden pointer to craft something that resembled nunchuks. Though the process was making O'Brien a giddy overgrown child enacting pre-adolescent male fantasies, Janice found herself thinking more about what Hank's strong hands could do with her.

It may be their last day on Earth. If the movies had taught her anything, it was that sex is appropriate to think of at times like this.

"So it may be our last day on Earth," Adam said, rolling his chair closer to Janice. He was speaking softly, as if he was doing a bad imitation of someone being seductive. "I know this janitor's closet that's probably unoccupied right now that we could sneak off to for a while. It's a little cramped, but we dim the lights, it could be pretty romantic."

"Yes, the janitor's closet!" Janice exclaimed.

"Really, you in? 'Cause I was thinking that we could grab some paper reams and try to make our way over there."

"The janitor's closet!" Janice stood up.

"I'm ready when you are," Adam said as he rose from his chair.

"There's gotta be a ton of viable weapons in there," Janice said.

"Yes, tools, mops, brooms. Lots of spear-type items," Hank said pensively.

"We'll go," Lillian volunteered suddenly. She and Will had been snuggling at the conference table, whispering sweet nothings into each other's ears that everyone else tried as hard as they could to ignore. But it was like a train wreck. Adam had surmised that they were planning to abscond, but he pretended not to hear, as he was all too happy to bid his team lead farewell.

"Could we please have the keys, Myron?" Will asked the seemingly lifeless janitor who had taken Judy's place under the table.

"Myron's not here no more," he said.

"Well, with whom am I speaking?" Lillian asked in a faux sweet manner used all too often by manipulative women.

"Hewlett Packard," came the voice from beneath the table.

"Okay then. Mr. Packard, may we please have your keys for a while?" Lillian coaxed.

"For a sweet lady, good ol' Huey Packard's willing to do just 'bout anything," he said as he unfastened the clasp that held the surprisingly few keys to his belt.

"Thank you, Mr. Packard," Lillian said.

"Much 'bliged, me lady," Myron said from beneath the table and closed his eyes.

"All right, I'm on board," Hank said. "Who else is going?"

"Dude, I'm in," O'Brien said, standing from his chair. "Gotta get some more photo ops."

"No, you're out of this one," Hank said.

"What? Don't do me like that, man," O'Brien protested.

"I'll go," Harold said, then turned to O'Brien. "But you ain't coming with me. I wanna keep all my limbs."

"Where'd you hear that?" O'Brien asked. Harold ignored him.

"I'm going," Pete said grinning. "I'll kill me some dead folks."

"I'll stay here," Adam said, reclining in his chair. "Call me for the big mission."

"You're not going?" Janice said. "Hank's been out there already, and you won't even go? What kind of man are you?"

"I'm in!" Adam said instantly.

"Okay, we've got a crew," Hank said. "Gentleman, grab your weapons."

2:02 PM

Marshall Owens now found himself in utter desolation. He had pulled off quite the performance by fooling Bill Callahan. Aren't politicians supposed to be adept liars? Or was there no truth in the expression "You can't shit a shitter"? Bill said he had called the police, but Owens could not see them yet, at least not from his vantage point at the rear of the building. He had spied several corpses, but no cops. For now, he was safe, both from the zombies and the law. Harold hadn't returned, so Owens was convinced he was dead. And even if he wasn't, would the establishment really believe the white millionaire philanthropist committed to curing all that ails mankind? Or the thug who could persuade Al Sharpton not to care about black people?

So Owens was able to sit pensively, mentally listing societal woes that he would heal when this current mess blew over.

Maybe he'd cure cancer. Nah, it received too much attention. Although he would be a hero, there was just too much competition, and he didn't want to be part of the race for that cure. Maybe he should stick with the diseases that didn't get that much media devotion. Herpes was a good one. And you never saw little girls jumping rope for that cure. There were no celebrity telethons. The neglected ailment didn't even have a colored ribbon. Marshall Owens would change that.

Yes, herpes it would be.

Then he'd work with the mental disorders. Maybe he'd market a pill to treat hypochondria. That one was quite brilliant.

Marshall Owens lit a Cuban cigar that he kept hidden in his desk drawer and puffed on it slowly and deliberately while plotting his new business venture. He shook off the worry that had crept in earlier. They can't arrest him. He had too many good ideas. And at no point in history were radical ideas ever silenced in prison.

2:14 PM

Led by Harold, the employees slinked against the white walls of the Pro-Well headquarters, armed with the most menacing office supplies they could craft into antiquated weapons. Except for Lillian, who held a very modern gun. The group of six seemed a bit excessive for the relatively short trip down the hall to the janitor's closet, but they needed as many hands as possible. And a couple members of the crew had no plans to return.

So far they had not faced any zombies. Indeed, they had faced nothing that could pose a threat to anything except Lillian's Easter egg-colored pumps. Human innards were strewn everywhere, and the spilled blood was gradually sinking into the gray-blue carpet and turning it a deep purple shade. It actually looked quite nice, Hank thought, but it was beginning to reek. They continued to slink through the elevator corridor that was noticeably devoid of the walking dead.

"Where did they go?" Adam whispered.

"I don't know, but I'd say this is worse," Pete said, his voice hushed.

"They're not discreet enough to hide," Will replied as he maintained the whispered tones.

"How do you know that?" Harold asked at full volume.

"What would they have to hide from?" Lillian snapped back.

"I dunno, but I know those fucks were here just a few minutes ago and they didn't just vanish," Harold said.

They surely did not. As the employees rounded the corner past the elevator bank, they were confronted by a veritable army of them. About fifteen were just standing there, staring with their empty eyes.

"Oh fuck," Hank said.

At that moment, like it was carefully choreographed, the Pro-Well workers turned abruptly and ran. They lost the zombies almost instantly as they ran past the elevators and turned back into the floor of cubicles.

"We're taking the long way," Hank said.

He assumed the lead, and they forged ahead, shuffling slowly past rows and rows that looked like a square canvas egg carton. They were like cells, small pods where the white-collar workers passed through their lives under fluorescent lights in drab coloring with the soundtrack of clicking keys and ringing phones. Seeing their 9-5 cages vacant and spattered in blood felt oddly liberating, like the employees had broken free of their restraints and risen up and slaughtered their master. But that was not the case, for Hank's peers were the ones who had been slaughtered and the actual liberation was performed by the dead homeless in the factory next door while the emperor was safe in his penthouse office. As much as Hank sympathized with the plight of the factory workers, he was committed to living as long as he possibly could.

So he pressed on, like fake nails, and led his co-workers and the violent ex-con to the maintenance closet. He turned around to check on his cohorts and saw that the zombies were coming nearer. They weren't making much progress, but they were in pursuit nonetheless. And they would be closer after the employees had raided the janitor's closet.

"All right, we've gotta ditch these assholes," Hank said.

"What do you suggest?" Pete asked.

"Trench warfare," Hank said. "Everyone hide behind a cubicle, collect everything you can from the desks, and launch it at them. We don't need to kill them all right now, we've just gotta buy some time."

"Got it," Adam said.

Will grasped Lillian's free hand, and they waddled quickly to an aisle desk. The cubicles were five deep against the wall, and most of the employees took the desks closer to the aisle. This strategy allowed for quicker escape but also gave the zombies easier access. Hank moved along the windowed wall and stopped at the fourth cubicle from the aisle. He reached his desk and grabbed the auxiliary pack of Marlboro Reds that he kept in the drawer in case of emergencies that he never anticipated to be of this magnitude. Shoving the cigarettes into his pocket, he turned to check out the locations of his troops. Adam was standing at the cubicle in the row behind him and had armed himself with pink, sparkly frames that showcased photos of Kelly's family.

"That's just cold," Pete said, while pulling an aerosol can of hairspray from Judy's desk drawer.

Harold, who didn't know anyone and in his own words, "couldn't give a shit about your shit" (he realized how stupid that sounded when the words came from his mouth, but silenced all mockery with an angry look), started violently ransacking arbitrary desks. Will could not tell what this crazed bodybuilder was searching for, but he stared at the back of his shaved head with disapproval. *This may be how you toss a prison cell or the house of someone who you believe has stolen your ho*, he thought, *but this was Pro-Well and no matter the rumored sins of Marshall Owens, it still had prestige.*

The line of zombies approached. Many were disfigured beyond recognition, but Will spotted Alonzo Alfredson amongst the mess. The mailroom worker appeared relatively unscathed, still sporting a button-down shirt and khaki pants. His gray skin and shambling gait were the only factors that denoted that he was one of the walking dead, until Pete hurled Judy's compact mirror, like a miniature Frisbee, into his eye and Alonzo went down on his face, taking what appeared to be Martine Garvey from the call center with him.

"I am the most awesome person you know," Pete proclaimed.

The rest of the Pro-Well employees followed suit, tossing various objects at their dead peers. Adam launched bottles of supplements and painkillers from Kelly's desk, which did little good on the ghouls, although he did manage to plant the corner of a jeweled picture frame into HR rep Lewis Donnelly's skull. As he fell to the ground, Kelly's son Jaden—or maybe it was Caden, Brayden, Hayden, Aiden, or Iron Maiden—smiled at them. Even Hank thought that it was pretty surreal and would have been ideal for one of that idiot O'Brien's photo ops.

Hank lobbed his own desk lamp at the oncoming zombies. As the cheap lamp left his hands, Hank realized how long he had wanted to do that. It was a release, cathartic even, to hurl the mundane relics of his stalled-out life. He hit a particularly gnarly zombie in the stomach that continued to advance, even though his jaw was mostly severed and his left eye dangled out of the socket. Hank reached down to his desk for another projectile to find nothing, and he realized that he had never truly moved into his cube like the rest of the employees. It had been a mechanism he used to never get too comfortable. If he started to become complacent in his misery, it would be like surrender. And Hank knew that he could never let that happen. But currently, his lack of desktop nostalgia was putting him at a disadvantage.

At Kelly's desk, Adam found himself with a full arsenal of flowers, photos, medication, scented lotions, and even a drawer full of 16-ounce bottles of vitamin water. Pete was busy tossing Judy's cheap cologne while Harold grabbed mini boom boxes from desks and launched them over his head, like radioactive basketballs, at the encroaching ghouls. He was quite effective. Meanwhile, Lillian was weakly tossing several stress relief toys and Rubik's cubes that fell yards short of hitting anything. Will continued to encourage her, repeating his "you can do it" mantra as she failed repeatedly.

The corpses fell one by one, hit with the projectiles lobbed by the office employees. None had met a true death, but the trench warfare had momentarily crippled the enemy, leaving enough time for the office workers to reach the janitor's closet, where they thought they would surely find the tools that could forever vanquish the walking dead.

2:20 PM

The General's army of corpses had swelled beyond his wildest hopes. The troops kept flocking to the Pro-Well parking lot, drawn to Ground Zero from all over the South Side and Oakland. They were an eclectic crowd of Yinzers, students, tattooed rockers, and white-collar professionals who were killed on the way to work. The plethora of volunteers was a testament to Pittsburgh's unique civic spirit: These locals refused to let death get in the way of a good party. So they united in solidarity, forming what at first glance appeared to be a tailgating extravaganza. And in a fortuitous twist of fate for the perpetually down-on-his-luck General, they brought props.

A posse of college-aged Pitt basketball fans had arrived a few minutes ago—apparently they had been nabbed late last night after a game on campus and had staggered around looking for a little fun until they came upon the party of their young un-lives—with an array of toys that the General immediately confiscated for the cause.

"Put the Revolution before yourself," he had shouted at the young enlistees, yanking a Pitt Panther towel from the shoulders of a shaggy-haired dead college boy and stealing an electronic megaphone from his equally dead friend.

Now the General could be heard, well, sort of, over the moans made by a chorus larger than a celebrity disaster relief fundraiser. There must be more than a hundred, the General thought. He had been having way too much fun concocting his hostile takeover to actually go into action. Now, the megaphone gave him a new-found motivation. It was finally time to make his demands.

2:34 PM

Rick O'Brien was definitely one to be played. He'd lost a fortune in one-dollar bills to women in g-strings and a fortune in hundreds to men with pyramid schemes. He'd fallen for just about every trick in the book. If it sounded too good to be true, O'Brien believed it wholeheartedly. Some called him an idiot, but he liked to think of himself as an eternal, unfaltering optimist. When some said the glass was half-empty, O'Brien said the bartender should hurry up.

Today, it had never even crossed his mind that he may not see tomorrow. He was already planning his next get-rich-quick scheme by marketing the photos from what would certainly be a historic ordeal. He actually felt lucky that he was a part of it. He would rather have been out with the men on a weapons run, hunting the most dangerous game along the way, but he would have to deal with the girls and the crazy old guy in the conference room for the time being.

He perused the photos on his Nikon. He looked brave in the one that he forced the dearly departed Doug to take in the elevator. Standing in the Captain Morgan pose, his foot on the chest of the eviscerated Omar, he looked so triumphant, a sex god to the mortal women he was sure to bed when they saw it. Damn, he thought, he needed more. Sure the carnage was nice, but he looked pretty handsome covered in blood.

"Hey, Preggos," he said.

"My name is Kelly," Preggos replied from the conference table.

"Yeah, sure," O'Brien replied. "Will you get a photo of me with all the blood on me?"

"Okay," Kelly said as O'Brien handed her the phone.

She was uncharacteristically willing to help someone with whom she had been locked in a small room for several hours who had never bothered to learn her name. Ordinarily, she would have admonished him, but her plan called for patience and cordiality. She was craving a chili dog, and as an eight-month-pregnant sociopath, nothing could get in her way. She had to leave, and she had to leave now. The urges and the hormones were taking over, but she was able to remain calm. She could not tell O'Brien that she needed him to risk his life for a chili dog with relish and onions. That would never do. So she'd play on his weakness for the flattery of women, and she'd make it to the Circle K in no time.

"You look so brave," she said. "Like a warrior returning from battle."

O'Brien hoisted his arm up and flexed his muscle, though it was not visible beneath his sleeve.

"Yeah, that's hot," Kelly said, smiling.

She continued snapping photos while O'Brien struck several ridiculous poses, alternating between a cheesy grin and mysterious glances over his shoulder. Janice looked on and rolled her eyes.

"Oh, that's a keeper!" Kelly said, enthusiastically as O'Brien gave the Shocker gesture with both hands. "I think we got some good ones there."

"Awesome," O'Brien replied as he took the phone from Kelly and immediately started perusing the photos. "Thanks, Carrie."

"No problem," she replied. "I know you want everyone to know that you're a hero, but I want you to know that I already think so."

"You don't think it was my fault about Doug?" he asked.

"Of course not," Kelly replied. "You were in the thick of it, fighting for your life. The weak don't survive."

"Yeah, whoever said that thing about the weak inheriting the Earth, right?" he replied, laughing.

Kelly played along, resisting the urge to correct him. "It's really not fair that they wouldn't let you go with them this time."

"I know. It sucks, right?" he said. "I'm ready to fight, get my hands dirty. But they don't want me, so what can I do?"

"You can show them," Kelly said. "Show them how much

they need you. You're the real leader of this group, not Hank. He can't even show up on time or quit smoking. How's he supposed to save us?"

"You know, I never smoked," O'Brien said. "Gotta preserve my—"

"Exactly," Kelly cut him off. "I mean, I don't understand why we're waiting here. You can lead us. You can get us out of here. You're the one with the fighting skills. We don't need the rest. You were out in this earlier. You know how to handle it."

"All right, stop," Janice said. "We're not going anywhere until the others get back. The four of us with no means of defense against all of them? It's a suicide mission."

"You know, some of us aren't trying to get laid," Kelly said. "Some of us are just trying to get home. I have a child. I'm sure that Myron can relate to that."

Myron was too busy doing crunches under the table to respond.

"I'm just trying to stay alive, and I think we all need to work together instead of sabotaging each other," Janice said.

"Oh, cut the crap." Kelly snapped. "You've just been kissing Hank's ass so he'll somehow turn straight and sleep with you. You're blind to what's going on. You've been here for one day; you don't know anything about how things work. If you were smart at all, you'd go for Rick here. He's obviously the better catch. And he gets it up for women."

"I'm not even responding to that," Janice said.

She continued praying to Gaia, Mother Earth, an artifact from her organic hippie days. She tried to remember the words to the prayers, but decided that since that ideology was all about freedom, it was perfectly acceptable to improvise. She blocked out Kelly's shameless manipulation of O'Brien and became lost in her prayers. She suddenly regretted having sold her soul to Satan two weeks ago for My Life with the Thrill Kill Cult tickets. This would have been a much better time.

2:46 PM

Wherever there was action, WTF News was miles away. Sometimes, if they were really motivated, the reporters arrived a day later when whatever had happened had been cleaned up, to ask the neighbors their thoughts on whatever it was that the public had lost interest in right after the first commercial break. In her two months so far at Pittsburgh's worst news outlet, Stephanie Stempniak had broken no stories, had delivered no headlines, and had not been near any action. So disconnected from contemporary society that they were practically in a different orbit, the station had recently broken a story about gay trysts in a certain section of Schenley Park, a phenomenon that just about everyone had been aware of for over twenty years. Decidedly behind the times, the station was a freak show with a camera and some connections that always lost the ratings battle, coming in behind even WWJD Christian Talk Radio and KRAP Hits of Today. *But that would all change today*, Stephanie thought as the WTF News van inched along the 10th Street Bridge.

There was some sort of melee in the increasingly chaotic South Side and Stephanie would be on the scene. Tensions between residents and weekend bar-hoppers had been mounting since before Stephanie had even moved to the western side of Pennsylvania and from what she could tell, there was some sort of anarchic outbreak of vigilante justice as the natives defended their turf from invaders of the drunk and disorderly kind.

"Cal, what is taking so long?" Stephanie asked from the back of the van where she fitted her earpiece and checked her WTF News microphone.

"You don't see this?" Cal, the cameraman asked as he eased his foot off the pedal to move six feet closer to the end of the bridge. "Whatever's going on over there's causing one hell of a backup."

"Well, let's just ditch the car and go on foot."

"Are you nuts? We're not leaving the van in the middle of the bridge," he said.

"Why not? We're WTF News!" Stephanie countered earnestly.

"I think you just answered your own question," Cal replied as the van moved another twelve feet before he pushed his foot back down on the brake.

Stephanie surrendered to the cameraman whose apathy was indicative of the station's general indifference. Most of the employees had simply stopped trying about a decade ago. After a drunken pilot crashed the news helicopter into a cornfield when he was supposed to be flying *towards*, not away from, the city to cover a fire in the Hill District, breaking news coverage was omitted from the station's repertoire. Indeed, WTF News mostly functioned as PR for the Steelers. Stephanie thought that this in and of itself warranted investigation. Did the higher-ups receive a cut from the team? Was the whole station being paid off? What was the arrangement to be a mouthpiece for a multimillion-dollar sports franchise? Or was it just easy ratings for management that truly did not give a fuck? And the on-air personalities were just as bad.

There was Nelson Keenan, the ventriloquist/weatherman who tended to refer to thunderstorms by their technical name: boom booms. And why the weekend forecast had to be presented with the help of a rather creepy dummy Stephanie had no idea. That was just the state of affairs at WTF News.

Then there was Darlene Higgins, the morning newscaster who tended to deliver reports on massive gun violence in McKeesport with the same sugary vocal inflections that she used to read her six children bedtime stories. There were a lot of "oohs" and "aahs" on the morning news, as if she was watching Internet videos of the zoo's baby panda. It was enough to make you diabetic. The evening news team didn't even bother to speak to one another or shuffle papers at the end of a broadcast. Instead they just stared, rather eerily in fact, into the camera, waiting for a commercial reprieve. Stephanie was a real newscaster, sticking her hairbrush into her father's face since she was four years old, demanding answers about why the chicken was cold again tonight. She was an acolyte to the faith of journalism, lived by the mantra to "comfort the afflicted and afflict the comfortable," that the people must know the truth. She was the devoted journalist in every movie that wouldn't let an earthquake get in her way of breaking the big story. There would be no city council cover-ups while Stephanie Stempniak was in town.

When she was hired, just a year out of journalism school, Stephanie had vowed to change all of the station's many woes. Actually, she vowed to get the hell out of this parody of the journalistic profession, but was finding that more difficult than she had imagined when she dreamed of being on TV as an eighth grader delivering her junior high's morning news. Of all her friends from the bachelor's in mass communications program at Mendenhall University, Stephanie was the sole graduate working in her milieu. Tracy the newspaper editor was waiting tables at her local TGI Fridays, Mike the sportscaster found himself no closer to the action than working security at the Wachovia Center, and Carla's weekly columns on sex in the dorms got her no action outside of, oddly enough, babysitting gigs for her parents' friends. Stephanie was the success story of her graduating class, hired as a field reporter in the medium Pittsburgh market, for a joke of a news station.

She'd heard about the South Side chaos over the police scanner she kept on her small desk in the corner of the open floor-plan office. While the rest of the on-air staff spent hours in makeup, trying to cover up those tiny wrinkles that hadn't been Botoxed yet, Stephanie was frantically searching wire services, desperately listening to the scanner, waiting for something that didn't sound quite right. She was waiting for something, anything, a mere blip on the radar, a pause in a CEO's speech where he should have been confident if he was forthright. Stephanie was the type to watch *America's Most Wanted* and actually keep on the lookout for the felons to show up in her upscale Shadyside neighborhood. She checked the Megan's Law website to locate all sex offenders within a fifty-mile radius, just waiting for an Amber Alert so she could expose the inherent flaws in the corrections system. She kept a database of financial records of nonprofit companies on her desktop, ready to scour them for inaccuracies whenever a dubious fact popped up on her far-reaching radar.

She would make this station respectable, damn it! WTF News would finally give a fuck.

The van was finally across the 10th Street Bridge. Stephanie smoothed her straight shoulder length dark hair and climbed up to the passenger seat in the front. Scruffy, overweight Cal took a swig from his soda bottle as he turned the van slowly onto Carson Street. Impatient after the thirty minutes spent on the bridge, Stephanie leaned forward in her seat, craning her neck as the van completed its laborious left onto the main drag of the South Side.

Stephanie's eyes went wide. This was the story she was looking for, the shocking tale that she would catch on camera, the scene of the most macabre urban destruction. The narrow street ran with blood, several partially digested human organs littered the curbs. Men, women, and children were running through the carnage, some making it to safety inside local businesses, but others taken down on the sidewalk by some cannibal mutants who immediately began to feast on their entrails.

"What the fuck?" Cal said, dropping the egg and cheese sandwich from his hand.

"I have no idea," Stephanie breathlessly replied.

She continued to stare out the windshield of the van, her usually quick, somewhat opportunistic mind blank. She didn't know how to proceed, what words she would be able to formulate when she stepped outside of the van. What could she possibly add to the scene? *Blood, guts, carnage, ghouls—now to Bob with sports?* She continued to stare at the human remains covering the street when she saw the soft foam of a news microphone lying in the street in a puddle of chunky blood. She didn't know if Cal saw the ominous object that had almost become alive in Stephanie's mind, if he seen it as a warning of what happens to ye who enter here. But he had definitely seen enough to decide to turn the van back to the right and aim to continue up 10th Street to the Liberty Tunnels. Stephanie sat in silence as the WTF news van backed up away from the story that would have made her career.

As Cal pulled the van out of reverse and hit the gas, Stephanie thought, "What the fuck?"

3:00 PM

"You know that between my plan and your bravery, we can definitely do this," Kelly said. "So let's go over it again."

"We make a run for it," O'Brien said. "I walk in front of you, swinging umbrellas in each arm in case one of those dead dudes gets too close, then we sprint to your car because it's closer as you're in the preggo chicks section. And I don't have my sweet Camaro cause I flew up here. Did I tell you that baby gets up to 120 miles per hour? Unreal."

"Exactly," she said, ignoring this last irrelevant bit of self-indulgent babble. "With your prowess, we can definitely make it. You just need to guard me. Saving a pregnant woman—that would be truly heroic. Especially since you were the lone survivor who would even consider helping me. You, Rick O'Brien, risked your life for the safety of another while the others stood by and helped themselves. You are truly selfless."

"Yeah," O'Brien said uneasily. *Where was she getting this?* he asked himself. He'd lived his whole life trying to collect as much ephemeral pleasure as possible. Selfless? That was certainly not him, but O'Brien was never one to reject compliments and tended to wear shoes that didn't fit. "I'm ready," he said, rising from his chair.

"This is a really stupid plan," Janice said.

"That's really not for you to decide," Kelly said. "Farewell, freak."

3:10 PM

The janitor's closet was a bit of a disappointment. True, the effort they expended to reach it had not been great, but it was still lacking in acceptable artillery. Blunt objects were in abundance, but there was nothing that could function like a railroad spike in the cranium for which Hank had been hoping. Instead, he wound up with a mop and a plastic, obelisk-shaped "Caution: Wet Floor" sign. Pete grabbed a spray bottle filled with Drano that he said he planned to use to light zombies on fire. *A bit dramatic*, Hank thought, but a viable weapon nonetheless. Adam took a broom and the custodial cart with a built-in trash can, which they decided could be useful to transport injured allies. Harold was left with a broom and a *"Cuidado: Piso Mujado"* sandwich board. He refused to elaborate on what he planned to do with it, but the others had the impression that it would be unnecessarily brutal.

While the four makeshift warriors grabbed as many items that could pass for weapons as possible, Will and Lillian stood in the doorway, their hands clasped, waiting for their moment alone.

"This is about as good as it's gonna get," Hank said, raising the mop to his cohorts.

"Then good luck to you all," Will said. "Hopefully we'll see you on the other side of these walls."

"You're staying in the janitor's closet?" Pete asked.

"We want some time alone," Lillian said.

"That was my idea!" Adam exclaimed, happy to bid his team lead farewell, but angry that the spot he'd envisioned for himself and Janice would be tarnished by these floppy, middle-aged creeps.

"Are you fucking kidding me?" Hank erupted seemingly from nowhere. He had put his life on the line in two expeditions amongst the flesh-munching dead, one of which to save this shrew, and now they were just going to leave? Just like the rest of his work at Pro-Well, it was now becoming apparent that Hank's efforts today were for naught.

"You guys will be all right. Today I've seen true teamwork. You can reach your goals with the help of others," Will quoted his email tagline.

"Yeah, well, if I were you I'd spend less time thinking about us and concentrate on finding the antidote to that gum you chewed at the Wonka factory," Hank said.

"Listen, Hank," Will said, ignoring the rather clever jest at his weight. "We've realized that we may not survive the day. And if we do not, well, I'd like to spend my last hours in the warm embrace of the woman I love." Will winked at Lillian, and she smiled back at him.

"Well I'm glad I risked my fucking life," Hank said sarcastically. "Have a great time in the janitor's closet. I'm sure there's some ammonia in here to set the mood."

He stormed away from the door, feeling the bravery he'd mustered in the past few hours fade back into apathy. No matter how many trips he made to the gym, product promos he added to his portfolio, zombies that he killed, or co-workers that he rescued from surely painful ends, it was quickly becoming clear to Hank that his life would never change. Maybe that was always the way it was and the distraction of battle had just made him forget during the past few hours, actually tricking him into thinking that he was worth something, that his life could be more than just mundane futility drenched in whiskey and peppered with senseless compulsions.

"Let's get the fuck outta here," Harold said.

"I'm ready," Adam said, itching to get out of the room and rid himself of the mental image of their flabby, pasty white flesh bumping around and knocking over bottles of Lysol.

"But first," Harold said in a menacing tone as he moved within inches of Lillian's upturned nose. "You better give me my motherfuckin' gun back."

Lillian handed the weapon to him. "I'm really sorry about that," she said. "I hope you understand."

"You do what you gotta do," Harold said.

He took the gun from her small hand, pushed it back into

his belt holster, and walked out of the closet. Adam and Pete followed, quickly wishing their team lead luck, either in survival or with his woman. Hank stared straight ahead, marching behind his work buddies, all too ready to cede control to them. As the three heavily armed employees exited the room, Harold discreetly stuck a paper clip into the outside keyhole, disabling the lock. If that bitch thought she could steal from him and get away from it, she was dead wrong.

3:13 PM

Kelly could barely reach her stumpy arms around O'Brien's slim waist as her swollen belly protruded into the back of his thigh. She decided to hold on to him in case she needed a human shield. Literally. That was his job anyway, to protect her from any hungry corpses that might decide that they want to have her for an early supper. She couldn't believe he fell for it: the moron. And all she had to stroke was his ego. It was so easy. She'd be home, eating her chili-cheese dog (because now there was to be cheese), and he'd probably be devoured before they reached the door. She didn't really wish harm upon the visiting client, but her life was definitely the one worth preserving. If he died today, there would just be fewer strippers complaining that some asshole touched them in the champagne room. Maybe Spencer Gifts would lose its biggest home décor customer. *No, this would not be a major tragedy*, Kelly thought.

She held on to her sleazy shield as they walked slowly past the cubicles towards the elevators. The coast appeared clear as they rounded the corner and approached the elevator bank. O'Brien hit the down button, and they waited patiently as Kelly stared at the bloody handprints on the wall.

"I did that earlier," O'Brien said, pointing to the red palm print.

"Did you get a photo?" Kelly asked, sarcastically. She could drop the façade now.

"No, I should do that now," O'Brien said, fishing into his pocket for his camera.

"What do you think you're doing?" Kelly asked.

"Just getting a shot of this," he said. He held the Nikon up to the print and snapped a photo. "Sweet."

"You idiot, you're going to get us killed by screwing around like that," Kelly snapped.

"I thought you liked the photos," he said, confused.

"Oh right, because getting souvenirs is exactly what's going to get us out of here," Kelly said.

"Well, I th—" O'Brien cut himself off as the elevator doors opened.

The interior was utter carnage. What was left of a completely eviscerated corpse lay on the floor while three standing zombies surrounded it. Apparently they had been locked in the elevator for quite some time and were now ready for dessert. They stared at Kelly and O'Brien with their glassy purple eyes. The female one in the khaki pants and torn cardigan with the half of her left ear missing was closest to the door and with her first step moved within a yard of O'Brien.

It was at this point that Kelly panicked. She had retained her composure for the whole ordeal even with her out-of-whack eight-month-pregnant hormones, because she had not encountered the ghouls face to face. Though they had taken over the office, the walking dead were still an abstract concept to her until what remained of Karen Adams of accounts payable stared at her from the elevator.

Karen took a step forward, and Kelly had no choice but to unload her baggage. She quickly removed her hands from O'Brien's waist and shoved him from the back into the elevator. Sliding in the sanguinary pool on the elevator floor, he managed to maintain his balance by leaning on the umbrella like a cane.

"What the fuck, Carrie?" he yelled.

"Sorry, but I thought you knew that everyone's out for themselves," Kelly said. "And the name's Kelly."

She eyed him with smug confidence as Jerome Simmons from the mailroom grabbed at O'Brien's arm. The buyer squirmed away from Jerome's hold and tried to bounce back over the corpse on the floor, but lost his footing and fell directly on top of the remains. The elevator doors began to slide shut as O'Brien struggled to stand back up in the puddle of blood, skin and bones.

"The doors!" O'Brien yelled.

Kelly was frozen, both in her terror of these menacing creatures and her inherent lack of compassion for others. She'd been protecting herself in this office by contributing to the downfall of others for years now. Why should today be any different? She had sabotaged several careers of those she viewed as a threat and of others that she simply did not like. She had honed her skills in the junior high cafeteria, guiding her clueless, insecure pals to ditch another member of the group on a weekly basis for being under suspicion of the high crimes of treason and her naïve impression of lesbianism. But Kelly had failed to consider that by trimming her kingdom to a select few, she would be unprepared for a battle royale of slanderous words with a veritable subcontinent of her exiles. Yet she had never lost her futile need for destruction. She was the epitome of schadenfreude, never advancing in the company ranks, but smiling when a co-worker was canned nonetheless.

Right now, she just needed that chili dog, and if she could appease the zombies with Rick O'Brien long enough to allow her to reach safety, it was all worth it. She stood in silence, watching the elevator doors close like a curtain on the final act of carnage, when suddenly the tip of an umbrella poked through the metal gates.

The doors slid open slowly to reveal a very angry O'Brien covered in blood, pulling the blue umbrella out of Jerome Simmons's eye. The mailroom employee fell to the floor as O'Brien avoided Karen's teeth and leapt from the elevator. Karen and the corpse formerly known as Sam Foster stepped into the office, free from their incarceration in this mobile metal cell.

"Good luck," O'Brien said as he stepped behind Kelly and started to walk back to the main work area, leaving Kelly frozen by the elevator. "And by the way, I think pregnant sex is hot, but I wouldn't fuck you with Tom Arnold's dick and that thing's got no standards."

He felt that he had made his point. Armed with his umbrellas, O'Brien walked towards the row of cubicles as a famished Sam Foster reached for Kelly's equally hungry belly.

3:19 PM

The janitor's closet had never looked so romantic. Certainly not under Myron's tyrannical reign. With Will's touch, it was soft, serene even. He had cracked several emergency glow sticks that were to be used in case the power went out. They glowed an eerie green, but they were reminiscent of candles and provided softer lighting than the harsh bulbs of the flashlights. He had found what he hoped were clean towels on the shelves and laid them down on the hard cement floor to make a small mattress. There were not nearly enough to function as blankets for their inevitable post-coital cuddle, but it would have to suffice. Will had swiped a miniature boom box from Laura Erickson's desk to provide mood music. He didn't really know much about this customer service rep, but hoped that Lillian would find her taste in music acceptable. He found himself doubting, though, that the 26-year-old had any Barry Manilow or Michael Bolton on a CD entitled *Feel the Steel*.

The smell was actually the most objectionable part of the room; a mixture of refuse, bleach, and mildew. Lillian drew breath from her mouth as she lay on the towel bed on her side, propped up on her elbow. She had removed her sea green Ann Taylor suit and eggshell blouse and was now clad only in her lace slip. The fact that she was the only woman Will had ever met who still wore a slip had always turned him on. Coyly she beckoned him while he yanked off his clip-on necktie and threw it on the floor. Will started to unbutton his shirt, giving Lillian the sexiest "come hither" look that a butter sandwich-munching, self-help addict could muster.

"Grrr," Lillian said, rolling her R. "Come to me, big man."

Will tossed his shirt over his shoulder and hit the play button on Laura Erickson's CD player that he had placed on the shelf next to a bottle of rat poison.

A loud guitar riff came blaring from the small speaker like it was bathed in booze and seasoned with cocaine. This certainly would not do for a lady of Lillian's class.

"Sorry," Will said, hitting the skip button.

"Are you ready, baby?" the unmistakable voice of a hair metal singer demanded before Will quickly hit the skip button.

"I'm really sorry," Will said.

"That's all right," Lillian replied. "Although I really thought much better of Laura Erickson."

The next track emanated from the speaker, a softer ballad with an acoustic guitar intro. It would have to do, as gazing down at his lover, Will could not contain his lust any longer.

"I would give you the stars in the sky, but they're too far away," came the voice from the speakers.

"My sentiments exactly," Will said as he smiled and crouched down on the floor next to his woman, his gut barely restrained beneath his undershirt.

"If you were a hooker, you'd know, I'd be happy to pay," the voice of Steel Panther frontman Michael Starr crooned from the speakers.

"I do have a surprise for you, though," he said, pulling a six-pack of waxy chocolate doughnuts from his pocket. "I'd been saving them in my desk for a special occasion."

"Eat them off my body," Lillian said, breathing heavily.

"If suddenly you were a guy, I'd be suddenly gay," Starr continued to sing.

Taken aback for a second by the song, Will smiled a huge, gaping grin and started to pull the plastic package open. He struggled, yanking the flimsy bag in all different directions.

"I always have trouble with these things," he said.

"Let me try," Lillian said.

Will handed her the package. Usually this happened when there was an erection on the line, so he was all too happy to let Lillian help. There was no hurry. They had locked the door of the closet and were lost to the world.

"My heart belongs to you, but my cock is community property," Starr sang as the love ballad reached a crescendo, but the middle managers were too enthralled with each other to notice this highly inappropriate lyric.

Lillian bit down on the edge of the wrapper and split the package open. Licking her lips, she pulled one doughnut from the package and placed it gingerly on her left breast. Will dove in headfirst, and thus was completely unaware that the door had been cracked open.

3:40 PM

They better get back here soon, Janice thought as she pouted at the conference table. The psychotic janitor had awakened from catatonia and was now talking to himself in rapid-fire Pittsburghese. If one of the functioning survivors did not return, she felt that she would soon become as crazy as he. The older man was mumbling something about libertarian lightning bolts and five-dollar footlongs, but the rest was mere gibberish. Left with nothing but a quickly degenerating companion, Janice began to think of all the things she had wanted to accomplish that looked like they may never occur. She wanted to drink absinthe on Edgar Allan Poe's grave, to memorize at least a few spells, and join a coven of witches. To be arrested, but not indicted, for allegedly stalking a certain werewolf of contemporary teen cinema.

Oddly enough, she still found herself wanting to visit Haight-Ashbury and live in a commune of free love and an endless supply of LSD. And someday, she even wanted to know what was so awesome about New Jersey. To dye her hair dark brown and iron it straight, visit tanning salons, and put on just that right amount of weight to make stuffing herself into chintzy animal print tube dresses socially acceptable yet ill-advised. She might even want to have a string of one-night stands with men who could only be accurately described as douchebags. To peel the Affliction T-shirt from his back and run her fingers through his gelled hair… No, she thought, that was taking it too far.

And it was in the future, anyway. She couldn't help but wonder whether she would still have one by the time this workday was over. She checked the gothic locket clock that she wore on a long pewter chain around her neck. 3:45. She would have completed her first day of work in a little over an hour. Suddenly, she heard the doorknob click.

"Hank?" she said hopefully, spinning her chair around.

"What, you've got no love for the Rick-Man?" a completely blood-soaked O'Brien said as he entered the conference room, spreading his arms open as the door slammed shut behind him.

"Back so soon?" Janice asked, disappointed. Her knight in business casual had not returned.

"Yeah, it didn't work out so well," he said.

"What happened to Kelly?"

"I don't know. Last thing I saw, she was in the elevator," he replied.

What O'Brien didn't see was the impromptu Caesarean section that the zombies performed in the elevator car. While the others devoured Kelly's arms and legs, Jerome Simmons went straight for the engorged stomach, ripping stretched skin with his teeth until he pulled out the premature child inside.

It was a girl.

And it was delicious.

O'Brien walked over to the potted plant in the corner of the room. He unzipped his pants, and Janice heard a stream of liquid entering the dirt that housed the four-foot-tall ficus.

"Oh, you've got to be kidding me," she said.

"What?" O'Brien said, turning his head around. "I'm sure you've seen worse."

"Sadly, I have," Janice said reluctantly.

O'Brien zipped his pants back up, tapped the air with his hand, and started to laugh.

"I forgot there's no handle to flush it," he said, returning to the table.

"Well, I'm glad you don't use a ficus on a regular basis," Janice said.

"That tree's a ficus?" he asked. Janice nodded. "Damn, I always that was a gay sex move."

O'Brien sat down on a chair and tossed the umbrellas to the ground. He sighed and thrust his feet on the table with a thud, just as glass of the conference window shattered.

3:46 PM

It was all in vain. All of his efforts, Hank thought as he walked away from the janitor's closet, *risking his pathetic life to save those morons.* Perhaps the whole day had been for nothing, but he had just been in denial until Wilbert and Lillian decided to surrender. Hank would not go that far—his worthless life was something that he was deeply committed to preserving. But he could no longer say the same for his co-workers. Sure, he would like to see Adam and Pete get through this thing as unscathed as possible, but once again found himself questioning his usual empathy that let him know that he was not a replicant.

The shattering of glass followed by a piercing scream jolted him out of his moping.

"The fuck was that?" Harold demanded, raising his gun.

"Sweet cherry pie," Adam said as he watched the remains of Charles Rasmussen crash through the glass window of the conference room. As the wall reached to about the mid-point of his thighs, Charles had tumbled, opulent gut first, through the window. Though he was now entangled in the Venetian blinds, it was clear that their hideout had been compromised.

Almost in unison, Adam and Pete broke into a run past the rows of cubicles while the zombies they had momentarily disabled with desk lamps and paperweights were slowly returning to their feet. As they approached the conference room, Charles Rasmussen's overweight dead body fell back out the window onto the main office floor. His disembodied head followed a moment later. Adam was not surprised when he looked into the shattered remains of the window to see Rick O'Brien brandishing the paper cutter blade.

"We've gotta move," Pete said. "Now!"

While Janice carefully opened the door, peering left and right to make sure she would not be suddenly ambushed by the walking dead, O'Brien awkwardly climbed through the window, trying to avoid the shards of glass. Armed with the telephone that she had wielded so effectively to kill the remains of Judy, Janice stepped out of the room, followed by a wild-eyed Myron. Hank and Harold, who had both moved lackadaisically towards the others to consciously display their apathy, had reached the conference room.

"Where should we go?" Janice asked, her eyes as they had been all day, on Hank.

"I don't know," Hank replied. "Where's Kelly? She's the expert on the building plans."

"She's gone. Long story," O'Brien said. "Man, that chick was a bitch."

"Well, we can't stay here," Janice pleaded. "And this is practically the only room I've even seen."

"Tragic," Hank said and lit a cigarette.

Janice looked at him, astounded as one could possibly appear when one is made up like an angst-ridden cartoon character.

"Greg Tombardi's office," Pete said, pointing to the small office hidden in the corner.

"All right, let's move, everyone," Adam said, waving in the general direction of the office. "Make sure you put your weapons in the overhead rack."

"What?" Pete asked incredulously.

"Sorry, man," Adam said, "Just seemed like the right thing to say."

"You meathead. How does fighting dead people possible remind you of airline travel?" Pete asked.

"I dunno," Adam replied.

With O'Brien and his makeshift sword leading the way, the employees quickly scurried towards the office.

One by one, they entered the room with Hank bringing up the rear. He closed the door behind him, locked it, and without even noticing, started twisting the knob back and forth and back and forth and back and forth, lulling himself back into the familiar comfort of compulsion.

3:52 PM

Marshall Owens wasn't worried about death. He'd survived a massive chemical explosion in a mechanism that usually couldn't even withstand a tornado. So he waited. Patiently, in fact, for someone to rescue him from his sumptuous office on the fourth floor, comfortably isolated from his flesh-eating subordinates. The fourth floor was the lab, a space for his experimentation to cure all that ails mankind. It was here that he spent most of his days, developing new products that would make him remembered as the hero he always knew he was.

Had it not been for the scars that covered two-thirds of his lean body, he would have parlayed his wealth into a second career as a ladies' man. But, due to the circumstances, he had to pretend. So he used his largesse to procure the most realistic synthetic female dolls from around the world and housed them in his other bedroom, the fantasy chamber that he would retire to about three times a week when he was feeling frisky. But the dolls didn't take up too much of his time. He did buy them the most expensive clothes—as they were perfect life-size replicas of the female form—but they never made him apologize or take them to the theater. So he thrust himself into his work. Tirelessly and alone, calling in the Men in Black when he needed test subjects. He performed the tests and documented the results with the stolen identities of former lab techs who had been repurposed in the factory so the quality assurance department and auditors wouldn't have reason to think that Pro-Well operations were anything but legit.

His methods may have lacked ethics, but Owens always felt that they were justified. He'd sacrifice the lives of a hundred more bums to ensure that one honest, hardworking man never again suffers the shame of erectile dysfunction. He'd force thousands of hobos to work under slave conditions to make male pattern baldness a thing of the past, a problem so archaic that children of the future would mock like it those with iPods do the eight-track. There would be no restless leg syndrome, no Down's syndrome, and, if he could help it, none of that goddamn left-handedness that forces potato peeler companies to waste money every year.

He wasn't worried about Hell. He knew that on Judgment Day, the community service would outweigh the murder. But Owens never looked at it as killing. It was more about cleaning up his city. And he'd heard that cleanliness is next to godliness. A few years ago, he'd even proposed an initiative to run sidewalk trash for fingerprints in order to identify and punish chronic litterbugs. It had been shot down due to what some members of the city council called "a colossal waste of time and money." And apparently there was absolutely no room in the budget to test discarded cigarette butts for DNA. But Owens had vowed that someday he would fund the program himself. What did the council know anyway?

Just as he'd attempted then, he figured he'd just go over their heads. He scrolled through his phone until he reached Bruce Dobson. Leaning back in his chair, he called the mayor.

3:54 PM

"Hank, Hank please, what's wrong with you?" Janice pleaded as Hank continued to suck on his cigarette, blowing smoke at the framed college diploma mounted on the wall.

"I can't believe this nimrod graduated," Hank commented, smirking. He turned away from the wall and tossed the cigarette butt to the floor and stomped it out. He carefully, deliberately ground the cigarette into the carpet until it was nothing but scattered pieces of tobacco and minuscule white paper remains. He looked up to see the rest of the group crowded in the corner, staring at him.

"What?" Hank asked.

"What's your fucking deal, man?" Harold asked sternly.

"Nothing," Hank replied, holding his own against the dangerous ex-con. "Just realizing where the rest of you people stand on survival."

"Just because that dumb fat fuck and his bitch gave up does not give you the right to put us all in danger," Harold said. "You draggin' ass could get me killed."

"And that would be a tragedy," Hank mused. He reached into his pocket, pulled out his cigarette pack, and lit another.

"Can I bum one of those?" Pete asked.

"Maybe if you ever made a sale, you could afford to buy a pack of your own," Hank retorted.

Pete threw up his arms in dismay and walked behind Greg's desk and set about firmly establishing a new ass groove in the presumably deceased supervisor's chair.

"Well, I guess it's all up to me then," O'Brien offered.

"You've got a plan?" Janice asked suspiciously.

"I need a plan?" O'Brien asked with genuine surprise. "Never mind."

"Hank, please," Janice said. "You're the only one who can save us. You're strong. You're brave. You're willing to risk your life to get out of here. You're not just going to stand around and wait for death."

"Oh yeah," Hank began sarcastically. "I'm not just going to wait here to die? Wake up! What do you think I've been doing for the past two years? What do you think that any of you have been doing? I've been coming here every day, without any plans of getting out. Wasting away in front of a goddamn Dell. What the fuck do you think we're all waiting for? At least today will make for a much better obituary."

Hank turned and walked towards the window that was buried under cheap, Venetian blinds on the wall across from the desk. Janice pursued him, a mere two feet behind.

"Come on, Hank, you know that's not true," Janice said.

Hank spun around. "Where do you get off telling me how I am? I'm not brave. If I was, I'd have moved out of the fucking South Side by now. I'd have just left it all, all the relative security I thought I had in this place and just start over. That's bravery. You don't know a damn thing about me."

He turned back toward the window and started fiddling with the blinds. It wasn't really to see what was outside, but because he felt that his hands should be busy. It might be a more effective way of conveying his lack of interest in Vampira's pleas.

"You're wrong," Janice continued. "Bravery is putting yourself in danger for the good of many. What you've been doing all day. It's a refusal to back down in the face of terror. It's—," Janice trailed off, at a loss for any more fabricated definitions.

"It's a bad emo band," Adam chimed in.

Hank continued to finger the blinds, as he leaned against the window with his other hand resting against the wall. He pulled one down with his thumb at eye level and let it pop back in place. Then he grabbed it again. A glimpse of what looked like a mass gathering in the parking lot had piqued his interest from his dramatic indifference. He pulled down the blind, and his eyes grew wide.

"Well, no matter the dictionary definitions of the word," Janice continued earnestly. "You have it. You can make a difference. We are all depending on you."

The cigarette dropped from Hank's lips to the floor, but this time he did not stop to grind it out.

"Well, rock me like a fucking hurricane," Hank said.

"You get it?" Janice said hopefully.

"It's the General," Hank said.

4:02 PM

Food, Nick Gordovsky thought. Well, if his mind had still been able to form words, that's what he would have thought. Instead he felt the concept of food. And to a zombie, that meant fresh human meat. The one just behind that door smelled particularly appetizing. Not that he discriminated. He'd eaten Gary, the call center guy with palsy, and he tasted just as good as that pretty Monica Toews who used to sit next to him. Not that Nick could discern between them. The only impulse that remained was hunger, and taste was really not a factor. His brain couldn't understand the images he saw or use any of his other four living senses, but he could tell when he was approaching a big meal. He didn't know how he knew. His mind wasn't that sharp anymore.

He moved blindly from the cubicle where he had been idling for the past few minutes. The smell was growing more intense. Flesh, ripe, and plentiful, ideal for his third dinner. He had forsaken the 1,500-calorie a day diet that he had observed when he was alive. Now that he was dead, he had no concept of such abstract principles. He didn't even know why he was moving towards the door. It was just instinct to eat, to destroy, and Nick could not fight it.

He shuffled slowly, because any self-respecting zombie moves slowly and laboriously, knowing that he is never in any rush to feast. The smell was growing stronger, and it certainly was appetizing. A juicy pancreas, a succulent appendix, several feet of the most tender intestines, the savory crunch of a gall-bladder; the scent of each organ rolled up into one tempting bundle for the recently deceased Nick Gordovsky. Fresh meat, that's what he smelled, and it was coming from behind that door. Guess who's coming to dinner.

If he'd had a more sophisticated understanding of his remaining senses, he would have smelled sweat, cheap men's cologne, and chocolate doughnuts.

4:03 PM

"You know that guy?" Harold asked, staring incredulously at Hank, who in turn stared incredulously at the friendly neighborhood vagrant in the parking lot.

"Yeah, he's just a harmless homeless guy," Hank said. "Although he does tend to get kind of touchy with chicks. But other than that, he's cool."

"Is this who you hang out with after work?" Pete asked.

"No, I just walk him to the after-hours bar so no one fucks with him. He can't really defend himself."

"He seems to be doing all right now," Harold said, squinting as he observed the massive size of the General's army.

"Is he saying something?" Adam asked, watching the General speak into a megaphone.

"That ain't possible," Harold said. "None of those dead fucks can talk."

"No, I'm pretty sure he's talking," Janice said. "Open the window."

"Aaaaah!" O'Brien yelled as he flew towards the window. The others quickly cleared a path while the visiting client smashed the base of Greg's phone through the window, shattering the glass that spilled out the two stories to the pavement. Shards struck a few zombies in their heads and shoulders, but only one went down from the blow of the phone.

"You could have just opened it with the latch," Hank said.

"Hindsight, 20/20 dude," O'Brien said in a semi-apologetic surfer tone.

Sticking his head out the window, Hank tried to make out the General's amplified voice over the full symphony of gargles and groans that rose like a noxious vapor from the parking lot.

"They look like they're having fun," Adam observed.

Indeed, from above, the parking lot looked like an outdoor summer concert. Polo shirt-clad convenience store employees were partying it up right next to suited businessmen who were heading for the downtown skyscrapers when some Hubbard squash-hued freak bit them at Starbucks. Dead folks of all colors and creeds alongside oen another; it was like a post-apocalyptic version of liberal utopia.

"Shut up, Adam," Pete said, his eyes never leaving the General. "Is he making demands?"

"Bring us Mr. Aarons," the General's voice crackled through the megaphone. A beeping, tonal version of "Hava Nagila" followed immediately.

"Mr. Aarons?" Pete asked.

"He means Owens," Harold said.

"Well, then let's get him," Adam suggested.

"These are zombies, not hostage-takers," Pete said in a condescending tone. "Do you really think they will refrain from eating us if they get their ransom?"

"It's worth a shot," Adam said as a series of beeps that sounded like Queen's "We Will Rock You" crackled through the electronic megaphone.

"We can at least use him as bait while we escape," Hank said.

"You're really going to use Marshall Owens as a sacrificial lamb in order to screen the goalie?" Myron asked, a bit more coherent, but still on his biblical hockey kick.

"He started that mess," Hank said, pointing to the zombie mosh pit in the parking lot. "As far as I'm concerned, he deserves it."

"Owens is goin' down, and if I have to facilitate that to save my own ass, then that's what I'm doin'," Harold said, sure never to let on that this was, in fact, his plan.

In prison, he had developed a valuable knack for picking winners, allowing him to stay alive while others were buried when the power that they craved finally betrayed them. Harold was a survivalist, never one to rise above the herd, but one who would be there long after the great ones had perished by the shiv. He applied that same logic to his current situation. The once powerful Owens was sequestered in luxury, waiting helplessly, biding his time until this whole thing blew over. These militant employees were armed, proactive, and willing to destroy the superfluous in order to survive. They would do what they had to do, and that was something with which Harold could empathize far too well.

Fuck Marshall Owens, the ex-con thought, because even his thoughts were highly profane. He had served his purpose in Harold's life, but now it seemed like "sentence" would be attached to that word. The man had to be put down. Six feet below, to be exact. Or, as today was going, probably his remains would probably be violently laid to rest in his reserved parking space in the lot outside.

"I say we grab that corporate swine Owens and throw him to the lynch mob," Hank said. He reserved his empathy for the innocents. Even that thug Harold, the overpaid terminator Lillian, and the strip club denizen O'Brien were mere victims of the greed of the man who signed their checks. *Kill one so that thousands may live*—that pre-guillotine battle cry sounded like a good mantra for the day.

"Do you think they'll know the difference if we feed them Owens or Myron?" Pete asked, trying to insert logic into a situation that truly defied it. "None of these flesh eaters has an ideology. It doesn't matter who they eat; they just want someone."

"Yeah, I don't think they keep kosher," Adam observed.

"Well, the General seems to be their leader, and he wants Owens, so I say we give him to them," Hank said.

"Listen, if you two dumb motherfuckers are gonna argue, you can just stay here," Harold said. "I operate by one rule: keep breathing."

"That sounds good to me," Pete said.

"Aarons, Aarons!" the General chanted into the megaphone.

"The Mexican Hat Dance" beeped up from the parking lot.

"Look," Hank said. "I just want to get out of here before they play 'Charge.'"

4:05 PM

Lillian's acid tongue was in Will's overactive ear when she noticed the fluorescent light infiltrating the dim green glow of the janitor's closet.

"Wilby, Wilby," she said, removing her mouth from his earlobe.

He looked up from her chest, half a chocolate doughnut protruding from his slobbering mouth. Lillian pushed his fat cheek, and he swiveled his head around to see the menacing figure of what was recently Nick Gordovsky standing in the doorway. Docker pants around his ankles, Will scrambled to stand up. He was a team lead, an office organizer. He would be damned if he let someone from another department eat his lover. Pro-Well held a contest every Halloween for best team costume themes. Since Will was stuck with Pete, whose idea of a Halloween costume was a T-shirt with an obscene handwritten slogan, and Hank, who refused to dress up at all, Nick's all-star customer service lineup beat them every year.

Well, not today, Will thought.

Gaining his balance, he assumed a fighting stance, or what he assumed to be a fighting stance as he had avoided confrontation for the first fifty-two years and seventy-three days of his life. Nick Gordovsky was no more than a playground bully who made fun of his weight and his tendency to pick his nose. But today he would not recoil in terror and suck his thumb. Wilbert Sarducci would fight. He threw his glasses to the floor and raised his fists to chest level. Eyes squinted, fists clenched, he spit half a chocolate-covered doughnut at the approaching zombie.

"You're gonna have to get past me first!" he yelled to the encroaching ghoul.

Will rolled his fists deliberately, then threw a mean left hook that would have dealt a concussion if the air had a head. *How did people in the movies fight without their glasses?* he wondered. In cinema, when a weak unlikely hero's spectacles were smashed, he got a burst of virile male energy and later, the girl. Will was just getting dizzy. His adrenaline was pumping, but he was still severely myopic. Nick continued to advance slowly, and Will began to flail, throwing punch after punch at the zombie, some connecting, but lacking the force to take down a hungry dead man. Will shuffled backwards and tripped in his pants. He fell on his cushioned spine onto the towel, barely missing Lillian, who had curled up in the corner under the shelf that housed several paint cans for emergency bathroom wall repair.

Laboriously, Nick knelt down atop of Will, who was scrambling backwards in a crab walk, and grabbed at him desperately. Finally, the zombie got a hold of Will's ankle and sank his teeth into the fat man's ample thigh.

Will screamed: the kind of shriek usually reserved for the adventurous girl in slasher flicks, the one who has lost her shirt when engaging in the type of illicit behavior that her more conservative friend bases her survival upon not doing. When she's hiding naked from a seven-foot-tall supervillain who has returned from a premature grave to chase her through the local woods with a tire iron soaked in the warm blood of her boyfriend. But Nick's hearing wasn't that great anymore, so he ignored what, to living ears, sounded like the shriek of a terrified, topless slut, and continued to munch on the team lead's quadriceps. Though quite tasty, the fatty tissue was difficult to chew, and Nick was more interested in the scent of the main course that was behind him.

His cognitive powers were obliterated, but there was something about that one that he just needed to devour. Could it be that he'd retained some inherent desire for retribution even in death? He didn't realize that this woman was responsible for making the last moments of his life an angry, anxious hell, but he wanted to destroy her nonetheless. Some electrical impulses remained in Nick Gordovsky's mangled brain that commanded him to "Eat this bitch!" It wasn't that far-fetched—mailmen in 1970s Manhattan had obeyed orders from far stranger sources.

Nick took another bite of his chubby appetizer and crawled towards the entrée in the corner. Lillian shuddered, attempting to retreat but looking more like a wind-up toy that continued to move in place after being thwarted repeatedly by a stubborn wall. The zombie pursued his advance, despite constant hits from that annoying first course. Will was losing blood rapidly from his severed femoral artery, and his hits had the strength of an accidental Pat Buchanan voter who'd missed her water aerobics class that week.

As Nick sank his teeth into Lillian's chest, all she could say was, "I'm so sorry."

4:12 PM

When they reached the mysterious fourth floor, Adam, Pete, and Hank had been transfixed by what appeared to be a colossal waste of space that held only tarp-covered tables and served to insulate a paranoid man with too much money. The walls were the sterile white of a hospital, and the center area—where the lower levels housed the conference rooms, kitchens, and weaponless supply closets—was vacant, making the entire floor one large, empty room. And, unlike the other levels, there were no windows, apparently in case rival pharmaceutical companies were using the old window-washing espionage ploy or had Spiderman on their side. Harold explained that this was the lab, that the tarps were protecting the equipment. He detailed how Marshall Owens develops all of Pro-Well's drugs himself through months of perfection and testing on subjects to whom the employees did not even need to ask about to know what happened.

"For someone so smart, how does he trust you with all this information?" Hank had asked.

"Never gave him a reason not to," Harold had said, still pretending there was no malice, no plans of vengeance. "But the days of Pro-Well are over, and I'm not gonna be here for the fallout."

The group had reached the door to the corner office that shone a rich mahogany in the midst of the sanitized laboratory bleakness of the floor. Hank knew that Owens had a reputation for enjoying the finer things in life, but he thought that the ivory-plated doorknob was a bit excessive.

When they heard the voice from behind the door, they knew, without Harold holding a finger up to his mouth, to be quiet.

"No, Bruce," Marshall Owens said, his voice muffled through the door, but still perceptible to the intruders. "It's been hours. Still no sign of them. I don't know what to tell you. I'm getting worried."

Without letting them do their token jingling, Harold pulled the keys from his pocket and put one in the doorknob that at least one elephant had died to create. Slowly, he twisted and pushed the door open. Harold entered the room while Adam, Pete, and Hank lurked against the walls on either side of the doorframe.

Owens stared at his bodyguard. If the facial reconstruction surgery hadn't left his expression somewhat frozen, he would have conveyed the shock and something like fear that enveloped his body when the door opened.

"Hang on a minute, Bruce," Owens said, and hit the hold button on his phone. "Harold, what took you so long? I was growing worried that you had become their latest victim."

"It's over, Marshall," Harold said, stepping towards the CEO's desk.

"It's never over, Harold," Marshall replied coolly. "You should know that better than anyone. It's never over. It just begins again as something else."

"I don't got time for your rhetorical shit," Harold said. "You're coming with me."

"I'll do no such thing," Owens said with a blind confidence that was usually bestowed only upon the dumbest of politicians and contributed to many memorable public gaffes. "Do you know who I have on the line right now? Bruce Dobson. The damn mayor. I have work to do getting this mess taken care of. I don't have time for this."

Owens hit the hold button again and spoke into the phone. "Bruce, I'm so sorry for the interruption. What were you saying?"

"Now," Harold roared as Adam, Pete, and Hank barged into the CEO's office.

Pete and Hank rushed to either side of the desk and grabbed Marshall Owens, pulling the CEO's arms behind his back. Adam followed and yanked the phone from Owens' hands.

"He'll call you back," Adam said and hung up the phone.

"What are you doing? Do you know who you just hung up on?" Owens shouted. "Harold, get them off me!"

"Nah, man, you did this to yourself," Harold said.

"Please, please," Owens pleaded, turning his head alternately between Pete and Hank. "I don't know what you've heard, but you've got the wrong man. I'm as much of a victim as you are. Please, Harold's the one you want."

"Don't you fucking think about it," Harold said as he pulled the gun from his belt and aimed it at the CEO's head.

"Yeah, don't you fucking think about it," Adam said from his position behind Owens, flicking the back of the millionaire's head with his finger.

He looked a lot taller on TV, Hank thought, *and a little less scrawny, but the scars were accurate.* There was really nothing television makeup crews could do to disguise such disfigurement. The omnipotent savior of the sick, the environment, and Pittsburgh's water polo league squirmed in the hold of these two low-level 9-to-5 drones. Owens flailed and kicked, but to no avail. Hank had started the binding process.

When you are being held against your will, there is no sound more ominous, more truly fucking frightening than that of duct tape ripping from the roll. And that is exactly what Marshall Owens heard as he played the victim to the renegade second-floor employees.

"You guys have nothing to gain by abducting me," Owens said. "As soon as he can, he'll betray you like he's betraying me. He'll lead you right off a cliff."

"Dude, just give up," Pete said. "We already know everything."

"Then you know that your good friend, Harold here is responsible for it all," Owens stated, staring at his once loyal soldier.

"Sorry, I don't think you can strong-arm chemicals into mixing together," Hank said. "The elements do not respond well to intimidation."

"Well, that's what City Council believes," Owens countered. "And that's the story that everyone will hear once this is over. You have a choice. You can go down with him or become a phoenix like me."

Hank rolled his eyes as he stretched a long piece of tape and wrapped it around Owens's arms that Pete held in place behind his back. *I've really got to shut this douche up*, Hank thought as Adam pushed his way back into the room with the janitor's cart, smiling.

"What is that for?" Owens asked.

"That's your ride," Adam said, pointing to the trash can.

Owens looked appalled, "I am not riding in a refuse bin."

"Don't worry," Adam said. "I put a clean garbage bag in just for you."

Owens appeared to be more aggravated than scared of his imminent abduction, more worried about tarnishing his suit in a trash can than facing the myriad flesh-hungry dead that had gathered in his parking lot.

"I gotta ask," Hank said, staring into Marshall Owens's eyes from mere inches away. He tugged at the lapel of the CEO's blazer. "Is this Prada?"

"Yes," Owens replied.

"Well, what do you know," Hank mused as he stretched the last piece of tape over the CEO's mouth.

"Good to have you back," Pete said to Hank.

4:22 PM

The elevators were in a state of bloody disrepair. Infested with zombies and corpses, the employees had no choice but to take the stairs. This proved quite difficult with the wheeled janitor's cart that contained a 160-pound millionaire in the trashcan. Pete and Adam led the way down the glass-encased stairwell, brandishing their weapons while Hank and Harold lifted the cart. Owens's eyes were wide and, unable to speak through the duct tape gag, he kept shaking his head to protest each step that his transporters took. Slowly, they descended the steps until they reached the third floor. Pausing to gaze through the glass pane, they saw a completely vacant level. *No survivors*, Hank thought. *That means the zombies are all on our floor, waiting for Thanksgiving.*

The employees continued down the steps until they reached the second floor. Marianne Leibowitz from payroll was standing by the glass doors, staring up at them, anxiously awaiting her first meal since being locked in the stairwell. Almost in unison, Pete and Adam swung their brooms and smashed Marianne's head from both sides at the ears. She lay on the ground, momentarily disabled until Adam shoved the handle side of his broom into her gaping mouth, shattering her skull. The doorway effectively cleared, Harold and Hank were able to put Owens back on the ground and, with Pete holding the door open, wheeled him into the main floor of the office.

And there they were. All the zombies that had worked in the office were approaching from the cubicles and the hallway and the group that had fallen during their attack from the trenches were now back on what was left of their feet, shambling towards the pulses that emerged from the stairwell.

"Battering ram," Hank said as he broke into a run directly into the wall of zombies, pushing Owens in the cart.

He ran through the throng of the dead, smashing them to the ground with the force of the maintenance cart. His expression a distorted grimace, he took down Tanya Atkins of sales and file clerk Wayne Evans.

Hank had cultivated his sinister, masculine image as a façade to cover his vulnerability, for his homosexuality and plethora of fears and obsessions would leave him open to ridicule. But you don't tease a guy you think will kill you, so Hank worked his physique and dark demeanor. It also came with the added benefit of mystique. Yet his bevy of weird phobias and illogical compulsions always made him feel like a fraud. But now he believed that he had earned his menacing persona. He was truly fearless in the face of zombies.

The others followed him. Adam and Pete using their brooms as spears while Harold calmly waited for Byron Eckman of the call center to approach him. When the dead man came within a few feet, Harold placed the "Caution: Wet Floor" sandwich board on his head so that the warnings were over both ears. Calling on all the force in his muscular arms, he pushed the sides together. And *SPLAT*—it was like a nutcracker. Byron crumbled onto the floor and Harold left the yellow sign on the remains of his head to follow the others. They reached Greg Tombardi's office, and Hank burst through the door, quickly pulling the gagged and helpless CEO behind him.

"Finally," O'Brien said, as they entered rolling Owens in the trash can. "Who's that guy?"

"That's Marshall Owens," Harold said. "That's who they want, and we're gonna give him to them."

Owens attempted to shout in protest, but his cries were muffled.

"What's that?" Harold asked, leaning into his boss. "Sorry, man, I can't really hear you. That's what you get, motherfucker."

Harold elbowed the CEO in the ribs.

"We're getting out of here, now," Hank said. "I'm off in fifteen minutes, and no army of dead people is gonna keep me in this office one second longer."

Adam reached his hand up to high-five Hank and received an honorary slap back.

"What's the plan?" Janice asked eagerly.

"Well, there are enough zombies out there to pack the Bat Cave," Hank said. "So we've got to use all the arms we've got and make a run for it."

"We'll make it to Owens's Escalade in his executive parking spot and run over as many as we can on the way outta here," Harold offered.

"But first we've gotta get out of this building," Hank said. "There's a whole shitload of those dead freaks on the floor, just waiting for a taste, and we've gotta get past them first."

Hank tore off his blood-soaked maroon shirt to reveal a white undershirt with several bloody splotches.

Janice was transfixed. Hank ripped the button-down shirt up the side under the left sleeve that had received the least secondary spatter. He tore a long piece off and tied it around his forehead like a bandana that soaked the sweat he'd worked up carrying the cart down two flights of stairs. Janice reached out and touched his bicep lightly, eyeing the full sleeve of tattoos.

"Where'd you have that done?" she asked.

"I got it in Nam," Hank said offhandedly.

He grabbed his black biker leather jacket from the desk where Janice had tossed it after thoughtfully grabbing before the conference room evacuation. She had naively assumed that he'd at least thank her for the consideration.

"Everyone, assemble your weapons," Hank said. "I'll be damned if I work overtime today."

As the rest of the survivors gathered their office supplies, Marshall Owens was twitching in the trash can. Pursing his mangled lips against the duct tape, he attempted to blow raspberries and slide his tongue out from behind his teeth, using the saliva to erode the adhesive. It wasn't working. The only sounds he emitted were monotonous hums from behind the tape as he jerked around in the confines of the trash can.

"Okay, that is getting really annoying," Hank said as he yanked the tape of the CEO's face.

"Thank you," Owens said, catching the breath he'd expended trying to blow into a wall of adhesive.

"You've got thirty seconds," Hank said. "What?"

"I just wanted to offer you an option," Owens began. "You appear to be the leader of this group. If you let me out of this trash can, I will grant you a spot within my empire."

Hank laughed, "Dude, you're gonna die on Elba." He started to pull the duct tape from the roll.

"Not if we do this right," Owens said. "We can get out of here. Get to my car. Save ourselves, and I'll make you my number two. You're smart, resourceful. You'd be a much better asset to Pro-Well than this goon." He nudged his shoulder towards Harold.

Harold responded by punching the CEO in the ribs again.

Owens leaned over in pain for a moment before quickly recovering. "See what I mean?"

"I'll be your number two," Myron offered.

Owens looked at the frail janitor, raised his one remaining eyebrow, and scoffed.

"See these tattoos on my arms?" Hank asked.

"How could I miss them?" Owens responded. "They are truly exquisite artwork."

Hank ignored the insincere flattery. "The reason I got them was to be unemployable. To never settle to be a white-collar drone. To never let myself fall victim to the mundane machine of the 9-to-5 culture. I figured that if I tattooed myself to the point of no return, I'd be forced to either succeed doing what I want or die in a gutter somewhere. It was supposed to be all or nothing. Over time I allowed myself to forget that. I became mediocre. I never admitted that until now. You think that after today, after fighting off the embodiment of the living dead that I have figuratively been for years, I'm just going to go right back to being a working stiff?"

"I can give you money," Owens pleaded.

"Don't want it," Hank replied, tearing the tape from the roll. "Never thought I felt that way, but I do."

"Women?" Owens offered.

Adam let out a guffaw.

"Not interested," Hank answered.

"I understand," Owens said. "Too high maintenance. But I do have an extensive collection of the most life-like female dolls. They cost over $10,000 each, but one can be yours."

"Eww," Janice exclaimed.

"You're pathetic," Hank said.

"I'll take one," O'Brien offered.

"What can I give you to get me out of this trash can?" Owens shouted, unable to restrain his temper any longer.

"Nothing," Hank said. "But I know someone who could use something from you."

"What does he want from me?"

"The General?" Hank asked rhetorically. "He wants you."

Hank pressed the tape back over the CEO's mouth.

4:42 PM

It seemed cliché to vow to change his life when he was at the brink of death, but that is what Pete did. If he lived through this day, he wouldn't be so lazy. He'd ride his bike that was now just taking up enough space in the kitchen to justify not cooking dinner. He'd join a softball team, learn how to play Frisbee golf. He'd even let his roommate sit in his proud ass groove on the couch. He'd stop establishing ass grooves at his friends' houses. Then he would find Jimmy Hoffa.

He'd go see his friend Tom's band play at the American Legion next Saturday. It would be a terrible event, but he would check it out, just in case it was his last chance to see Exploding Tomato Death Ray. He'd run for mayor and persuade Adam to do the same, and they would orchestrate a massive smear campaign against one another. "Adam Kaplan is a jaywalker," "Pete Nicks uses money from UNICEF boxes to buy scratch-off tickets." And he certainly would not work here anymore. Maybe he'd go to law school. He could see himself litigating. Sales just didn't seem to be working out for him.

Along with being forgotten by the rest of his team, Pete's lack of commissions was seriously putting a damper on his lifestyle. He would like to have money at some point, even if for no other reason than to waste it, but he would like some nonetheless. Preferably, he would like to pass the time in his ass groove, pondering the inherent contradiction in Descartes' "I think therefore I am" hypothesis after this day of interaction with many brain-dead creatures that "are." How could he amend it to encompass zombies and the Hollywood illiterati? I walk therefore I am? No, that left out Stephen Hawking. I eat therefore I am? Nope, then he omitted anorexics and the entire population of Ethiopia. He could think of no philosophical mantra that was truly all-inclusive. He reclined in the ass groove he'd established in Greg Tombardi's chair and assumed The Thinker pose. Maybe that would help.

If he lived through this day, he may be stronger, but if he winds up severely injured, the loss of blood would probably make him weaker. It was all too much to be spinning through his head while he could still hear the groans of his recently deceased co-workers on the other side of the office wall. So he blurted out the one thing he could come up with.

"Coiffism," Pete said.

"Excuse me?" Janice asked, confused.

"Coiffism," Pete explained, rather irritably for someone who had just blurted out an invented word. "Discrimination against people based on hairstyle."

"Is that what you've been thinking about all day?" Hank said.

"Dude, I'm the smartest guy you know," Pete countered. "I can kick zombie ass while inventing my own language."

Marshall Owens started squirming in his bindings, attempting to speak through the duct tape.

"Goddammit. I thought he was done," Hank said. He walked from the window where he was surveying the madness in the parking lot to the CEO in the trash can. With no sympathy for the devil or his skin grafts, Hank ripped the tape from what was left of Owens's lips.

"I just want you to know that Pro-Well does not condone discrimination, based on hairstyle or anything else for that matter. Do you feel you have been treated unjustly based on your looks? I know how that is. People always looking at you, behaving differently based on physical appearance. I can help. Believe me. I have been there. If you let me out of this trash can, we can combat coiffism together," Owens pleaded.

"That's it?" Hank asked incredulously. "That's all you've got left? A feeble plea to prevent an inside joke?"

"Yeah, it was just hypothetical coiffism," Adam interjected.

"Would you people shut the fuck up?" Harold shouted. "The more time you spend talking about hair the less time we got to get outta here."

"Harold," Owens began in a condescending tone. "You of all people should be sensitive to prejudice. And look at this situation now. We are all being marginalized, segregated from our own society that has become overrun by those monsters outside. They are the tyrants we need to overthrow! Not me. I am a victim just like you."

"You know, we all agree that we want those things dead," Hank said, unrolling a fresh piece of duct tape for the rather loquacious CEO who was becoming quite the annoyance. "But you're the Marie Antoinette of this revolution. And we'll let them eat you."

"I'm still interested in those dolls if you want to give 'em to me," O'Brien offered from behind the desk where he leaned against the wall, trying desperately to see his reflection in his voluptuous curves of his flask.

Owens rolled his eyes.

"Now, if you have nothing of importance to say, I ask that you stop the squirming and the squealing," Hank said, holding the duct tape in front of Owens's active mouth. "This tape should be used for fashioning weapons, not as a gag."

Owens stared stone-faced as Hank started to pull the tape over the CEO's mouth. But, as his hand brushed against Owens's face, the scarred millionaire seized the moment to clamp his capped teeth down on Hank's index finger.

"Fuck!" Hank shouted.

Janice leapt to Hank's side and inspected the wound. Marshall Owens's bite was a defense mechanism, his use of the only weapon still available when hogtied in a trash can. It was not the ravenous chomp of the dead outside, but an instinctual urge to fight against his captor. Hank's skin wasn't broken. Instead the only mark was the perfect impression of thousands of dollars in dental work.

"Well, of all the people to bite me today, I'm actually glad it was you," Hank said as he rolled the rest of the tape over Owens's now dually dangerous mouth.

4:45 PM

Tasha Daniels had always considered herself one hell of a fighter. If you fucked with her or her man, she was not afraid to go all *Flavor of Love* girl on your ass. She'd yanked out more hair than chemotherapy. She'd been starting and ending fights since she was three, but the nineteen-year-old had never been in a situation quite like this. Hairejullah was usually a peaceful store, a place for all wig-wearing women, and some fabulous men, to purchase their weave. Tasha was a phenomenal salesgirl and provided the customers with excellent insight into how easy each specific brand ripped out when the wearer had been acting a ho and was put in her place. "No matter how hard you smack a bitch, these nails won't break," she was known to say, and, "This ring is almost like brass knuckles for when you need to deck that waiter who disrespected you like that. Didn't even ask if you wanted more diet soda before taking your glass and filling it up again. That's what his ass gets for being all presumptuous and shit."

Located in a shopping plaza on the edge of the South Side, Hairellujah had the largest selection of fake human hair in Western Pennsylvania. There were aisles and aisles of wigs, enough synthetic hair to make several hundred thousand My

Little Ponies and roughly 14 million fake mustaches. This was the place to get a realistic weave if you were, in fact, a Barbie doll. These wigs were nothing more than cheap female toupees.

The oddly spacious specialty shop was sandwiched between an automotive supply outlet and a state-run liquor store in a shopping center that was usually forgotten when one referenced the South Side. Indeed, when locals thought of the district, it was bars and independent shops specializing in everything from skateboards to imported swords to vintage furniture to magic. No one associated the unique, vibrant South Side with the cultural abyss of this strip mall that contained discount chain stores and cheap hair products. There was a dollar store, a Popeye's Chicken, a Payless Shoe Source, a Sally Beauty Supply, and a Rainbow Fashions. The Supercuts housed within was an almost ignored corporate refuge for those who could not afford the stylish haircuts from the five independent salons on the main drag. The sole reason most residents even ventured this far down towards the river was to visit the grocery store.

The shoddy Hairellujah was Tasha's dominion that she ruled over with tyrannical glee. She had been promoted to manager because, for some strange reason, the shop had a high turnover rate. Seemed that a week working alongside Tasha was too much for most to handle. Even working above her proved too stressful. So when the latest manager resigned, Tasha quickly assumed her post. Under Tasha's reign, the store was cleaner, but she found herself working nearly 60 hours a week due to the ever-dwindling employee count. But the more hours worked, the more the store was under Tasha's control. If she caught one of her underlings lazing on the job, the lovely and talented Miss Daniels wasn't afraid to unleash verbal hell on her ass. She emptied her arsenal on the unsuspecting sales associates, not ashamed to personally insult her co-workers with a barrage of unsubstantiated claims. That was just how Tasha worked, and if they couldn't handle it, she didn't need them.

And one of the few remaining employees who had been able to handle being referred to as a fat, disrespecting bitch had just been eviscerated on aisle four.

The usually organized store that Tasha minded with an obsessive eye was in a state of disarray. Several grayish-tinted superfreaks had stumbled through the aisles, knocking over wig-sporting mannequin heads and cheap jewelry display wheels. Tasha's co-worker—that fat lazy bitch who was always texting instead of helping stock the shelves—was lying in the middle of one of the seven aisles. A blond Farrah Fawcett wig had fallen onto her dead face, and the insides of her giant gut were spilled onto the tiled floor. Skinny Tasha was hiding in the back of the store, in the supply area where they kept floor-to-ceiling shelves stocked with the shrink-wrapped wigs displayed on the main floor. Though the partition covered most of the width of the store, there was a doorway-sized portion cut out and the only thing that separated Tasha from four approaching zombies was a lone metal chain that got less respect than Rodney Dangerfield from even the living customers.

Tasha shivered in her tight pink jeans as a young man in a wife beater, his arms covered in tattoos, approached the chain, dragging a curly black wig with red streaks under his skate sneaker. Last year, she had been convinced that lying, cheating bastard Larry had been running around with some weave-wearing slut named Courtney. So Tasha accosted not one, but three weave-wearing sluts named Courtney until she found the right one. She'd slammed fourteen heads into the lockers before her high school principal decided it was enough and insisted that Tasha be institutionalized, *for the good of everyone, God damn it.* But she wouldn't let anyone disrespect her like that, so she attacked a nurse and got the hell out of there. Clearly, Tasha Daniels was not one to back down, so she grabbed the metal rod that she used to pull wigs from the high shelves and held it like a lance.

"You better come get me, mother fucker!" she shouted. No dumbass freak fucked with her like this and got away with it.

Some dude had touched her hair on the bus a couple weeks ago. He said it was an accident, that the rush hour crowds just packed the bus too tightly to avoid physical contact, that he was sorry if he'd offended her. But she wasn't buying that crap, so she kicked him in the groin until she could tell by his pained moans that he was truly sorry. Shit, she'd beaten some dumb ho's ass just for looking at her ex-boyfriend, then she'd beaten him for looking back. Now this freak thinks he can try to eat her and get away with it. She'd tear his ass up before that happened. She was ready to fight at any perceived disrespect, and eating her underlings, well, that was definitely not permitted. Help did not that come easy around here.

She stared into his dead eyes as he walked right into the chain and bounced back, unable to figure out how to get through this barrier.

"Well, what are you waiting for? You pansy-ass bitch," she shouted.

The tattooed zombie lifted his head, and his milky lifeless eyes seemed to sparkle as he glared at her. The zombie sneered and let out a low growl. Tasha tightened her grip on the five-foot-long grabber and broke into a run, aiming the metal pole straight at her would-be attacker's forehead.

4:56 PM

The employees were as ready as they could be when facing the most bizarre array of hungry corpses fathomable. Outside the office was a festival of college kids, drunken buffoons, hobos, yuppies, and even the pierogie mascot who runs circles at PNC Park during Pirates games. He had bitten his linen pasta exterior and was currently writhing on the ground as his arms were stuck in the potato innards. The living employees stood outside the doorway of the conference room, armed with every pseudo-weapon they could find. Pete held what were once brooms in both hands. He had snapped off the parts that were useful for cleaning to create sharp, splintered tips that were useful for stabbing. Janice almost made a run to her desk for her letter opener but thought that the disturbance she'd create to the team would not be worth a three-inch dull blade. Instead, she held the phone cord nunchuks at her hip and had a full arsenal of projectiles in her large purse. *This thing really would have been quite valuable when I used to steal beer from parties,* she thought.

But that was in her punk rock days, and she would have looked ridiculous in her Exploited t-shirt holding a lacy torso-shaped bag. Yet it was serving its purpose now. Three staplers, two tape dispensers, a framed photograph of a couple she had only seen when their skin had started to fall off in leper-like chunks, and a paper weight model of downtown Pittsburgh's PPG Place. It really was quite a pretty structure, and Janice wondered if she would ever see it again. After years of complaining about the monotony of the mid-sized sports-obsessed city, she now found herself missing its predictability.

Harold jammed his handgun into Marshall Owens's temple and used his free hand to hold the CEO close to him in case he tried to make a run for it. They had decided that the maintenance cart was too cumbersome for this journey in case they needed to take the stairs again. Owens was allowed to walk, but remained a prisoner. He was simply easier to transport on foot.

After hearing much protesting and self-promotion from the newly self-dubbed Rick-Man, the ad-hoc council of reason (made up of Hank, Pete, and Harold) had finally allowed O'Brien to carry the paper cutter blade. When it was placed in his hands, the CDC buyer cradled it with orgasmic joy, coveting the weapon and hugging it against his chest.

"I feel like I've done a good deed," Pete had said as he watched the emotional reunion between warrior and weapon.

It was like reuniting Beowulf with Hrunting, Arthur with Excalibur, Colonel Mustard with the candlestick. Truly a heartwarming scene if ever there was one in the midst of a blitzkrieg of the dead.

Outside the conference room, O'Brien held the blade in his left hand while snapping pictures of the approaching dead.

"The fuck's wrong with you?" Harold barked.

"This is gonna get me so much ass," O'Brien said as he continued to capture every glorious moment on camera.

Even Myron had agreed to carry a weapon, but could not be trusted with anything that could seriously injure the living. He was granted a phone book, which he proceeded to read. After the janitor managed to bore the rag tag warriors by dictating random business slogans from advertising insets in the Yellow Pages during battle preparation, Hank had taped the book shut. Now Myron was silent again and held the phone book under his arm and stared at the approaching zombies.

Leading the charge was Hank, pushing Adam in a wheeling desk chair. Adam held two umbrellas with sharp tips that Hank had merely explained were to be used as lances, leaving the rest of the group quite confused.

They were a motley army; a disheveled, blood-spattered crew of disgruntled white-collar employees, a hogtied millionaire, a janitor, and a felon with a firearm. And they, like the Wu Tang Clan, weren't nothing to fuck with. The clock was running out and they would all be damned if they died in the office.

But this wasn't Hell. At least not Hank's vision of it. He was never afraid of the Hollywood versions because they always looked a lot like an Alice Cooper concert, and anyone who knew anything knew that the devil has better musical taste. The flames made it look like an eternal bonfire party that the police can never find. Maybe that's Hell for the dirty cop: an urgent call to bust an underage party that he will circle for eternity. Hank could not have fathomed spending forever in a lame version of Cloud City set to incessant harp music. Zombies were not part of Hank's Hell. Drunk middle-aged women in sequined sweaters hosting open houses were, along with every man who ever went to Jared, life coaches, Tipper Gore, Philadelphia sports fans, and stubborn idiots that forced society to condone the misuse of the word "impact." The zombies he could handle. He could take them out with a laptop if need be. It was a lot easier than stopping the infectious pandemic of celebrity news. With umbrellas, a phone receiver with its cord duct taped to a table leg, and a spray bottle filled with Drano all hooked into his belt, Hank felt completely secure. He was born to do this. Vigilante justice was swift. He wouldn't stop until those dead cannibal freaks were dead again.

But there were a lot of them, covering all the stages of decomposition that were possible to reach in just a few hours of death. The eyes and ears appeared to be the first casualties of their violent state of limbo. Either the virus had similar effects as leprosy, or these parts were destroyed when their victims resisted being repurposed as lunch. Hank stared at the thirty approaching zombies.

"Well, at least this means that this is probably all of them," he said.

"Least till we get outside," Harold added.

"We'll worry about that when we get there," Hank said. "Everyone ready?"

"Fuck yeah!" Adam shouted. "Pour some sugar on me!"

Hank jumped into a breakneck run, pushing Adam into the mob of the dead. His arms outstretched above his head, umbrellas pointed forward, Adam held steady while the force of the chair propelled him. An eye socket, an aorta, a carotid artery, a mouth, Adam stabbed through several zombies as he flew forward. Blood soaked the cubicles and the customer service poster on the wall. The man who had just reached the top of the mountain with the help of his team was now a sanguinary horror story. Once through the horde of zombies, Hank stopped the chair and swung it around abruptly, preparing for Round Two.

"Fuck like a beast!" Adam yelled as Hank launched into a run, ready to trample the remaining brood.

The scrawny Web designer was a jousting machine. Flying swiftly through the cumbersome corpses, Adam held his arms steady as the unsuspecting dead walked right into the sharp ends of the umbrellas. They kept coming, slowly, awkwardly until Adam had a zombie kabob. Hank wanted to remark on the irony of the hunters becoming the hunted, the compulsively overeating corpses becoming food-like objects, but there was no time.

"How the tables have turned," he stated quietly, hoping that none of his cohorts heard the cliché.

And they didn't, for they were far too busy waging the second line of the battle. Janice lobbed the miniature PPG Place at a particularly rabid zombie wearing a flowery blouse and part of an a-line skirt that was now almost a micro-mini. Except for the whole dead thing, she looked like a stripper at a corporate function for AIG execs. Her arms outstretched like a mummy about to trip over its bandages, she sluggishly ambled towards Janice until the sharp towers of the Pittsburgh skyscraper were embedded into her skull. She fell to the ground as Janice reached into her corset purse, without a pause, to retrieve another projectile and lob it at Herb Jorgenson from HR. She would have hit him if he'd still had a jaw, but the stapler whizzed past his depleted chin and smashed what may have been QA associate Lauren Michaels in the ear.

O'Brien led the tertiary charge, spinning and slicing and chopping through the line of the dead. Grasping the blade with both hands on the handle, trying his best to look like a maskless Zorro. Meanwhile, a safe twelve feet away, Pete was prodding, pounding, stabbing, and whacking (none of which was in a sexual way) the advancing front of zombies with his broom handles. Between the two, it was like watching half the Teenage Mutant Ninja Turtles.

Dodging the makeshift weapons and the arterial spatter, Harold quickly shoved his boss through the battle while Janice stabbed a fallen Lauren Michaels in the cheek with the six-inch piece of splintered wood that made up half of the nunchuks. She smiled, proud of her first kill in an official battle. She was now a hardened zombie slayer. She watched Lauren gurgle, blood spilling from the hole in her face. As the slain quality assurance worker lay on the ground, her lifeless eyes blindly staring at her killer, Janice realized that being dead may not be that cool.

For the past month and a half, she had been infatuated with the idea of rising from the grave, to return as a pallid, red-lipped succubus. But looking at the gray skin of this creature, her cloudy eyes and the gaping hole in her cheek, Janice thought that un-death may not be that glamorous. Could she risk some boring vigilante like Rick O'Brien staking her in the heart? Even Lestat had his fair share of embarrassing moments and disfiguring incidents. Watching her grotesque kill slip into the abyss of true death, Janice decided that a decadent coffin might be a waste of money. That was the problem with switching ideologies for the fashion; she eventually found herself to be a non-believer.

She did not want to die.

Glam seemed like fun. The practitioners had interesting hair and festive outfits. They always seemed to be having a party, and their only ideology was Dionysian excess. If death came, it was a surprise and probably because a friend crashed the car during an ill-advised beer run.

A full-fledged zombie attack was probably not the best time to be pondering lifestyle choices, as it left one open to someone else making the decision. In Janice's case, it was sales rep Mark Lidstrom. And he wanted her to be a late-afternoon snack. Slowly he approached Janice from behind, dragging a broken leg that had been crushed in an earlier incident involving the elevator door. As it turns out, zombies are not good with buttons. Shaggy brown hair hanging over his blind eyes, he limped towards Janice, his teeth bared, ready for an oral strike. He came closer until he was inches from the second-guessing Goth, standing a full head higher than she. He bent down slowly, but his motor skills were not what they used to be and his chin clunked down on Janice's skull.

She flinched, jumping away from the dead man who was practically on top of her when—WHAP! Mark fell to the floor to reveal Myron standing behind him, grasping the Yellow Pages. The janitor had awakened from his mighty slumber, And just in time for Janice.

"No need to thank me, dear," he said. "Just protectin' my own."

Janice nodded as a way to alleviate her shock. The babbling maintenance man had saved her life. She would have to thank him on her Facebook page later. If there was a *later*. She pulled the remaining part of the wooden pointer out of Lauren Michael's face and ran through the relatively clear path that Pete and O'Brien had created, dodging the walking dead along the way.

Unfortunately, it turns out that Myron was as inept at zombie killing as he was at everything else in his life. As a teenager, he attempted to emulate his heroes by trying out for the high school football team. He was cut in the first round and never looked back. It didn't cross his mind to try out again his sophomore year, or to work on his game in a county league. Where did he get off thinking that he could ever be a Mean Joe Green? No, great deeds were not in his future. If at first he didn't succeed, he gave up.

As he stepped over what he presumed to be the lifeless remains of Mark Lidstrom, the temporarily incapacitated salesman—whose ease with customers had always upstaged Pete's self-deprecating rants—latched onto Myron's ankle like it was a new account. Myron kicked and squirmed and freed his right leg, but not before Mark took a quick nibble from the skin that covered his Achilles tendon.

Better not to say anything, Myron thought. As often as he failed in life, he had never asked for anyone's sympathy. Though unsolicited co-workers and bar buddies tended to console him when the Steelers failed to make the playoffs and when his eldest daughter died in a car crash, he'd never asked for their sympathies. Stumbling away from the corpse, Myron figured he'd just let his ankle bleed. He staggered past the fallen zombies in the mass grave that was once the office to join the others outside of the stairwell doors. The trail of dead did not end until about four feet from where they stood. And some were beginning to rise again.

With the other employees crowded behind him, Hank calmly held the spray bottle Pete had looted from the janitor's closet at eye level. His arm outstretched, he waited patiently as Brooks Henderson of accounting slowly rose to his feet. Wobbling slightly as he stood up, he soon regained his equilibrium and moved towards Hank. The valiant technical writer smirked at the approaching zombie and unleashed a spritz of whoop-ass into the dead man's mangled face. He pulled the trigger a second time and a third, coating the recently deceased accountant's nose and eyes with Drano. Without noticing, the now shiny zombie continued his advance. Hank pulled his silver Zippo lighter from his pocket and opened the flame. He waited the few seconds until Brooks' chin passed through the hand-held fire.

It took less than a second for his head to become a fireball. Flailing, trying to regain some sense of composure that would give him one last meal, the zombie fell face first onto the floor. The flame started to spread slowly on the cheap carpeting.

Then the fire alarm sounded with a piercing piccolo-pitched beep. O'Brien nearly Van Goghed himself with the blade while attempting to cover his ears from the audio onslaught, which he somehow found more threatening than the hungry dead. But that flaming zombie was pretty damn sweet, he thought, so he'd better memorialize the event. O'Brien pulled his camera from his pocket and snapped a quick photo of the fiery mess. It was just in the nick of time before the sprinkler system kicked on, killing the flames almost instantly.

"Fuck me with a fork," Hank lamented.

"Ow," Adam said.

"Sorry, man," O'Brien said, wrapping his arm around Hank's shoulders in consolation. "That would have been awesome."

"I'll say it again. Hopefully tomorrow will be better than today," Pete said.

"No shit," Harold snapped. "I'm gettin' the fuck outta here."

He grabbed Owens and kept the gun pressed squarely into the CEO's spine as he opened the door and entered the stairwell. Myron followed, but once on the landing, he caught a glimpse out the glass wall. Just when he was starting to gain clarity, it all slipped away with one glance at the parking lot. Hundreds of the dead freaks were congregated outside the office, and even from this height, he recognized Elaine. His favorite bartender, she had been serving him Iron City beers at Cordy's for the past twenty years. The teased black perm and the Beadazzled, sandblasted denim jacket. She was gone. And so was probably everyone he knew. Myron had made one gallant effort to stay alive, and now he was ready to give up again. He based his life on those around him, on the habitual. If everything he knew was gone, what was the point of existing?

Pete was not ready to surrender so quickly. He shoved Myron from the back, and the janitor easily obeyed his command and started to walk down the stairs, his head hung low in mourning of his fair city. The others followed, stepping over materials purchaser Mara Lancaster's lifeless body on the third-floor landing.

4:59 PM

The General's original army was now scattered in a crowd of a hundred or so like-minded rebels. He had tried counting them earlier, but gave up when he covered the twenty-four in his immediate area. He held the megaphone in hand, and a ladies' handbag he'd picked up from the lot hung on his shoulder. He may need to assume a new identity when this was all over. La-Toya Thomson, age 28, organ donor. It may be a difficult one to pull off, but the General had done some amazing things in his life. Once, a long time ago, he'd organized a successful labor union of the dead that overthrew a pharmaceutical giant.

"Owens, Owens!" he chanted into the megaphone, finally having recalled his nemesis's name.

He pressed 58 on the buttons and the first bars of Beethoven's "Fur Elise" mechanically beeped from the horn. *Now this was a call to arms*, he thought.

"Let them eat cake!" he shouted into the megaphone, "Hail Caesar! Can I get a witness?"

As militant as he was feeling, the General was also growing quite hungry. The rest of his troops had been feasting all morning, but the General did not have the taste for human flesh. He'd once grilled a rat and had even swallowed live goldfish when he'd gone to collect empty beer cans at a frat party, but eating a fellow man was not an option. He had standards.

The General rifled through LaToya Thomson's gold-studded purse, searching for something edible. He opened what appeared to be a compact mirror and found thirty individually wrapped candies. Though their plastic packaging labeled them by the day, the General was starving and he popped each candy out and tossed them into his mouth one by one. He chewed the remainder of October's orthotricyclin, finding it quite bitter. *Maybe this is that sugar-free candy,* he thought. The taste was acrid, but it was sustenance nonetheless. While the twenty-three days worth of birth control digested in his system, the General threw the compact on the ground and resumed command of his army.

"Off with their heads!" he shouted from his post directly in front of the office's front doors. "Let sleeping dogs lie! Testify!"

Then he spotted them. A group of living humans standing directly behind the glass panes. Now was the time for action. He just needed to be heard above the moans and gurgles of his troops.

"Quiet!" he shouted. "There is nothing to fear but fear itself!"

No, that didn't work. He had officially lost control of his army. But he had demands to make and it wouldn't let noisy troops get in his way.

5:03 PM

"Fuck me Amadeus, there's a lot of them," Adam observed from the Pro-Well lobby.

"The Escalade's right there," Harold said, pointing to the huge, black SUV parked about twenty feet from the door. It was barely visible behind the veritable wall of zombies.

"We give them the creep, then we run," Hank said. "Kill as many as possible along the way."

As the words rolled off his tongue, Hank couldn't believe that he had uttered them. He had been living an uncomfortable existence of minimal release for years, and it bothered him a bit that he was so at ease with the task at hand. Of course, he'd thought of shooting up the office before—who hadn't?—but was truly amazed that he was given what appeared to be a legal, and actually necessary, means to do so. Killing zombies was therapeutic for Hank. He needed to clobber something more challenging and fulfilling than a punching bag. He needed something that could fight back. Actually, he needed to get out of his rut and find a new career. But violence would be a better temporary release than beer. And somehow, the stars had aligned and afforded Hank the ideal outlet for his pent-up aggression.

There was no law about killing the dead. Hell, there wasn't even a ruling against fucking the dead until some sick freak made it absolutely necessary. If they were tried, the case would truly set a precedent, an example for all future zombie warfare. They could all claim self-defense, and Myron would certainly be acquitted on a temporary insanity plea. Shit, so would Vampira. Hank couldn't imagine what kind of outfit she'd show up in at the trial. It would definitely get her booted from a jury. And of what would that be composed? Locating twelve living locals who knew nothing of this mess would be difficult to say the least. The majority probably possessed the same repressed desires to go on a workplace killing spree. And the rest would be in severe withdrawal from Pro-Well's sedatives.

And where were the police anyway? The city had been known to bring in the National Guard for extreme weather, but where was the law now? Hank looked at the orgy of dead in the parking lot. If these people were living, they would have been immobilized by sonic weapons and rubber bullets by now. And then he saw the red and blue lights of six squad cars. A young officer stood on a roof, attempting to kick away the gray arms grabbing from the sides of the Crown Victoria. One of the corpses was also wearing a blue uniform, and his badge gleamed in the sunlight. *So much for the law*, Hank thought. Well, they'd probably just get in the way anyway. Damn cops, always spoiling the good parties.

He looked out the window and locked eyes with the General, who looked quite confused with a studded red purse hanging from his shoulder.

The employees stood behind the revolving door, ready to make their offering to the crazed homeless commander of the dead. Janice crowded behind Hank, her hands resting on his back. He shook her off.

"When we leave, try to stay close together," Janice justified her proximity to Hank. "They'll probably come in the door after us, and I think we should try to get as many as possible caught in here."

"Andy!" Myron shouted suddenly.

The group turned to him. He had officially snapped again.

"It's Andy Mason!" Myron shouted, pointing to the tall zombie with the shaggy bleached-blond hair that stood on the front line.

"Yeah, I think he's right," Pete observed. "Probably got wasted after the game last night. No pun intended."

"No, no!" Myron shouted as he jumped around the lobby in a panic. "Not Andy! They've taken everything!" He stopped suddenly and gazed longingly out the window at the Steelers punter. "Please Andy, say it ain't so."

Myron ran to the receptionist's desk and picked up the Dell computer monitor. He carried it towards the clear walls.

"What are you doing with that?" Hank asked.

Myron didn't reply. He just stared straight ahead, his eyes on the oft-intoxicated football star. Janice opened her mouth to plead with him, but clammed up when she saw the tears streaming down the gray-haired man's sallow, sunken face. A moment of rare pity took hold of her. As someone who morphed identities on almost a seasonal basis, she had no experience with the complete loss of familiarity that Myron was going through. Her attachment to any of the fringe subcultures had been as fleeting as her friendships within them. But Myron had lived each day the same as the last, forging lifelong bonds with both close friends and local icons he had never met. The idea that his heroes had fallen was too much for Myron to handle. He approached the window, laboring to carry the monitor in his thin arms.

"Don't even think about it!" Harold commanded, but Myron kept moving closer.

He raised his arms in the air and Adam flung himself onto Myron's back, tackling the janitor to the ground. But it was too late, for Myron had flung the Dell through the window-paned wall of the lobby, shattering the glass. Adam leapt to his feet, his arms bleeding from minor cuts. Myron stood up and brushed himself off, shards of glass sticking out of his shoulders and back. He didn't seem to notice as he ran through the window into the throng of the dead. He had almost reached Andy Mason when they attacked. Seven zombies pushed and stomped and encroached. They shoved him on the ground, grabbing and chewing and noshing on the skinny janitor's insides. Myron surrendered to death just as he had surrendered to every aspect of his life. Now, as seven ravenous corpses tore him limb from limb, each with about as much self-control as an Oprah fan at a Russell Stover factory, Myron let it happen. He tossed his head back like he was relaxing, before a particularly greedy zombie wearing sea green hospital scrubs bit into his throat and tore out his esophagus. Blood spurted from the mortal wound, and Myron was now officially nothing more than a mess on the ground for his successor to clean up.

The remaining employees watched as the ghouls closed in. Myron had let in a veritable tsunami of the dead. Slowly the corpses shambled through the shattered floor-to-ceiling window, smashing into one another as they all tried to wedge themselves through the four-foot-wide opening at once. One zombie stumbled over another very tall ghoul's leg and fell into the lobby. That was an advantage that the living humans had: self-control. They also had patience and cognitive abilities. So while the dead pushed and stumbled to cram through the shattered window all at once, the employees turned to their original exit strategy—the now neglected revolving door.

Hank pushed his way out first, with Janice clutching his back.

"Dude, if we make it through this, we're definitely doing that burlesque show," Adam said to Pete as they pushed through the door.

"Oh, hell yeah," Pete replied, cramming his lean body against Adam.

Harold followed, pushing the gagged Owens in front of him at gunpoint like a human shield. Stepping backwards to avoid the encroaching zombies, O'Brien snapped one last photo before throwing himself into the revolving door with such force that it trapped Harold between the panes. Owens, finally freed of the gun to his back, made a run for it. He shuffled against the outside wall of the building, his hands still taped behind his back. Just as quickly as he was spun into the office, Harold spun back out.

"The fuck's wrong with you, man?" he said, smacking O'Brien in the shoulder with the gun.

Owens stepped directly in front of Hank, and the tattooed copywriter shoved him towards the General.

"Arrivederci, douchebag," he said.

The General grabbed Owens and began to speak over the screams and groans of the crowd.

"These men, they are your brothers, your sisters, your second cousins," the General began, but was cut off by the reappearance of one of his original battalion members. "Admiral Green Hair!" he exclaimed to the apparently promoted punk who was now mere feet from the CEO.

But the officer was ravenous, so he bit into Owens's neck, and several other new troops joined in the fracas. Maybe he should have skipped the introduction and gone straight to the main point of his speech, the General thought. His arms around Owens's back, Admiral Green Hair gnawed on the CEO's neck, blood dripping from his gray skin onto the hospital scrubs. He noshed away while three newer members of the army clawed and bit at the man's lower body. The first appendage to drop to the ground was his left leg. His right followed seconds later. Admiral Green Hair continued eating the neck, greedily gnawing on the flesh, literally biting off much more than he could chew. Chunks of skin fell from the zombie's mouth to the ground as he continued to feast on the Pro-Well founder. When he had ripped off all the flesh and the spinal cord that ran through Owens's neck and it looked like the remains of a freshly eaten chicken wing, Admiral Green Hair let the body drop to the ground where the other troops were still feasting.

As Marshall Owens's lifeless corpse hit the gravel, the remains of his neck cracked and the CEO's head rolled a few feet away from its body. The General pushed around the feasting zombies and picked up the head by Owens's short, stylish businessman's hair. He held the head up like he had just slain Medusa and shouted to an increasingly chaotic crowd.

"Aux armes, mes citoyens!"

The troops failed to notice the General. He wasn't that tall, so the head was barely visible in the veritable melee, and his shouts were almost inaudible. The General pulled his arm back down, lowering the head to his eye level.

"Mr. Aarons. What you have done to us is wrong. We are not slaves. We are the righteous street men," he began. But as the General turned the severed head around to face him so that they could enjoy a true tête-à-tête, he dropped it to the ground.

The sound that came from the General's throat was something between an "Eww" and an "Ugh." He had engaged in an intense monologue to Goggles one night before he realized that his fellow street dweller had died of hypothermia earlier in the evening, but he could not bring himself to participate in something this macabre. He was a man who feasted on garbage, but some things were just too much for the General. After all, this was the first time he had actually witnessed the atrocities of war.

Marshall Owens's head rolled several feet from where the General had dropped it, nearly tripping Harold as he fended off attacks from three dead Pitt students. After smashing the final zombie with the "Caution: Wet Floor" sign, he knelt down and quickly picked up the severed head.

"Damn," he said smiling. "Ain't that a bitch, boss?"

He laughed and propped the sign on the ground next to him while he held the head with both hands and lobbed it as hard as he could at an approaching dead construction worker.

Narrowly avoiding several sets of rotting teeth, Hank shoved towards the Escalade, hitting and stabbing zombies along the way. He sliced a tall one in a tattered suit and jabbed at the eyes of a young woman holding a leash for a dog that had long since departed. He didn't even see the small zombie until it wrapped its tiny arms around his leg. A sudden rush of pained sympathy came over him for the first time since he was initially greeted by hundreds of his dead co-workers. Even if its teeth were bared, ready to sink into his calf, Hank did not know if he could kill a kid.

The little zombie looked up at Hank to reveal a full goatee above his yellow teeth.

"Oh thank fuck," Hank said, relieved.

He swung his left leg back and kicked the dead dwarf right between the legs, sending his attacker flying over the parking lot melee like a perfectly punted football. It was a damn shame that Andy Mason was one of them.

Now a lone ghoul blocked his way, though it had the weight of about ten times the dwarf he had just punted. A morbidly obese dead woman stood directly in front of the driver's door. Clad in beige stretch pants and a purple polka dot shirt that could not hide the fat that formed in rolls like a gelatinous, terrifying cinnamon roll of doom, she took a small step towards Hank which, to a dead woman of such magnificent girth, was a giant leap for her kind.

Hank froze. He suddenly remembered his swimming teacher. As a child, he was convinced that her weight was a disease that could be spread by the water. He remembered standing at the side of the pool, shaking and crying, prompting his parents to believe he'd developed a strange case of hydrophobia (that was actually not unlike the illogical fears he would fall victim to twenty years later). He stared at the hulking, jiggling mass that was slowly inching towards him, ready to swallow him whole. He felt like whatever was in a hot dog right before it was to be put in its casing. Unable to move, Hank stood still as her hungry mouth hung agape above her three pillowy chins. She was a mere foot from his face when a gunshot rang out and her skull shattered, pieces of bone and fluffy red hair flying through the air. She fell to the side, her bulk landing with a squish onto the asphalt.

Breaking out of his catatonia, Hank shook his head and turned to his left to see Harold brandishing his firearm. The ex-con tossed a bundle of keys and Hank caught them. He jumped over the fat corpse and scrambled to stick the key in the driver's door.

"Jesus, Hank, you just keep getting gayer," Adam said, running past Hank to the passenger side of the car.

Hank fumbled for a second, then stabbed the key into the lock and twisted. He pulled the door open, leapt into the front seat and slammed the door behind him. As he started the engine, Janice joined Adam in the back seat, followed by Pete. O'Brien jumped onto the hood avoid the clutches of a legless zombie who was pulling himself from under the car. A dead convenience store worker in a long green vest approached, with the name Phil embroidered on his chest. O'Brien brusquely rolled onto his back, his legs splayed above his head. He thrust his body forward and in one swift motion, swung the blade into Phil's neck. His head still half attached, the zombie fell to the ground. O'Brien rolled off the hood of the car, and Hank popped the trunk.

O'Brien ran to the back of the SUV, slicing the temple of an elderly zombie who was still using her walker. He hopped into the trunk and pulled the door down behind him. Hank revved the engine, and Harold turned his head. He was punching a teenage emo zombie right in his angled bangs, trying to conserve his bullets, when he heard the car ready to go.

"Fuck it," he said and shot the eyeliner-wearing adolescent square in the forehead.

Skipping over the bodies of the dead and the truly dead that littered the parking lot, Harold reached the passenger door and jumped into the front seat. Hank put the SUV in reverse and slammed his foot on the gas, leaving a trail of flattened corpses in his wake. He switched gears to drive and turned the wheel, spinning the car towards the parking lot exit that would place them in the closest proximity to the Hot Metal Bridge.

O'Brien sat backwards in the trunk, peering out the window like a child whose major thrill in life was sticking his tongue out at drivers at red lights. He held his camera to the tinted glass, maniacally snapping pictures of the desecrated parking lot. These would definitely need to be digitally manipulated, he thought, as he checked out the latest show of a dark scene covered by the magnified defroster lines on the rear window. He reached his arm out and snapped an image of his face when the car ran over a particularly solid corpse and O'Brien's head hit the ceiling.

"Watch out!" he yelled. "I don't have a seat belt back here."

"Deal with it," Pete said. "You're cargo now."

Hank drove the car at warp speed, Mr. Sulu, out of the parking lot, swerving it every so often to mow down pedestrian zombies. They were sparse, but most were still traveling in the direction of Pro-Well. Hank turned the car right onto the Hot Metal Bridge where the fleeing zombie slayers were immediately met by three corpses who were in the midst of tearing apart a bike messenger whose Schwinn lay to the side of his ravaged corpse. Hank floored the gas and ran over the unsuspecting diners. A zombie head flew off its zombie body and landed on the hood of the car.

Janice screamed. On instinct, Hank flicked on the windshield wipers, but it only served to smear blood over the glass as the head was a foot from the windshield. Hank swerved, trying to dislodge the macabre new hood ornament, but it stubbornly remained on its neck, staring at the passengers. Its hair was cut short, with three days' growth on the cheeks and chin and its mouth was open as if it was trying to tell them something that no one in the car wanted to hear.

Hank gunned the SUV down the narrow Hot Metal Bridge, under its arachnid-like overhead beams and up to the intersection with East Carson Street. When he reached the blinking red traffic light, Hank turned right onto the main drag of the South Side. After moving no more than four feet, Hank slammed on the brakes. The severed head flew from the hood, smashing onto the double yellow line on the street while O'Brien was tossed around the trunk.

"Damn, dude," he said, clutching his head.

The rest of the car's passengers ignored him as they were all transfixed by the scene on Carson Street. It was a true infestation.

Hank watched the zombies fill the street, ripping flesh apart while the few survivors tried to run through the throng, only to be eaten alive. A tiny, emaciated punk of a girl was winding her way through the crowd, using her small frame to slip through the flailing arms of the dead. They watched as she nearly made it through the mob, running towards the salvation of a running Escalade when a heavily muscled zombie with a shaved head and goatee, clad in all black knocked her to the ground. *Definitely a bouncer from one of the ninety-something bars on this stretch*, Janice thought, *the most threatening of any South Side subset to be turned into a flesh-eating ghoul.*

Hank stared ahead with an odd sense of déjà vu. He had seen this before. Actually three times in the past several years, for the street had the same crowded, anarchic look after the Steelers won the Super Bowl. And again when the Penguins won the Stanley Cup in four months later. Hank had watched the drunken celebration from the corner of his street, more curious as to how the riot squad would respond than the final score of the game. He had stood on the corner, slightly removed from the gloating spectacle, hoping that he could witness what would surely become excessive force lawsuits. Not to testify in court against police brutality, but merely for the entertainment. Now there were no authorities to keep the rioters in line. And in lieu of a sea of black and gold, there was red. Blood red that flowed down the street and into the drains. The violence was a lot cooler to Hank when he imagined it. After a day of mutilating hungry corpses, he was just jaded.

"You live around here?" Adam asked Janice.

She stared straight ahead at the bloody crowd of dead cannibals decimating her neighbors. The street was overrun, leaving no room to wiggle through the throng, and she could not imagine the scene at any of the bars. The zombies started passing a large intestine over their heads like the obligatory giant inflatable penis at outdoor rock festivals.

"Actually, yes," she replied and grasped Adam's hand.

He nodded and smirked as he held onto her hand.

"Your eyes," he said. "Your eyes look like root beer flavored candies."

"Just shut up before I change my mind," Janice said.

"The fuck we gonna do?" Harold asked.

Still staring straight ahead, Hank revved the engine.

"We're going for it," he replied.

With both hands on the wheel at the 10 o'clock and 2 o'clock formation that he hadn't employed since learning the optimal steering position in high school Driver's Ed, Hank pushed his foot down hard on the gas pedal. He sped the Escalade up to the dense zombie riot and maintained velocity as bodies flew through the air. Bones crunched beneath the car like, well, crunching bones, as they passed from 27th Street to 26th to

25th, leaving a trail of bloody remains in their wake. A flattened human pancreas decorated with tire impressions was far more interesting road kill than a deer.

"Yea!" O'Brien cheered, thrusting his arm in the air and smacking his fist against the ceiling.

Hank kept driving, eyes staring straight ahead while bodies flew to the left and right and collapsed under the hood of the car.

"You're a fuckin' maniac, man," Harold said.

Hank ignored him as he passed the 24th Street intersection where three college-aged zombies were devouring a Jerseylicious twenty-something. He smashed the SUV into a long-haired zombie in an Iron Maiden shirt whose middle and ring fingers had been bitten off, giving the lucky metalhead permanent devil horns. The force of the side-view mirror severed the tanned head of a young douche right at the popped collar. Corpses launched into the air as Hank continued to drive, destroying everything in his path.

Hands on the wheel, eyes on the road, leaving a trail of dead. Yes, today was Hank's day.

EPILOGUE

The South Side was considered a war zone until the next Monday, during which time, the remaining law enforcement officers cleared the completely dead from the streets and terminated the walking dead with guns, machetes, and batons. The attack was almost completely isolated to Carson Street and its surrounding blocks. A few suburbanites managed to make it home before dropping dead and attempting to eat their children, but those sporadic outbreaks were easily neutralized by local police and the neighborhood watch.

Lillian and Will were discovered days later, their decomposing bodies locked in an eternal embrace. The photograph of their partially eaten, rotting corpses hugging half-naked on the floor of the janitor's closet is now distributed in corporate offices to illustrate the dangers of work romances.

Adam and Janice stayed together for exactly three days before they realized that they were not the last living people on Earth. More specifically, it was the moment that they woke up in bed and Adam asked, "You come here often?" Janice didn't need this idiot; she had herself in her future. Her future, it felt good to say those words again. Let alone to believe them. After coming so close to death, Janice was no longer fascinated by it. A week after the ordeal, she stripped her walls of the upside-down crucifixes and let the white walls go as bare as her skin. She figured she'd give herself a chance again.

After the town calmed down, she quickly found a job in quality assurance work for a title company on the North Shore. As there was no one left at Ground Zero (Pro-Well) to verify, her résumé stated that she had been there for three years and was, in fact, promoted to manager of her section. Though she had done actual work at Pro-Well for a little less than two hours, she had gotten the gist of it and was able to move with ease into her new role and ample salary. She promised herself that this was the last time she'd be a fraud.

Adam decided that Web design was far too dangerous and joined the Army, parlaying his newfound skills as a warrior to quieting insurgents. He told his fellow enlistees that the war casualties had nothing on what he had seen at the office one day. Pete remained in Pittsburgh, but after spending a day quarantined with Rick O'Brien, decided that the sleazy life of a salesman was not for him. So he enrolled in law school. He has established a magnificent ass groove in a couch on the fourth floor of the University of Pittsburgh law school's library.

Though Marshall Owens was never officially declared dead, his lawyers decided to honor the requests of his will so that they could make sure to grab their pay from his estate. He donated his life-like doll collection to Jerry's Kids, but left Pro-Well Pharmaceuticals to his most trusted and loyal servant, Harold. Had he been born a different man, Harold would have felt remorseful guilt about betraying the man's trust and effectively feeding him to a mob of hungry corpses. But Harold never looked back. He took the hand that he was dealt and counted the other players' cards to ensure that he'd leave with the pot.

Though the factory had been seized by the police, the office condemned, and the developing chemicals in the lab mysteriously vanished, Harold decided to continue with the development of Owens's organ superstore that he had planned to unveil in the year 2015. After riding high with Pro-Well for several months, he could not return to small-time street crime and he saw first-hand just how much money could be made by dealing drugs legally. Of course, Harold had no concept of subtlety, and his version of the business endeavor manifested itself quite differently than Marshall Owens had imagined. Harold filmed a few ads in which he sported tight Wranglers, an oversized belt buckle, and a cowboy hat and boots, proclaiming the great deals you can get on organs at Harry's House of Hearts, Route 22 in Delmont.

"We've got livers, ovaries, hearts, valves—you name it! More blood than Dracula could ever want! For the best prices, come to Harry's House of Hearts, Route 22 in Delmont. Need a kidney? We've got 'em pre-owned for no down payment and 12-9 financing on all healthy models under the age of 40!"

The pitch did not go over well as, surprisingly, the public was reluctant to buy organs from an ex-con who operated out of what used to be a 24-hour Taco Bell. Unfortunately for Harold, folks with renal failure were unwilling to purchase organs from an angry thug in blinged-out spurs who ended his commercials by walking away from the camera into the sunset, then quickly turning around and pulling a gun from his holster like an Old west gunfight. He pointed the pistol at the camera and pulled the trigger, and the commercial was over. Harold could not understand why, but for some reason the general dying public construed being shot as a threat. With business lagging, Harold burnt down the building for the insurance money. He was quickly apprehended and thrown back in jail where he became the loyal henchman to Olivia Divine, Queen of the unfathomably brutal and rapidly expanding Transvestite Nation.

Rick O'Brien quickly landed a publishing deal to release his coffee table book depicting photography of his adventure inside Ground Zero. Entitled *My Day With the Dead*, the hardback became a best-seller that received rave reviews for its gritty, in-depth look at the zombie uprising in Pittsburgh. The only criticism was the inclusion of memoir-type diary entries by Rick O'Brien, printed as insets at the corners of some of the full-page images. All too often, the type gave little explanation of the action or the terror he and his compatriots felt, except to proclaim O'Brien's heroic nature and a graphic description of zombie tits. The book made him a fifteen-minute pop culture sensation à la the Balloon Boy, and O'Brien quickly exhausted the talk show circuit. He is currently appealing the restraining order that the entire cast of *The View* filed against him.

And as for Hank, well, he's just about the same. He never speaks of that day, letting his actions become rumors and folk legend in the South Side. To Hank, it was not so much an adventure, but a way of getting things off his chest. He felt better now, knowing that he was incapable of hurting himself. No longer did he hide the scissors to protect his eyes from somnambulant paranoia. He still locked his door, because he knew quite well what kind of freaks were out there. But if they were to somehow get in, well, *good luck*, he thought. For now his arsenal not only included the most metal, yet archaic, weapons, but bloodstained office supplies that had actually seen battle. Though many residences in the neighborhood were on the market because of the sudden deaths of their owners, Hank remained in his subterranean apartment. It was comfortable and familiar, and it housed his souvenirs of the war that had changed his life. He never washed the blood off the phone flail, the pointer harpoon, or the umbrella lances. These were the only items from his collection that had ever been in combat and if anyone ever came to his house, he wanted them to know that he knew how to use them.

He chose to stay in the South Side because the whole zombie apocalypse thing had weeded out some of the neighborhood's more annoying residents. Indeed, several groups of jocks tried to impress anorexic bimbos by engaging in valiant, yet ultimately ill-conceived, battle with sporting equipment and empty beer bottles. And most of the hipsters were anti-gun, so they were eaten in the streets while the blue-collar Second Amendment defenders emerged from the chaos in their Pirates caps and plumbing company T-shirts.

Thanks to the oversized mouths of his fellow survivors from that fateful day at the office, Hank had become somewhat of a folk hero in the South Side. His exploits were legendary and he had signed more bar napkins than he ever thought he possible. Local low-budget horror filmmakers had approached him to write the movie version of that day, and he had agreed. He was currently living on the workmen's comp he and the others had received for their massive inconvenience and work-related injuries while he finalized his Shakespearean farce about 16th-century child-killer Gilles de Rais. But mostly, he tried to keep a low profile, hanging out at his favorite haunts.

Hank stabbed his cigarette out in the ashtray, gulped the rest of his beer, and slammed the pint glass down on the Bat Cave bar. Exhaling the last bit of smoke from his lungs, he turned to his left.

"You ready to go to the Vets?" he asked.

"Oh yeah. Yeah, 'course, Hank," the General replied.

Hank rose from his seat, shoving a napkin into the glass. He picked up the teddy bear from the bar and handed it to the General.

"No, leave it," the gray-skinned homeless man said. "For the ladies."

Hank shrugged and placed the stuffed purple bear back on the bar. The General stood up from his chair and walked towards the door. Hank followed, and the unlikely duo walked from the bar into the bright sun of high noon.

By getting *Working Stiffs* published at 28, Lucy Leitner accomplishes her rather dubious goal of being on the same career timeline as Hunter Thompson. She has worked among the (brain) dead in web writing, print media, and the Japanese machine tool game. She finds long walks on the beach tedious and filled with sand. On warm summer nights, she enjoys a glass of red wine and a symposium on the impending zombie apocalypse. This foresight has elevated her to being the entire Board of Directors at breaking news site DailyGhoul.com. Lucy loves movies about phone booth time travel and bands with an unnecessary amount of X's in their names. Known by many aliases, she has parlayed the dollars she won betting on hockey games into an impressive collection of groceries.

WELCOME TO THE END OF THE WORLD!

Disease-K has decimated the world leaving its victims shambling homicidal maniacs. And nestled along the warm Gulf waters sits Gulf Shores...the last outpost of civilization. With looters and thieves preying on the shocked survivors, it's up to the retirees and bank tellers, phone repairmen and charterboat captains to put the town back together.

THE SHADOWS ARE GATHERING OUTSIDE OF TOWN!

There, in the sands and marshes of the Gulf of Mexico, the citizens of Gulf Shores along with scattered military units, a downed Air Force pilot, and a lone Coast Guard cutter form the last line of defense against the amassing horde of the infected marching its way toward the sea destroying what is left of humanity along the way.

As summer gives way to the fall and the cold winds blow off the sea, Gulf Shores draws the line and prepares to make the...

THE LAST STAND ON ZOMBIE ISLAND!

WWW.NECROPUBLICATIONS.COM

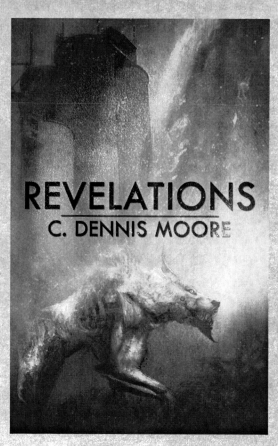

REVELATIONS
C. DENNIS MOORE

FRESH FLESH SERIES BOOK 1

A MAN FROZEN IN TIME...

Geoffrey was an experiment in cryogenics. But someone forgot to wake him up...fifty years ago! Now he's awake and finding out the world isn't exactly the way he left it.

HELL ON EARTH...

The Lord led the righteous to Heaven and left Hell to literally open up on Earth. And Hell is spreading like an infection. Unfortunately it's inside that infection where Geoffrey has to go in search of answers, the most important being: Why wasn't he taken?

Geoffrey must face the worst that Hell can throw at him as he sets out on an epic journey taking him through The Garden, The Cavern of God's Silence, the Island of Wails and more as the answers to all of Geoffrey's questions reveal themselves and at the end of his journey his final revelation can have the power to change the world...if he's man enough to pull the trigger.

WWW.NECROPUBLICATIONS.COM

WHEN FRANKIE RED COMES TO TOWN...PEOPLE ARE GOING TO DIE!

It's fall of 2012, and Dan Suppers is lost. Abandoning his broken down vehicle, he's been walking through the woods for hours looking for something – anything – that resembles civilization. What he finds is a smoking pit of Hell – a large building filled with what Dan soon realizes are the remnants of hundreds of human corpses.

AND DAN THOUGHT HE WAS HAVING A BAD DAY!

Red Town Lost chronicles the efforts of a terrified man to discover the secret of what happened the night the building burned, and in the process unraveling four harrowing tales revolving around four unforgettable individuals and their own unique trials and tribulations that are somehow connected to the burned out building. Unfortunately, the man will discover very quickly that the stories are not just connected with his morbid discovery, but in fact may hold horrifying implications for the man and his very soul!

WHO IS FRANKIE RED AND WHAT DOES HE HAVE IN STORE FOR DAN... AND MANKIND?

WWW.NECROPUBLICATIONS.COM

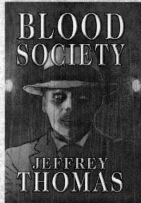

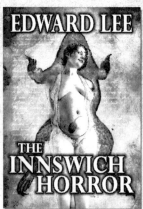
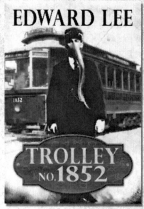

CPSIA information can be obtained at www.ICGtesting.com
Printed in the USA
LVOW130032040912

297230LV00011B/95/P